Acclair
Listening to th

Nan's second book *Listening to the Silen...* .. a collection of stories of the people who have benefited after reading her first book (*Sounds of Silence*)... (it) is already flying off the shelves and many are waiting for her third book..."

G2 Magazine, Aug-Sept. 2010

The book (*Listening to the Silence*) comprises about 30 heart-touching stories. They all belong to people who have perhaps walked long miles to find the light at the end of the tunnel.

Society Magazine, July 2010

The book (*Listening to the Silence*) wraps itself around the heart of the reader from the first page, drawing you into a world of silent communication with God and the spirit world... It is an outpouring of the heart that will touch your soul... This is not a quick read. It deserves to be read slowly, every word to be savoured as a gift of Grace."

Life Positive Magazine, Sept. 2010

Her first book, *Sounds of Silence*, published over a decade ago, created ripples as it challenged set concepts about life after death... her second book (*Listening to the Silence*), the sequel, was launched at an out-of-the-ordinary book reading event."

The Times of India, Mumbai, April 8, 2010

"Pain is inevitable, suffering is a choice," says author Nan Umrigar... *Listening to the Silence* chronicles experiences that various people have had with the spiritual world and the influence of Baba's teachings on them."

DNA, Pune, June 20, 2010

"*Listening to the Silence* is compiled after extensive research by the author that re-tells tales told by people of how in their deepest moment of despair, their misgivings and fears have been redeemed by Meher Baba, spiritual guide to the author."

DNA, Mumbai, April 9, 2010

LISTENING TO THE SILENCE

TRUE STORIES OF A HEALING LOVE FROM THE SPIRITUAL REALMS

Nan Umrigar

YogiImpressions®

LISTENING TO THE SILENCE
First published in India in 2010 by
Yogi Impressions Books Pvt. Ltd.
1711, Centre 1, World Trade Centre,
Cuffe Parade, Mumbai 400 005, India.
Website: www.yogiimpressions.com

First Edition, March 2010
Fifth reprint, June 2017

ISBN 978-81-88479-50-4

Printed at: Repro India Ltd., Mumbai

Message from Karl

Darling Mummy,

Baba has a lot of happy thoughts about the new book.
He is always so very involved in the welfare of the world,
always hoping that, with His compassion and
active participation in the lives of His people,
all their troubles can be successfully wiped out.

So you can imagine the happy thoughts that come to Him
when He sees how so many have begun to really love
Him, and because of this love have been impressed to
write their experiences so beautifully, with their own
hands, and from their own hearts. It pleases Him
immensely and He goes through even more joyful
moments when they continue to reach out to Him, and
He is able to share Himself inwardly with them.

But, He wants you to convey His love and thanks
not only to those who have written but also to those
who have worked so hard to make this book happen.
He wants to reach out His hand more so to all those
who now, and in future, will share and help spread His
Love by making this book more available to the world.

– Love, Karl
June 16, 2009

5th April, 2010

My Dearest Mother Nan Umrigar,

I am so happy that this is your second book.
What a gift you have received from your son Karl!

I went through a few pages of your new book 'Listening to the Silence' and they are written very well. It is good that you are writing. This is a gift you have received from Beloved Meher Baba.

Because after your son's death, he sent you a message to go to Baba's Samadhi. Since then, you have been writing, and what a gift you are giving to the whole world.

The pictures from Meherabad are so beautiful, and these pictures have been taken and produced with great detail! I see that there are many things about Beloved Meher Baba and Meherabad in the book. It is simply beautiful.

You are doing Beloved Baba's work.
Thank you, thank you, thank you.

With all love and Jai Baba to you.

In His Love and Service,

Bhau

V. S. Kalchuri, lovingly named Bhau by Meher Baba and respectfully referred to as Bhauji, is the present Chairman of Avatar Meher Baba Perpetual Public Charitable Trust, Ahmednagar, India.

Contents

Appendix

Acknowledgements

I was excited…

In January 2007, I thought that my book *Listening to the Silence* had finally taken some shape. So I copied the rough manuscript on a CD, packed it with a bottle of red wine and some sweets for my publisher and his staff, and marched off to his new office at World Trade Centre in Mumbai, to give it all to him.

But guess what happened? Instead of the seventeenth floor, the lift took me to the eighteenth floor. The liftman apologised for the mistake, and requested me to walk one floor down the staircase. So, armed with all the goodies – my mobile phone, my purse, and the CD, I took the first step down.

The next thing I remember is me saying, "Oh my God! I am falling." I went head first, down a flight of fifteen huge stone steps, and found myself sitting at the bottom. My left leg was bent inward at the hip, my right ankle was swelling visibly and blood was flowing down from my head. Everything lay scattered on the landing. I looked around for help. My hellos resounded and echoed in space. It was three o'clock in the afternoon, and there was not a soul in sight. I looked up at the steps looming above me and thought, 'My God, did I actually fall from there and am still alive? Baba, now what?'

A patter of feet answered my question, and a stranger came running down to me. He tried to help me, saw that I was not in a state to get up and ran to find someone. He soon located my publisher, who arrived with some of his staff. I was rushed to the hospital. The result was a broken femur, a fractured ankle, and a deep gash on the head. The bottle of wine, the sweets, the mobile and the CD, were all intact. Nothing broke except my bones.

I tell you all this because I want to show you that the fall was responsible for much more than just pain. It put me out of commission, physically and mentally, for more than three months. It took me back to a time in 1994, when I had fallen down the steps of the home of the renowned medium Mrs. Rishi, just before my first book *Sounds of Silence* was completed. I remembered how I had struggled with a broken ankle to sit for hours at an ordinary old typewriter to finish the manuscript. Most importantly, both times it resulted in so many positive things.

It proved to me that my book was not yet ready to be published. The time was not right, and there was much more to be done. My enforced stay at home resulted in many meetings with those who had written their stories, and provided the opportunity for innumerable changes. It also resulted in a deeper friendship with my publisher.

It took almost two more years and three more surgeries for my bones to heal, and yet more time for the new CD to be completed. I sincerely hope that Baba will eventually be happy with it.

So, here I want to really thank my publisher for patiently standing by me for so long. I thank him for his encouragement and for his conviction that the book was worth publishing. I thank you Gautam, for the amount of calls you made to me through these difficult years to keep me focused, for going through the manuscript chapter by chapter, and for sharing your knowledge and insights with me.

I want to thank Kim Verma for spending so many hours going through the manuscript in the initial stages of editing, helping to decide titles, and which story to keep and what to put where. My grateful thanks to Shiv Sharma, who took it on from there and has done such a wonderful job of fine-tuning, editing and completing the book.

Nisha Ghosh, thank you for your friendship and support. You came over so many times to my home to help with the writing, the structure and the contents. Kamal Mulla, thank you for all your assistance which not only came from the mind, but so spontaneously from the heart.

There are many others who have offered their unswerving assistance in the making of this book. Amie Rabadi, Gayatri Bathija, I value your comments and suggestions. Priya Pardiwalla, Steven

Mathias and Firoza Bhabha, dear friends, I appreciate all your inputs which helped me put my thoughts into perspective.

Soumya and Cyrus Khambata, my heartfelt thanks for your support, your wealth of knowledge, and for your detailed editing of Baba's quotes. You have supplied me with so many beautiful anecdotes and photographs of Baba.

I am deeply indebted to the Bhau Kalchuri, Chairman of the Avatar Meher Baba Trust; to Ward Parks and Ted Judson for helping me so much with the necessary permissions and details.

I am extremely grateful to Dot Lesnik for her beautiful description of the Tile Wall at the Meher Pilgrim Retreat in Meherabad, and even more so to the unknown artist whose tile is used for the book cover. Your vision is beautiful. So also, to Homyar Mistry for photographing it all so perfectly and working so meticulously on the details.

A very special thank you to Sweety and Bozo of Hyderabad, to Dinesh Chibber (Budda) and all Baba friends from Chennai, to Lisa and Jehangir Jeejeebhoy, and to Sunita Garware and Leila Bilimoria, for their generosity, trust and support in helping turn this book into something special.

But most of all, I want to offer my thanks to all those who have shared their stories with me. For me every story was most important but, as much as I would have liked to, it was impossible to include them all. I want you to know that I deeply appreciate the effort.

The creation of this book has been a partnership – a wonderful journey together. I am sure that all those who are walking it with me will look back to remember Khorshed Bhavnagri with gratitude. She has now passed into spirit, but I will forever remain beholden to her, for it was through her connection with her departed sons Vispi and Ratu, that I got to know about Karl – and so to Meher Baba.

Beloved Baba, it has been a very difficult climb up those huge stone steps again. At this stage I am still climbing, knowing full well that only with Your help will it be possible for me to get there.

Thank you my Karl, and my dearest family, for helping me to achieve it.

Nan Umrigar

Introduction

"When the tongue is silent, the mind speaks;
When the mind is silent, the heart sings;
When the heart stops singing,
The Soul begins to experience its original Self."[1]

The journey I have travelled from *Sounds of Silence,* my first book, to *Listening to the Silence,* has been a beautiful one. A journey that started alone is now our story and our journey together. This book is about all of you who are now with Baba, and for those of you yet to come, or rather, whom Baba will draw to Himself. As He describes in His own words, ***"I am the Thief of Hearts."*** Each story here describes the Divine Thief at work, and after so many years and countless incidents, I still do not cease to be amazed at the perfection of the Perfect One.

My own journey into the Silence began the day my son Karl fell from his horse, one April afternoon in 1979. On the 3rd of May, he passed into the spirit world, and the silence of a great grief fell upon my soul. Then, just when I thought that life would never be the same again, the unbelievable happened. Karl reached out from the beyond and began a chain of communication that described his love for a Master, his "Father in Heaven," and his beloved Meher Baba in the spirit world. He said that he had a new mission and that while the communication between his world and ours may be understood, justified, or interpreted as an experience, this was "no barrier to the energy that belongs to pure selfless love." Meher Baba was going to show us that life, in general, held no barriers to a love that is in our hearts.

Karl said in the earliest of his urgings, *"There will be many people who will call on you for help. You must take them all to Baba and know that once they come to Him, He takes care of them and never lets them down. All you have to do is to bring them to Him. Tell everyone that He has made them a part of His Love, and that Love will never fail them. Happiness and joy are waiting for them. Just be with Him. That is all I have to say."*

Karl's love for his beloved Meher Baba has reached out to me and to countless others. It is this spirit of love that prompted me to write my first book *Sounds of Silence*, and now this second book too. This is a book that will tell you more of the love we have and the struggle to love the One who makes it all possible. You may call that One by any name you wish, but for me everything is Baba's. It is Baba's love that has helped me on my way. It is His love that has helped me to emerge from the shroud of silence that had engulfed me and to begin listening to the inner driving urge of the soul; to hear the sounds that have healing messages, the echoes of which still resound in my heart.

Today, I too just listen.

In all this time, I have heard many sad and heartrending stories of accidents, tragedies, broken hearts and troubled marriages. Many, whose loved ones have crossed over to the other side, have come to Baba in order to make a connection with them. Through Baba's grace, I have had the chance to help lift their lives by giving them beautiful messages of love and hope, messages that come from Baba, through Karl. I have had the privilege of taking so many to a paradise called Meherabad, to take some of them over the threshold of the Samadhi, and deliver them into the warm and loving embrace of Meher Baba. I have been a witness to the way so many lives have changed. It has given me much joy to see how Baba has washed away sadness and pain, turned lives around, and I have never ceased to be amazed by the way Baba has touched each and every one with His Love.

> ***Baba says, "Consciously or unconsciously, every living creature seeks one thing. In the lower forms of life and in less advanced human beings, the quest is unconscious; in advanced human beings it is conscious. The object of the quest is called by many names: happiness, peace, freedom, truth, love, perfection, Self-realization, God-realization, union with God. Essentially it is a search for all of these, because all of these and all other noble concepts, no matter what their name, turn out in the end to be one. Everyone***

has moments of happiness, glimpses of truth, fleeting experiences of affinity with God; what everyone longs for is to make them permanent... My function is to indicate the direction of the path that man has to travel, point out the pitfalls on the way, lessen the hazards of the difficult passages, and lighten and ease the final lap that ends in the culmination of his quest.

I bring to man divine love and the life eternal."[2]

Since the time *Sounds of Silence* has been published, many people have asked questions about my continuing journey and of the unusual experiences of all those that have come to Baba. I am not qualified to explain the spiritual insights that appear with some of the communications but, within my limited understanding, I have tried to put down faithfully all that I have learned over the years, watching as life unfolds. I have to tell you how meeting so many people, interacting with them, hearing their stories and seeing the change in their lives, has affected my own thinking and helped me enormously to discover myself. I know now that when you are sincerely searching, Baba always somehow finds a way of answering your queries.

So, in answer to all these various questions, interspersed with some of my own learning experiences and a few more of Karl's mischievous activities from the spirit world, here is interwoven a collection of stories of this wonderful journey we have all undertaken. There is an outpouring of the heart by all those who have been fortunate enough to make their own connection with the Beloved, and who have had the faith and the courage to continue to walk hand in hand with Him. This book is the combined effort of the many that have come forward to share their sounds with you. Some have only heard whispers, some loud echoes, while a few have really heard the thunder that is God.

My husband, Jimmy, was sceptical and said, "Waste of time... no one will allow you to tell their story or to use their names." But he was wrong, for not only did everyone readily agree, they also decided to write their own little stories, and believe me they are really written from the heart.

May all their stories reach you, awaken you and help you to know, understand and realise that there is really so much more to life than just living it. I am sure that somewhere, something will touch a chord in your heart and that, maybe, in some small way it will create in you a sense of knowledge and wonder. It may also give you the strength to triumph over adversity, to evolve on your own path and to fulfill your own destiny.

All those who count their blessings must know that God is Love and there is a reason for everything. Those that look to their own personal growth must also know that this change in their perspective will guarantee them a new and better passage through life.

I hope this book will help everyone find that passage.

The picture of Meher Baba that came as my birthday gift.

CHAPTER 1

The Ocean of Love

It was the 3rd of June 1996, and my birthday. I woke up in the morning to a beautiful cloudy sky, a cool breeze, and a light but steady drizzle. Greeting calls from family and friends, and messenger boys bearing baskets of fruit and bunches of flowers became the order of the day.

In a happy mood, I took up my pen and began my daily morning communication with Karl. *"Hi mum,"* he said, *"those in the world want to wish you a happy birthday, and so do we. Baba, your mum, dad and sister, your uncle and aunt, both your grannies and grandpas and so many others who all love you from here; all of them want to wish you Mum. Baba especially says, 'Bless you'."*

Grateful for Baba's special blessings and attention, I jokingly asked whether I was going to receive a gift from Karl himself. Hardly had the words been uttered, there was a knock at my door. My servant Ishwar, who normally would never disturb me at prayer time, said in Gujarati, "Bai, ain koi aapi ne gayoon che" (Madam, someone came and left this for you). Saying this, he put an envelope on my table and departed. Staring at the blank white envelope, I could not resist interrupting my morning routine by opening it.

I gasped, for out came a big beautiful picture of Meher Baba!

Holding my precious birthday gift close to my heart, I strolled around my new home in Pune. I went into my little garden, resplendent with its hedges of pink and white hibiscus, and sat down on the bench to think about it all. The years had passed by. Everything was different.

I looked at Baba's picture in my hand and wondered what life had in store for me. At this time, my family was scattered all over the globe. My son Neville and his family in Dubai, my daughter Tina and her family in Mumbai, and my husband, Jimmy, and I, alone in Pune, away from the place we had called home.

Yes, it did feel a bit strange. Was Baba trying to show me something? I had a sneaky feeling that in His own way, He was trying to convince me that a place called home was really nothing but a space between four walls; that home is really where the heart is, and that those whom we dearly love and call family, would always be with us no matter where we lived.

Loosening my strong attachments... is that what He was up to?

However, these thoughts being too much to handle, I got myself busy settling into my new surroundings hoping very hard that whatever it was, I would be able to learn the lessons well and that Baba had a few lovely surprises around the corner for me.

They were not long in coming. The very next morning the words of Karl's new message leapt out of the pages of my *auto writing* book, *"Mummy, I have already given you the greatest gift of love, the gift of Baba. What more can you ask for? No matter where you are, Baba is with you everywhere, and loving Him is all that matters."*

This made me think and look back at my life. When I was a little girl, I was terrified of losing my parents. I loved them dearly. My prayer to God was that He would always keep them safe. I cried in fear whenever my father had to leave and go anywhere. I prayed that my sisters and I would always be there for each other in spite of our differences, weaknesses and strengths, especially the smallest one who was born a handicapped child. I prayed for my pets.

My prayers were answered.

When I went to school, I wanted to be as pretty as my house captain, as popular as the head girl, and as clever as my neighbour on the next desk. I kept asking God for that. I also prayed to be able to win all the sports events I took part in, and so make my father proud of me. But most of all I prayed at exam time.

My prayers were answered.

I graduated and went to college, when boyfriends were the objects of my earnest supplications to God. I wanted to become a drama queen. I prayed for popularity, fun at parties, to be allowed late nights, and not to get caught bunking classes. I prayed for a car of my own, so I could zip around like all the whiz kids around me.

My prayers were answered.

I married my childhood sweetheart and became the mother of three lovely children. Although the deliveries were not easy, I prayed my way through all that, constantly asking God to help my babies to grow up strong, healthy and happy. To have all their dreams come true.

My prayers were all answered – till the day Karl had his accident and fell from his horse that April afternoon. Then I prayed as I had never prayed before. I not only prayed, but I begged of God to let him live.

My prayers were not answered. I prayed no more. The door was shut.

It seemed as if we had all moved into a bottomless pit that had no sunshine coming through. It was a time when the family lost all faith in God and in the goodness of the world. As for me, I was miserable and heartbroken; in fact a complete wreck. I struggled to understand why this had happened. What had we done to deserve this? What was God's role in our suffering and why had He decided to take my son away in the prime of his life? What and who was God really? Was He the Zarathustra I had pictured in my young life, dressed in long white robes and finger pointing towards the sky? Was He a man? Was He light? Was He energy? Was He there at all?

This went on for almost four years till Baba entered my life and everything changed. I will never, ever forget that blessed day when I first stepped over the threshold of the *Samadhi* and into Baba's loving care. Life took a different turn, and in spite of the inner conflict of whether Baba was God, I trusted my son's communication with me, and the very fact that Karl said he was with Him, under His care, and considered Him to be his 'Father in Heaven' began to have some meaning for me.

Then every trip to Meherabad, every new person that came, every new experience I went through, made me understand more and more. Whatever came my way, however small, made me realise that everything that had happened – be it a sign, an appearance, or an incident – had been orchestrated to bring me closer to Him. My constant prayer became, "Let me know the Truth, God, so I do not spend my days blaming You."

> In His own way Baba answered, ***"The mind cannot be turned to the Truth by sheer force. In the beginning it has to be coaxed and won over from its usual rambles, just in the same way as it is necessary to coax children in order to induce them to give up their play and take to study. The Master wins over the aspirant to the Truth with infinite dexterity. When the mind is won over to the Truth, all the senses automatically follow."***[1]

So it has been with me too. Like that child, I have been coaxed by Baba into accepting His Truths.

Somewhere along the line I learned that God is not the creator of our pain and suffering. It is our own *karma,* the fruits of our past actions which automatically and spontaneously – though at times at a sub-conscious level – create such situations to balance out our karmic debts and dues. Hence it is our soul that chooses the experience of having to go through happiness or tragedy, to soar in ecstasy or struggle through a period of horrible pain. And through it all, God's presence is always at hand to help us, guide us, and lift us out of our self-created maze, if only we care to call out to Him and experience His ever-flowing and unconditional Love for each one of us.

In other words, it is only through experiencing the ups and downs of our karma and the impressions that give rise to it, that we at last arrive at balance. Only when balance is achieved can we become free and know God.

> Baba says in His book, *God Speaks,* ***"It is only through these diverse opposite impressions and their respective opposite experiences, that the gross-conscious human soul in the gross world could possibly one day, after millions of births and deaths, and through these opposite experiences of births and deaths, be able to balance or thin out the residual or concentrated opposite impressions."***[2]

Slowly I began to understand the role in our life of such periods of trials and turbulence as a part of growth, a balancing act of the past deeds and a move forward towards the goal.

As soon as I began to accept all this, I changed. I began to heal. I started to listen to what God had to say, through Karl, through books, through His followers, through people around me. Although most of it went over my head, I guess somewhere along the way, just a little did sink in, then more, and still yet more. It gave me something to think and ponder over, and to know that when the difficult times come, it is then that God steps in to hold our hand to help us get through it all.

God began to be my friend instead of my enemy.

So where was I now?

Yes, Baba's presence was certainly more alive to me since I had relocated to Pune. Unbelievable as it was, I was actually in the very city where Baba had been born. His family home called 'Baba House' on Dastur Meher Road was just around the corner, and by now He was in possession of more than just one corner of my heart. Baba had definitely become more to me than just my constant companion and the centre of my life.

I closed my eyes in gratitude and looked again at the words in my auto writing book. They said, *"Baba is with you everywhere and loving Him is all that matters."*

Baba's home in Pune.

CHAPTER 2

The Family Grows

That Baba had a great respect for family had a further impact on me. He always encouraged His followers to put the family first. There are many stories that have been told about how Baba always said that family obligations must first be fulfilled, and that the role that mothers and fathers were born to play as parents must be first completed successfully before any other thoughts could be entertained. Yes, even of joining Him.

> He said, *"Though the children are the beneficiaries of the married life of the parents, the married life of the parents is in its turn enriched by the presence of the children. Children give to parents an opportunity for expressing and developing a real and spontaneous love in which sacrifice becomes easy and delightful. And the part played by children in the life of parents is of tremendous importance for the spiritual advancement of the parents themselves. It therefore follows that when children make their appearance in married life, they ought to be wholeheartedly welcomed by the parents."*[1]

In my adult years, it never occurred to me to look at the spiritual impact my children had on me, or that there was any significance beyond the responsibility of nurturing them with love and giving them the best education, values etc. My parents had taught me that by spending time in prayer and in the remembrance and gratitude of all that had been graced or given to us, was a way to love Him. I remember encouraging my children to do the same; to pray by rote the *Avestan* prayers of our faith as written in our books, and then maybe to add a little more to it by just talking to God and asking for the favours that were needed at that particular time.

As time went by, I continued the visits to the fire temple. I respected and revered God but was not overly religious in any way. It puzzled me that there were scholars and religious heads who urged us to rediscover our religion by keeping up with rituals, and reading and delving into discussions on topics written by modern-day authors. If we were principled and conscientious of having good thoughts, good words and good deeds, then we were following the basic tenets of our religion and loving God at the same time. That, to my mind, was enough. It made us good human beings. That was my firm belief.

When Meher Baba entered my life, little did I realise that there was to be an awakening and that Baba was not only reaching out to me but also to other members of my family. Many other stories have come about which have all added to my own growth and learning.

What am I going to discover while writing this one?

My niece, Zia Cama, says:

The greatest gift that I have ever received is Baba – Avatar Meher Baba – and it was presented to me by Karl.

Karl is my cousin and so it was natural that we spent our childhood together. Being very dear and close to me, it was natural that all of us were very affected by his accident and untimely passing at the young age of eighteen.

Six years later, on one of the occasions when all the family had gathered around our big dining table, my aunt Nan or Nanny as we call her, told us about her amazing communication with Karl. Sitting next to her, looking out at the sea and listening to her story, I was not at all surprised, for her words just confirmed what my father always said. As a devout follower of Ramana Maharshi, he believed in the immortality of the soul.

I wondered how and why it was my aunt Nanny who was telling us all this, for she was seemingly the least religious or spiritual-minded of the whole family, always fond of good clothes, fun-loving and party-going. This kind of confused me, until I learned that you don't need to be sombre to be a recipient of such unusual experiences. I also remember feeling extremely happy that Karl was back with us again. Karl had not only returned, but also brought with him one 'other' whom he called his 'Father in Heaven'.

It was in this way that Karl introduced our family to Avatar Meher Baba. Thereafter, Meher Baba became a sporadic influence in my life. Gradually I accepted Him as becoming a part of my everyday existence. As the years went by, the yearning to be with the Baba fold was constantly growing within me. I wanted Him to be more tangible, not just by way of signs and visions, but to experience the peace that existed just by reading, discussing and listening to stories about Him. All of this got slowly fulfilled till eventually I knew and was convinced in my heart that for me Baba was God.

A few incidents in my life were responsible for my growth and conviction.

One of my trips to Meherabad with friends culminated with our visit to the Pune Baba Centre where I was strangely drawn to a Baba locket which I purchased instantly knowing full well that I would wear it forever, and that it would be a symbol of Baba's constant companionship through my life.

By this time I had developed a severe pain in my neck which I continued to ignore and went for a holiday with my family. Swimming in the sea and stretching my arms out to ride the waves gave me a shooting pain, and I decided to come out of the water. As usual my hand went up to feel the pendant – it wasn't there! It had fallen off! I was devastated. Knowing how much it meant to me, my little family spent the entire evening trying to find it. We hunted desperately in the sand, in the waves and amongst the pink and white shells, but there was no Baba pendant. I was in tears. I slept fitfully through the night. I kept looking out of the big open window of my room, looking at the dark branches of the huge tree outside, at the sky and the stars, and thinking of Baba. When I awoke the next morning, my eyes immediately went again to the same open window and to the same tree just outside, and to my surprise I saw a clear image of Baba among the branches of the tree. I did not wish to move lest I lose sight of Beloved Baba's image. I was in awe of the fact that He would manifest Himself to me in this way.

We dressed to go out for a morning drive with the children

and made our way to the car which was always parked right under that same big tree just outside my window. In spite of the lovely vision, there was still a certain heaviness in my heart and all through the drive, I was restless and sad. When we returned, we parked the car in the same place again, under that very same tree. I opened the door and as I stepped out, there was my Baba pendant lying upside down in the sand right next to my feet! I couldn't believe it! I picked it up and held it to my heart. Though Baba humoured me by giving me back the pendant, I gathered that I had limited Baba to the locket when, in fact, He is all around me.

By now the pain in my neck was getting worse, making it unbearable most of the times. No one could diagnose the cause of the pain. This made me turn more and more to the only one who could really help me cope up – Baba! Much later, I was diagnosed for compression in the 6th, 7th and 8th vertebrae, and an immediate operation was recommended. Karl's message said, *"Zia, your neck will take long to cure only with healing. An operation will be a much faster way to get better so go ahead, but listen for the voice of Baba when you are put under. He will be by your bedside and cast His light over you. Do not be afraid."* I was more than excited that Baba, Karl and Dr. Lang, the spirit surgeon, were all going to be present by my side. Having resigned to Baba, I was confident of the outcome of the operation. It was a success!

Looking back, being with Meher Baba has been a process of Him growing on me. There have been countless instances, happenings and events in my life where He has established His divinity to me, subtly, and at times, obviously. Words seem inadequate to express the beauty of these experiences. Maybe, the subtlety of the experiences are for me to relish and savour for life.

Karl gifted me Avatar Meher Baba and Beloved Baba has gifted me life – to live it to remember Him, to be resigned to Him, and to please Him. Thank you Baba for this gift!

It was a learning experience for me. Every new person that came along, and every new incident that took place, Baba was driving home a point. In this case, I was astounded that in so short a time Baba had reached out so beautifully to Zia, and that she had responded so readily to His love – I myself had taken so long to get there. Baba had led her to all the vital spots of His existence on earth, and introduced her to many who served Him with love. He had taken her to His Home, His Samadhi, and made her aware of His Majesty. By practical examples, He had made her understand that you do not have to be religious or spiritual to get closer to Him. He had taught her that she should not equate Him with something tangible, that He was as limitless as the ocean, and all rivers were welcome to flow into Him. For the waters to merge there gracefully, all you had to do was just love Him from the heart. These were all lessons for me too, and I began to listen to what He said very carefully indeed.

Very soon, there was a new addition to my Baba family.

It was the 14th of September 1996. The monsoon, with the thunder-clouds and showers of rain, had withdrawn, and the mornings in Pune were beginning to turn crisp and cool. I sat down for my normal communication with Karl. Usually he would begin by giving me some preliminary advice but today, somehow, he got straight to the point: *"Hi Mum, today a small puppy will come to your door, and when he comes, you must not turn him away. He needs you, and in turn will become a good friend to the family. You will find him in the course of the day."*

How very unusual! I prepared to go marketing for the weekly groceries, and after quickly going through the list, I drove to Shivaji Market, the main shopping centre of Pune. I was cruising along on my way home through a one-way street which incidentally goes past Baba House on Dastur Meher Road, when the pathetic figure of a white dog ran in front of my car. Involuntarily I said, "Oh God, poor thing!" The dog was in a pitiable condition. He was practically hairless, full of eczema and flea-bitten. Flies hovered around the innumerable sores and wounds on his poor emaciated body. He was in such a sorry state that he could hardly walk.

Before I could gather my wits around me, I was almost halfway home. As I drove on, I began to wonder if, maybe, this was the dog Karl had talked about this morning. I was feeling really guilty – should I stop and turn back? But then I imagined the horror on my husband Jimmy's face if I had saddled him with a flea-bitten stray dog that was about to drop. I further excused myself by arguing that Karl had mentioned a 'small dog', and this was quite a big one. Although I felt really terrible about not being humane enough to stop and help the poor thing, there was nothing I could do, for by then I had almost reached home. It was too late to go back.

I blurted out the whole story to Jimmy as soon as I got there. "Are you crazy? Do you want to get rabies? You are damn lucky you did not bring the thing here, because do you know what would have happened?" He paused, and then shouted, "Both you and the mongrel would have been out... out!"

October 1. It was Jimmy's birthday. Our daughter Tina rang to say "happy birthday," and after the good wishes she said, "Oh by the way, have you heard the news? Neville has a new puppy." I hardly had time to digest this, when the phone rang again. This time it was our daughter-in-law Sabita to wish Jimmy. After they had spoken, I took the receiver and asked about the new dog. "Oh yes, mummy," she replied, "that is a long story. You see, one afternoon, I was sitting on the steps of my porch waiting for the children to come home from school, and my mind pleasurably drifted to thoughts of Karl. I was also missing Baba very much and feeling a little lost, so I asked Baba for a sign – just something, anything, to show me that He was close to me. The garden gate half-opened, and a small puppy walked in. Although he looked lost, yet he had a kind of ferocious look about him, and so I called the servant to shoo him out.

Ruffles – the puppy who walked into our home and our hearts.

At 4 o'clock, the children, Zahan and Zara, came home from school and following them again, in crept the fluffy, white, little puppy.

"Looking at him closely, he did not really look like a stray, for he was well-brushed and clean, but was so obviously lost and scared and so much in need of love that my heart instantly went out to him. However, the safety of the family came first, and not knowing where he came from I thought it would be better to keep him at a distance till we could be sure. So, we kept a bowl of milk and bread for him in the garden and closed the house door. Guess what, the next morning when we woke up, he was still there. He looked at us longingly, and slowly walked into the house. The children took pity on him and begged to keep him. Now what do you know, he just refuses to leave us and everyone just adores him! Till today he is still with us. He has become one of the family, mummy, and his name is Ruffles."

I listened to the whole story, but it only struck me as incidental after I disconnected the line, so I rang up once more and asked just one question. "Sabita, on which day did this dog come?" And I knew the answer even before she said it, "On September 14!"

But that is not all. A year later, my children came back from Dubai and, of course, Ruffles came along with them. And guess what? He entered my home in Pune on the 14th of September – but just one year later!

And to think that if I had not been aware of how Baba works, I would have surely missed the connection. It only goes to prove that 'Baba signs' do not always come the way you expect them to, that you have to give them a much wider perspective and look much deeper than mere words for the veiled signals therein.

Now Ruff is part of our family and our life. But most surprising of all is the fact that of all people, it is my husband Jimmy who cannot do without him! Also surprising is the fact that he is loved by all except a close follower of Baba, who lives down my road, and is more than terrified of him. Very often Ruff hides in a corner until she comes, and then rushes like a demon at her, till the poor lady freezes by the side of the road, closes her eyes and invoking Baba's protection, just keeps repeating, "Jai Baba – Jai Baba – Jai Baba." Ruff, he just stands there and barks and barks at her. I really do not know if for him it is a game, or maybe he just likes hearing Baba's name?

CHAPTER 3

Pune

Pune was certainly a change from my old life. I was now in a new green city with open spaces, a small market place, and quaint little homes inhabited by quite a different set of people. As compared to this quietude, the hubbub of Mumbai, the traffic, the car horns, the congestion, the milling crowds; it all seemed so far away. Although Pune had its own graceful charm, I missed the familiar smell of seaweed that came in from the sea just below my bedroom window in Mumbai. I missed the sparkle over the waters of the ocean as the sun danced over the swells and ripples that swept the shores near my home. But life carried on.

One day, I was invited to the opening of a new stud farm at Nanoli, near Lonavala. Among the busload that travelled from Pune that day was Leila Captain, a schoolmate I had not seen or associated with for many years. During that two-hour ride, we sat together and caught up with all that had taken place in our lives. She told me all about herself, her hopes and ambitions since the last time I had met her.

Ever since I can remember, it was human suffering that always drew her. All through school her dream was to become a doctor, but although she tried, she did not make it. So, attempting a few other things like joining an airline, and training to be a vet, she finally got married, and in time shifted to Pune. Here she had a chance to do what she always longed to do – spend her time going to hospitals, sitting by the bedsides of those struggling in pain and helping those who had no hope of survival. She just wanted to hold their hands and give them something more than medicine – something from the heart.

I believe that her life went on this way for quite some time and she was happy, but nothing lasts forever. Come 1994, she had grown much older, her back began giving her trouble and so, bedside nursing was no longer possible. Hence her hospital visits became few and far between. By then her husband had passed away, her daughter married, and her son was busy with his own work. Now her life needed some motivation and a new direction. As she talked, I could see that her energies had reached a low level, and she was feeling rather lonely and confused.

Then, in the very next sentence, the conversation seemed to suddenly turn around, the subject changed and out of the blue she quizzed me about *Sounds of Silence*. It took a while for me to explain everything in the rattling bus but I need not have worried. It turned out that auto writing was not something new to her, for she had heard about it from her mother. But something new and wonderful did happen.

This is the first time she heard about Meher Baba and, as always, His timing was perfect.

After our talk in the bus that day, Leila suddenly began to take a great interest in Baba. Reading *Sounds of Silence* further activated her. As always, she so readily came forward to help. She took it upon herself to keep in touch with me. She helped me to organise the many trips we made to Meherabad, to make newcomers comfortable, and to feel Baba's Love. For her it was a change in lifestyle and she began to love it almost as much as I did.

This went on smoothly for a while till one day, in December 1997, I left with Jimmy for my usual three-month stay in Mumbai for the racing season. I picked up the phone and said, "Leila, I am leaving. I have with me a few ladies who are new to Baba and need some help and guidance, so I am leaving them for you to look after. They are now 'your guys'." And, I left.

From that moment on, everything miraculously changed for her. Baba so cleverly changed her lifestyle from helping the ill and the dying, to helping the living to live again. Instead of sitting by the bedside of those about to die, she began helping living human beings to deal with their lives on earth. They all became her friends. Her loneliness vanished overnight and she went back to being the Leila I remember – a strong, wonderful organiser, not ready to tolerate any nonsense, and yet the most kind and compassionate person I have known. I tell you all this because till today Leila always stands by my side, and is a constant source of support to me.

What happened next? Carrying a handful of my books that had just been published, Leila took it upon herself to help in the distribution in Pune. Since the Blue Diamond Hotel bookshop was closest to her home, her first step was to leave some of the copies there for sale. A few days later, as we walked in to conclude a few sales details, we were confronted by two beautiful eyes, a striking young face, and a hushed voice that said, "Are you Nan Umrigar? Oh my goodness, I cannot believe that you have actually walked in through this door. I have waited so long to meet you. Do you have a few minutes to spare?"

Her name was Scherry Commisariat and what followed was a story that took my breath away!

For Scherry, it all began way back in the 70s when Karl was a known jockey and she a teenager with a crush on him; very ordinary and very natural as in the teen years with every girl and boy. She had never met Karl personally, yet always felt like she knew him. Although she was never an ardent race-goer, she yearned to meet him some day. But that was not meant to be, for one morning, newspapers flashed the crushing news of Karl Umrigar's tragic accident and death, and her dream came to a rude end. 'This is it', she thought, 'I'm never going to meet him now'.

In 1996, about six months before my book *Sounds of Silence* was published, she had a dream that had a great impact on her. She dreamt that she was woken up from her sleep by her grandmother (who had passed on many years ago), and was taken to another dimension where she found herself in a big hall where there were many happy-looking spirits having a great party. She looked around and suddenly came face to face with a young man who stood before her with folded hands and a mischievous smile on his lips. She stared at him, trying to recall if she had met him before, when he asked, "So, don't you recognise me?" She clapped her hand to her forehead and exclaimed ecstatically, "Karl! I forgot you were here!" They embraced like old friends and she instinctively knew that this is what she had waited for all those years. Needless to mention, she refused to leave his side and begged to stay with him as long as she could. "No," he said, "You must go back now and when your time comes, I'll come for you. But you must go back now." She woke up with a start, her mind racing with bewildered feelings. She relived the dream whilst talking to her husband who recognised that something significant had happened to her that night.

Talking about coincidences, sometime later, a friend lent her a copy of *Sounds of Silence*. The moment she saw the cover, she reacted with shock! This was the same face that she had seen in her dream!

As fate would have it, she met Leila Captain soon after and struck a bond that became a beautiful and loving friendship that still exists today.

After her chance meeting with me at the bookshop, she told me more about the difficulties of her present life and received a lot of heart-warming messages from Karl. That led to many beautiful visits to Meherabad and she felt as if her life had begun to have some kind of meaning. But it did not last long. She faced many personal crises and found herself contemplating her plight and her future with a heavy heart. That was the day she saw a vision of Meher Baba at the foot of her bed. Dressed in a long, white, robe-like garment, Baba smiled at her compassionately and said (in Gujarati), "Take My hand in yours, My daughter, and I will take care of all your worries. All will soon be well." She felt so overwhelmed by His love and compassion and by His appearance, that she became a follower overnight. She knew that she had found the love and the light she was looking for. It was Baba.

In 1999, she lost her husband suddenly and tragically, and found herself in a state of shock. There were days of deep despair but her faith in Baba helped her to recover quickly. Meher Baba looked after her and her children in ways only He can. Connecting with Him internally, and trying her best to love Him unconditionally, helped her make the right decisions and choices and kept her focused towards the higher path, proving to her that faith and trust never go unrewarded. Baba showed her that love is the greatest healer, in any situation.

As of now, Scherry's life has changed radically and she has moved on. She says, "Though life has its difficult course of ups and downs and brings with it its hurdles and rewards, my deep love and absolute faith in Baba has brought me a new experience of peace, tranquillity, joy and gratitude. Today I have become older and much more has happened in my life. Baba has helped my horizons to expand, and now I have become a grateful instrument for bringing clarity into the lives of others. I am now able to see the world with very different eyes and hold a finer understanding about life's truths. Meher Baba has been for me a most wise, loving and compassionate teacher, guide, Master and, above all, a friend. Baba is and always will be there for me."

This was how my life in Pune took shape. After Scherry, there came Jayaa Shetty and then Raju Chaudhry. I mention these names because Leila soon became their 'mother figure', and all of them became my staunch Baba support group in Pune. It is over ten years now and we still remain steadfast in our love for each other and for Baba. From then onward it snowballed – a friend brought a friend, and then another and so on. Baba reached out to the multitude and many started making their way to Meherabad. Surprisingly, I even came across some who had lived their lives in Pune and till now were not even aware that Baba was actually born here or that His home still existed. Suddenly, Baba took on a new significance for them. The Baba Centre at Rasta Peth in Pune grew in stature, and became the visiting place for so many more.

But as always, Baba was the 'Silent Master' and took His time to awaken Himself in all hearts.

CHAPTER 4

Piloting the Uncertainties of Life

Although we now had our home in Pune, horses and racing continued to be a draw for Jimmy and me, and the racecourse at Mahalaxmi, Mumbai, had its own special charm. We could not stay away from it for long. So, we decided to spend the few months of the Mumbai racing season at a club there.

Baba continued to hold my close Baba-circle together and hardly a day passed when my friends – Amie, Freny, Kamlu, Jenny, Sushilla and I would not call each other and share everything with one another. In this way we managed to meet up with all the demands of people who, after reading the book, wanted to know more and more about Baba. And there were so many.

Sounds of Silence became a signpost: 'This way to Meher Baba'.

More and more people read that signpost. More and more people began to discover for themselves how Baba loves, how hard He works to draw everyone closer to Him, and just what it means to have Him in one's life.

There are scores of stories that crowd my mind, each testifying to Baba's all pervasive love and reach. It is impossible to put them all down in this book so I will keep them for another day.

Here is one story from two Mumbai friends that may touch your heart. Adil Gandhy tells you all about his introduction to Baba and what happened thereafter.

Nan gave her book *Sounds of Silence* to me on the very first day it was published in December 1996. I read the first half of it pretty soon as it concerned Karl who had been a dear friend all through his childhood, and also because it connected with everything and everyone I knew. However, when the book began going into details regarding Meher Baba, a man who claimed to be God, I was astounded by the fact that not only did He once exist amongst us but that I had not heard of Him before. Amazing! I closed the book and never opened it again until much later.

In October 1997, one of my dear old friends, Zaraius Dastur, a senior pilot with a well-known airline, became the victim of circumstances and cruel fate found this innocent man being prosecuted and ultimately put behind bars.

Deeply saddened, I attended every court hearing just so that I could demonstrate my support for him, and also with the prayer that by some miracle he would be released, if not completely, at least on bail.

It was during one of these times that I noticed a sudden change in my poor, innocent, imprisoned friend. In spite of him being in such an unfortunate situation, he was piously calm and serene. He did not have the hatred, bitterness and fatalistic uncertainty he had begun with at the time of his arrest. All he would do during our brief meetings in court is talk about a Meher Baba! How had he come to this point, I wondered?

He had been given *Sounds of Silence* by a dear common friend, Anita Lawyer, while he was in jail. Many other kind friends had come forward with help in the form of other books, prayers and so on, but in his bitterness he had rejected and turned away from everything, refusing to even look at them. However, seeing the face of Karl on the cover, he remembered an old childhood association with the Umrigar family who had at one time lived in the very same building as him. So, with little else to do, he just picked up the book as a matter of interest. Soon, he found himself completely absorbed in the pages. Zaraius read chapter after chapter and in the process felt himself drawn very strongly to this *Guru* – this Meher Baba that Karl talked so lovingly about. He began to love His face, His strength, and His beauty.

To add to this, another very strange incident took place. The man who created the circumstances around which Zaraius was arrested, happened to be lodged in the very same cell. Coincidently, his daughter, an ardent Baba follower, gave her father a book entitled *Discourses* by Meher Baba, hoping that it would help him. He didn't want to read the same and threw it to Zaraius saying, "I don't believe in Babas... you may read it if you wish."

For Zaraius, this book became his gospel and changed the course of his life. He read about the beginning and end of creation, the formation and function of *sanskaras*. He thought about everything Baba said about good and evil, and the nature of the ego. But above all, he began to meditate on Baba and search for answers from within. Having all the time in the world at his disposal, he became absorbed in Baba, studied the 'Seven Realities' in real earnest, struggled hard to understand it all and to implement it in his own life.

The Seven Realities by Meher Baba

1. The only Real Existence is that of the One and only God, who is the Self in every finite self.
2. The only Real Love is the love for this Infinity (God), which arouses an intense longing to see, know and become one with its Truth (God).
3. The only Real Sacrifice is that in which, in pursuance of this love, all things, body, mind, position, welfare and even life itself, are sacrificed.
4. The only Real Renunciation is that which abandons, even in the midst of worldly duties, all selfish thoughts and desires.
5. The only Real Knowledge is the knowledge that God is the inner dweller in good people and in so-called bad, in saint and in so-called sinner. This knowledge requires you to help all equally as circumstances demand, without expectation of reward; and when compelled to take part in a dispute, to act without the slightest trace of enmity or hatred; to try to make others happy, with brotherly or sisterly feeling for each one; and to harm no one in thought, word or deed, not even those who harm you.
6. The only Real Control is the discipline of the senses to abstain from indulgence in low desires, which alone ensures absolute purity of character.
7. The only Real Surrender is that in which poise is undisturbed by any adverse circumstances; and the individual, amidst every kind of hardship, is resigned with perfect calm to the will of God.[1]

Whenever the prisoners had time for a breather or for a spot of exercise in the courtyard, Zaraius took his books and his learning and shared his newfound wisdom with others, hoping to also give them the benefit of his knowledge, sharing with them little pieces of Baba's loving heart. In the process, he himself learned many things. He learned to tolerate his enemy, how to deal with the fear, the terror and the atrocities of being in jail. Although there was not much hope of release, for dealing in drugs is known to be a non-bailable offence, in spite of that he learned how to face the thought of getting through each day with a positive attitude. He devised a set of thumb rules, some for spiritual growth, others for interaction with his fellow human beings, but all centred on one simple concept – Love.

He found time to send loving messages to his lovely young wife and three children, and to assure his old parents that everything would soon be alright. In fact, he began to try his best to see the brighter side, having faith that Baba would help right to prevail over wrong. Of course there were times when he despaired over any hope of freedom but those times were rare and, by and large, with Baba by his side, he began to handle himself with courage and fortitude. At the end of it all, he even found in his heart to feel forgiveness for the one who had caused all this upheaval in his life.

On the 12th of January 1998, Zaraius's daughter Sharmaine went to Meherabad on *dhuni* day to beg Baba to 'hurry and have her beloved father released'. It was a very moving moment for many there.

A few days later, the prisoners were ordered to clean up their cells. Zaraius, armed with sponge, soapsuds and water, prepared to scrub the walls of his room. As he lifted his hand to the wall, he fell back in surprise – he could not believe what he saw! There were three faces on the wall. A beautiful likeness of Jesus, one of Mother Teresa and the third was… Meher Baba! His cellmates also saw these images. Some of them bowed down in wonder while others fled in terror. This vision was the beginning of many such instances in Zaraius's life, so much so that he no longer attributed them to coincidence.

Although there were many harrowing days that followed, what with the frequent hearings and visits to the courthouse, Zaraius focused on the visions and the regular encouraging messages from Karl, *"Baba is with you – Baba loves you – Baba will always do what is best for you"* and so on. This kept him strong in his faith and trust.

It was March 1998, almost five months after my pilot friend's arrest. Anita offered to take me to Meherabad. Since so much had already happened to impress Zaraius, and he had been so incessantly talking about it, I felt encouraged to see what this place had to offer and what this so-called God was all about! So we made a day trip to the *ashram* and arrived just in time for the morning *aarti,* which is at 7 am. I must admit that I found it to be a lovely, calm and peaceful place, which certainly gave me very positive vibes but nothing more… at the time.

It was on that day that I knelt down at Baba's Samadhi and said, "If You are such a great Man or God, as many say, then please help free my friend from this unfortunate predicament, or at least help to release him on bail. And if You do, then I promise to come back with him to personally acknowledge and thank You."

Four months later, after over ten long and seemingly endless months of imprisonment, the day of the High Court bail appeal finally came up for hearing. Karl's message to Zariaus's daughter said, *"The man responsible for putting him in will be responsible for getting him out."*

We waited with bated breath. The man who was responsible for Zaraius's predicament walked in and made a judicial confession of his guilt. Zaraius was given the benefit of doubt and, if I am not mistaken, it was the first time that a person indicted for a supposed drug-related offence was granted bail by the authorities.

I then thought to myself, 'This Baba has really been doing His work and fulfilled His promise, and it is now time that I fulfilled mine.'

So, it was a couple of weeks later that Anita, Zaraius and I went to visit Meherabad. It was the Captain's very first visit and naturally his excitement was palpable. He could hardly believe he was on his way to a place he had read and dreamt so much about while in captivity, and that he was actually going to bow down to the One whom he now loved and believed in so deeply.

As for me, that weekend at Meherabad became probably the worst period I went through in my life. A few days before the trip, my own world fell apart. I was confronted with the news that my wife wanted to leave me after twenty-five years of marriage. It was with this terrible knowledge and ache in my heart that I now had to visit Baba with my friends as promised.

But strange to say, once I reached there, my resentment dissipated. I thought about my friend, about his terrible predicament and of how Baba had helped him with His love. I thought about how sometimes there seems a point of no return, but of how Baba always finds a way out for you if you really love Him. I began coming close to Baba with all that had happened. In my deep pain and sorrow, I truly opened my heart and let Him in. I knelt at His Samadhi and asked Him to help and guide me to do the right thing.

It was there, when I was sitting at the Samadhi one morning, that I got an intuitive message from Baba through Karl saying, "Do not try to fight, take revenge, or to keep your wife back. Allow her to go peacefully."

I sat quietly allowing the choice to seep through every cell of my body. There seemed to be no struggle or resistance, but in its place, from deep within me, I felt a sense of great power and freedom.

After that, I visited Meherabad very often for a while, for I knew I was drawing spiritual strength from Baba who was helping me in every way to cope with my loss, and in the process getting to love Him more and more.

There was a period around that time when I also wanted desperately to see some proof of His presence, just like Zaraius had and many others too. I kept asking Baba to somehow show or manifest Himself to me in any which way.

It was on the 25th of February 1999, Baba's birthday, that my wish to see Baba was finally granted. Lo and behold, I suddenly discovered a gorgeous three-part face of Beloved Meher Baba in a pensive, meditative posture with one eye closed, exactly on the wall in my bathroom! There was no mistaking this – the same identical, longish nose with the pointed centre and the thick moustache. Oh, there was absolutely no doubt! My exhilaration and my joy were indescribable.

It has been many years now since Baba first entered my life.

The picture of His image (albeit now fading) remains on my wall and I am very much at peace with myself and with life in general. I know that the lesson I have learned is that everyone's life has to have its share of ups and downs but, in my experience, Baba helps us to grow mentally, spiritually and emotionally to eventually become stronger and better.

As it stands today, Zaraius's case is yet not over but he loves Baba regardless. He is still out on bail living quietly with his family. He still visits Meherabad and the Samadhi as often as he can and when asked why, he says, "I pay homage to Baba at the Samadhi every moment I have to spare for I still have something more to learn. Besides, I may have to go back in again."

My dear friend has taught me an important lesson – to love Baba without any expectations and to continue to love Him from the heart, and to believe that 'whatever my Master does is of the highest benefit to all concerned' – (Hafiz). Jai Baba!

CHAPTER 5

I Am Here

"I am never silent. I speak eternally. The voice that is heard deep within the soul is my voice ... The voice of inspiration, of intuition, of guidance. To those who are receptive to this voice I speak."[1]

Heavenly messages do not always come in Godly ways and are not always delivered by angels. A meadowlark can sing, so you can listen. Thunder may roll, so you can hear. A star may shine brightly, so you can see. A life can be born, so you can notice. God can reach down and touch you, so you should not brush the butterfly away. He talks to us all the time. The question is not how or to whom He talks, but who listens.

So the message really is, "Do not miss out on God's blessings just because they are not packaged the way you expect."

God communicates to us in different ways – through feelings, through thoughts, through experiences, through images and pictures. God awakens us through love. Some may see Him in significant dreams and visions; some may even feel an actual presence or feel an overwhelming sense of love. He also reaches out to us very often through signs. Words are not really necessary. He responds to us in direct proportion to our ability to comprehend and in a language that He knows we will understand. Things suddenly fall into place, extraordinary coincidences, signs that have no rational explanation. Words uttered by a friend, a write-up in a magazine, or a telephone conversation that comes out of the blue.

I have seen that Baba uses small, simple things and very casual moments to reveal Himself to man. He can meet us in the most common ways – if we have but eyes to see and ears to hear.

He uses no great sign, nothing spectacular in the seemingly incidental, along-the-road-of-life meetings which He orchestrates. There are "no miles to walk, no long journey to travel, no strange language to learn, no state of ecstasy to be experienced. Just meetings by the wayside."

I don't really remember the day, but I know that it was sometime in the September of 1996 that Don Stevens came into my life. You might well ask, "Who is Don Stevens?"

He is a retired international oil executive who has been a life-long spiritual seeker. Don became a member of the *Sufi Movement* in the USA, in 1943. It is this that brought him under the guidance of Meher Baba. At present he lives in Paris, France, and is one of the few westerners alive today who had close and frequent access to Baba. He now devotes his full time in writing about Merwan Sheriar Irani, later known as Meher Baba. He arranges translations of Baba's writings and works closely with several Meher Baba groups in Europe, the United Kingdom and India. He is best known as the co-editor of Baba's book *God Speaks*.

I cannot recall what prompted the meeting with him and his books committee at the Sun-n-Sand Hotel in Mumbai. I cannot remember whether I called him or he called me. I only remember that I was not only nervous, but absolutely in awe of having an opportunity to meet up with such an august personality. I needed a great deal of courage to sit there and discuss the then almost completed manuscript of *Sounds of Silence* with a literary genius. For sheer support, I took along my friends Amie Rabadi and Freny Pedder. What would he think of us? Would he dismiss the book as ridiculous? Would he think that our way of coming to Baba was a figment of the imagination? What would be his reaction?

But I needn't have worried. His initial loving 'Baba Hugs' and his friendly and gentle ways, endeared him to us immediately. To add to this, his slow, deliberate manner of speaking and his precise way of thinking deeply before answering any questions, put to rest whatever doubts we had as to how we would relate with him.

He took my manuscript to France from where I was delighted to get a lengthy phone call from him. In response I could only stammer the words "thank you, thank you, thank you for your loving response and positive reaction to my book."

Since that day he has been a dear friend to all of us. He is always ready to give us the benefit of his knowledge, to lend a helping hand. He makes it a point to be present on almost every important occasion connected with Baba that we organise.

He is now over ninety-one years of age but as active as ever, and his devotion to Baba is absolute. That is the most touching and endearing part of him.

It is on the occasion of one of his recent visits to India to promote translations of Baba's major works such as *God Speaks* and *Discourses* into Hindi, Marathi, Gujarati and Telugu, that I had the privilege of meeting up with him once again. It is at this time that he presented me with his new publication *Meher Baba – The Awakener of the Age.* I read through it slowly, savouring all the personal touches of Don's long association with Baba and in the process came upon a chapter entitled 'The Avatar' that almost made me cry.

In this chapter, Don tells us about a typical day spent in Meherazad with Baba, and a little about his own close relationship with Him from 1952 to 1968.

Don says: A relationship with Baba was always intensely personal. You felt that you were the centre of the universe. In fact you were. Baba never put on. You were unique and there was never anything to suggest that you were anything other than the most important thing before Baba. This was not good *avataric* relations. It was Reality.

... Somewhere around 9:30 we were all assembled in Mandali Hall. Then Baba would arrive. More often than not, the first order of business was an inevitable sequence of questions: 'Don, how did you sleep last night?' 'How is your digestion?' The proper care of the body was always a matter of great concern for Baba. Baba also had a way of spotting an old friend and seeing that all was not completely right, "You look pulled down," Baba would gesture.

... Perhaps one thinks that living with a great Master is necessarily filled with inspiring dissertations on the nature of God, and the practices necessary to win through to His presence. This was not the usual diet with Baba. On occasion, He would bring up a fascinating point in the spiritual realm but it was not the usual topic.

... Quite often there were amusing diversions such as playing the game of seven tiles or occasionally a special game of cards. (He mostly won.) Baba had a fantastic sense of humour, and whenever things got tense, almost always Baba found an amusing point, which relieved the tension.

... As the clock on the wall opposite Baba began moving towards 5 pm, we could not keep our eyes off it as sometime about now, Baba would announce His intention of leaving for the day. And by 5.30 pm it was almost always time for Him to start moving towards the double-door facing Mehera's garden and the house where He spent the night. Baba would then move towards the porch of His home mostly on the arm of one of His followers.

... Once, in later years during a visit, He asked me to take His arm. At the steps, one of the women was there to take Him inside the house for the night. On this occasion, as I turned to go back, I heard His clap and turned at once to see that He wanted me to return for an embrace. I felt the warmth of His arms about me and then it was evident that I should leave. I started back but the *mandali* in front of me called out that Baba wanted me to return again. I walked back and He enfolded me again tenderly in an embrace and kissed me on the side of the cheek. I turned once more and made my way, almost in tears, to Mandali Hall. But still again He clapped, and wonder of wonders, again He embraced me even more tenderly. It was the last time I saw the form of Meher Baba inhabited by His soul.

Here I must mention, once more, the suffering of these last years of Baba's life in physical form. During the final days, at the slightest movement, great jerks would rack His physical frame, which He would describe as His 'crucifixion'. In one of His final spasms, Baba managed with great effort to show by signs to Eruch, His close disciple, "But I will come back." It was Baba's last message to him and to the physical world.[2]

Don Stevens was in London on the 31st of January 1969, when the telephone call came. All he heard in the beginning were noises that sounded like someone choking. "Who is it? What is wrong?" he asked. The choking and gasping continued till finally he made out the words, "He's gone. He's left. Baba has dropped His body."

Don was thunderstruck! Baba, whom he had known and loved

for twenty-six years, had dropped His body. It simply could not be. When it all actually sank in, all he could think about was that he wanted to rush to India to see the form of his Beloved Baba one last time. He just had to get there. But how? Americans had to have a visa for entry to India and it was a procedure that took a few days, to say the least. However, he resolved to give it a try. So, he set off to the High Commission office. No luck – everyone was away for the weekend and unavailable. He was sick at heart. A friend advised him to try the Air India office at Bond Street and that is where he went. Intuition led him to a desk placed at one side of the room. Sitting down, he noticed a small nameplate – Miss Irani.

To find someone there with the same family name as Baba's was quite a shock for Don.

When Baba's name, Don's destination and the urgent situation were explained to her, Miss Irani promised that she would treat this as an emergency and try her best to get him there on time.

She immediately drafted a telex appeal to be sent on priority basis asking for humanitarian special permission for Don to land at Bombay airport. She assured Don that with some luck he could expect a reply in time for him to catch the 3 pm Air India flight to Bombay en route to Pune. So, with his heart in his mouth and trembling hands, Don called again at 1 pm. To his delight the order had just come in and his eyes filled with tears of relief and joy.

Through passport control and a few moments of waiting in the lounge, Don was on his assigned seat in a half-empty plane and skimming through the blue sky towards Baba. Some time later, the loudspeaker system came on and a pleasant voice said, "Sorry for the delay, ladies and gentlemen, in welcoming you aboard. This is Captain Irani, your pilot. We are now flying over Geneva." His voice was drowned out by Don's heartbeats as once more he was caught up in a great wave of bemusement. Another Irani! Two people important to his mission, and both named Irani! He burst out laughing.

"It's okay Baba, I get the message," he said, and knew for sure that he had not been cut off from his companion and Master at all; that Baba was actively present now more than ever before.

As the passengers deplaned for refuelling in Delhi, he read in a Delhi edition of The Indian Express that Sarosh Irani, a trusted Baba disciple, had made the decision to postpone the internment until Sunday, 2nd February 1969, to allow for those coming from abroad.

Incredible! What luck!

Then he was standing in one of two check-in lines where each person had to call out their names for a flight manifest check. As Don's turn came and he was about to give his name, he happened to overhear the young man in the line at his side call out his name. Also a Mr. Irani!

At last Pune, then on to Ahmednagar, up Meherabad Hill, then to the Samadhi, and on to Baba. For Don, the journey was over. He walked slowly to the familiar tomb. He had come in time.

One would think that here Don's story would be complete, but it was not. A while later as he stood in contemplation with his eyes closed, he sensed someone by his side. There was a tall, elderly, gentle-faced man whom he could not recognise, but who reminded him that Baba had introduced them some years ago. And when he knew that Don had just flown in from London, he said, "Then you must have had my son as your pilot, Captain Irani."

I would like you to know here, that on inquiry some months later, it was found that at that time there was just one London staff member in Air India with the family name Irani, and just one pilot, too.

Don had been given both of them on the same day!

Don concludes his story by saying, "There is no way to describe the grace and exquisite thoughtfulness of a Perfect Being. It surrounds one with a total, encompassing knowledge of love and security. To find this confirmed so completely and with such humour in its elegant expression, was entirely unexpected. I knew, and I was deeply touched."

Do you know why, reading about all this in Don's book almost made me cry? It was because I realised with a shocking certainty that what Baba did from the very moment that He dropped His body, He is still doing even now. That the little signs that so many of us had experienced then and since were not just imagination or wishful thinking, nor was it the subconscious mind playing games. It was just Baba's way of showing His love and that is the reason why I want to share them with you.

Baba and Don Stevens, with Eruch in the background.

The incident with Don Stevens described to you was way back in 1969. Now we move forward to the year 2001.

Lively, vivacious and charming, Anita Roy read *Sounds of Silence* and could not contain herself. She was so taken up with the contents that she called me for an appointment. We spoke about Meher Baba at great length. Who was Meher Baba? Why was He not so well known? Where was His Samadhi? But in spite of all that I had to say to her, I guess she needed some answers of her own.

She went to Meherabad and that is how her life changed.

Anita continues: I got married on the 29th of December 2000 and before I knew it, I was on an Air India flight from Bombay to London on the 15th of January 2001. I said my goodbyes and settled myself in my seat but it all hit me just as the flight was about to take off, and I began to sob. I thought of all my memories in Bombay as a child and those growing-up years. I thought of all my family, my friends and loved ones that I was leaving behind, and I could not but help wondering what my new life had in store for me – would my life ever be the same. If not, would I be able to cope with the new one, and how? I did the only thing that I know to do in situations like that.

I closed my eyes and began praying to Baba. As I prayed, a terrible thought struck me – what if Baba was with me in Bombay and what if He didn't continue to be my constant companion in London? How would I survive? I began to weep furiously. I said to Baba, "Please, please give me some sign that You are coming with me to London... give me a sign now!" Then again, pleased with my question, thinking to myself that how will Baba ever give me such a sign on an aircraft that is about to take off, I wiped away my tears.

But even before I could finish thinking that, the voice over the flight's PA system said, "Good morning, ladies and gentlemen, this is your Captain Zaraius Dastur. Welcome aboard." I was stunned and shocked. Just a name, but I didn't need anything more for I knew that those few words were meant just for me. My heart jumped and skipped a beat. The sign Baba gave me was so absolutely perfect, for Zaraius is an ardent Baba follower, whose own story of how he came to Baba is so powerful and mind-blowing that I could hardly believe that he was actually my flight Captain, taking me on my journey from Bombay to London. I wrote a note to him and sent it along with the airhostess. He actually came out to meet me, and we talked for a while about Baba and some of the wonderful experiences, signs and messages that we had received from Him.

I forgot everything, my tears and my diffidence, and knew that Baba had done this for me to be constantly aware and assured that He is indeed with us every minute, even if we are not consciously aware of it.

I arrived in London to live there without knowing anybody; no family, no friends, nobody except a new husband and one of England's coldest winters to keep me company! I called Nan in desperation. "Hold on to Baba," she said, and gave me the name of Susan Biddu who was in charge of the London Baba Centre. She advised me to contact her so that she could guide me to the London Centre. I found my way there only to see not a single familiar face. In my first week in London, I had already got to the stage of hating every moment and now to top it all, I was standing in front of a room full of people I did not even know.

It was the 31st of January 2001, *Amartithi* day – the anniversary of the day Baba 'dropped His body', and the Centre was full of Baba lovers who had all come to pay their respects. I took a seat in a corner wondering if anyone would notice me except maybe Baba, and the programme started. I was praying hard to Baba to send me a message to prove to me that He was there amongst us on that day. I even said to Him threateningly, 'I will never come to this Centre again if You do not let me know that You are here.'

Just then, a box containing Baba sayings was being taken around. Each person was asked to pick one and then read it out aloud. The box came around and I picked one. Until now, Baba had never failed to answer my call so I did not know if I could say that I was shocked or just surprised, but I was both surprised and shocked! My slip read, "I am here, I am here, I tell you – I AM HERE!"

CHAPTER 6

Other Loving Signs

Baba's signs continue. The wonder of most, and the sheer audacity of some, often leave one gasping for breath, making me wonder how Baba has time to think of so many beautiful ways to reach the heart.

Raynah Tayabali was looking for answers about her mother, about the life beyond. Her mother had passed on when she was very young. She had no recollection of her but felt her loss keenly throughout her life. Her search led her to me. She wrote to me hoping to receive a message from her mother through Karl. Her mother did have a message for her.

While I waited for Nan to send me a message from my mother through Karl, I was having second thoughts. How can this be real? Me, getting a message from my mother? How will I know if it is truly my mother? I may get a beautiful message, but what good will it do me if I can't be sure it is her?

So, I prayed earnestly. "Mummy, please give me a clear sign" I said, "give me proof that it is you."

Finally, the letter came. I opened it with trembling hands and when I finished reading it, I wept with joy. It was the most beautiful message I had ever received from anyone in my life. It spoke of our deep connection with each other, of an undying love that transcends life on earth, of me finding her henceforth in Baba and in His love. Towards the end, Karl added, *"She wishes to make no demands on her daughter – just a ray of sunshine sent to bring her, her mother's love."*

I knew without a doubt that the message was for real. I had got my sign. The sign had to do with my name. My name is Raynah. In my christening certificate it is Ray(Nah). This had always puzzled me. I was told that I was called Raynah Elizabeth because I shared a birthday with the Queen of England, and 'Raynah' is an anglicised version of the Portuguese word for queen. I remembered that about four years ago, a cousin visiting me from abroad had casually mentioned the fact that my mother wanted very much to call me 'Ray', and that while she was expecting me she often used to say, "If I have a girl, I shall call her Ray. She will be my ray of sunshine." I remembered also that at a party, just a few months before I got my message, someone happened to be singing the old song 'You are my sunshine' and an aunt had said to me later, "By the way, that was your mother's favourite lullaby and she used to always sing it to you kids."

I could not have got a more beautiful sign. Nan was, of course, quite unaware of the significance of 'Ray'. In fact we had not met at all. While some may say that this was sheer coincidence, I know in my heart that I had been given the sign I had asked from my mother.

Thus began my journey on the path of love and surrender. I went to Meherabad quite often after that and spent many hours in the little cabin at the side of the Samadhi – I love that cabin. I spend a lot of time sitting there on the floor and just being with Baba. The energy I receive there is awesome. I feel as if I have just plunged into an Ocean of Love.

I sense myself, in this cabin, in the very depths of my being, one with love and from there I am learning to look at my life in all its aspects. I see my actions, my emotions, my thoughts, my faults, everything, and I let them happen, and when I remember, I bring them all to Meher Baba. This 'letting them happen' is a wonderful experience. I feel so much more at peace, I sink more and more into the awareness that He takes care of everything and only Baba matters. I am discovering more and more, in depth, the meaning of the words 'Don't Worry, Be Happy'. The more I surrender, the more I experience this.

For me, the sign from my mother has truly been a gift and sometimes I can hardly believe how my life has changed since I turned to Baba in faith, and acknowledged Him as God.

Gita Budhiraja received a message, through Karl, from her son Amit one day: 'Mum, look for the butterfly – the butterfly is me.' As always, after you receive a message like this, imagination tends to take over. So when she called me hysterically from her home in Delhi to tell me that an army of butterflies suddenly surrounded her, I decided to be happy for her and help to hold on to her sanity. It could well be that the butterflies had always been there and that she began noticing them for the first time. But strangely enough, from what she described, wherever she went, and whatever she did, she suddenly found butterflies flying straight into her, sitting on her fingers, on the icing of her cake, or just flitting in the corner of her room. She was totally dazed. Could this really be Amit following her around? She thought that it was too good to be true. "It was on my birthday," she says, "that I asked Amit to show himself to me. I had just returned home in the evening when my daughter Anjali asked me to come quickly into the room. As we enter the hall, on the wall there is a lovely picture of Amit. There on the photo, sitting on his forehead was a tiny black and yellow butterfly – a real, live butterfly! It stayed there for a while and then what do you think – it flew into my purse!"

Karl tells us that *"Butterflies are God's creatures and it is possible for us to make our presence felt through these gentle souls. We find it easy to relate with them because they have an extra-sensory ability which transcends human emotions and desires. We can get them to obey our silent wishes. So whenever you do have a relationship with one, you will know that you are now in the aura of Baba and it is Baba who finds ways and means to get through to you. He wishes you to be aware of it. So just go with the feelings you get and I am sure you will begin to feel an inner happiness with any experience you have with the butterflies."*

What about the time when Kim Verma asked Baba for a sign that He was listening to her? She looked over at His book *God Speaks* which always lies side by side with *Sounds of Silence* on her bedside table, and then suddenly had an overwhelming urge to turn up the volume of her TV set which was on mute. On TV was a live performance of an old Simon and Garfunkel song, one that she loved and remembered. She tried hard to understand what the song was trying to tell her till she realised that Karl' s book and the song were both called *Sounds of Silence*!

Salome Roy Kapur, I remember as a pretty little girl who danced professionally with her brother Edwin at receptions and wedding parties. She caught my eye not only because she was so small, but because she was as graceful then as she is now. Much time has passed since then, time in which Baba has reached out to her through the pages of a book to show her His love.

Salome says: One lovely morning, in the year 2000, I was singing *Begin the Beguine*, Baba's favourite song, thinking deeply about Meher Baba and how wonderful it would be if I could somehow, anyhow, go to His Samadhi in Meherabad.

It was uncanny the way it all happened. It was as if Baba actually heard my thoughts and wishes, for at that very moment my friend Ranjana phoned to tell me that she had included my name to go with them to Ahmednagar to the Samadhi, and that too, actually accompanied by Nan herself. It was too good to be true. Without thinking, I said "Oh yes!"

I have to tell you that obstacles did come up and I did have second thoughts, but I desperately needed to go and repeatedly told Baba, 'please, please make it possible'. As the day approached, everything just seemed to fall into place and I was on my way.

It is important for you to know that six years earlier I had a dream. In that dream there was a man dressed in white, surrounded by fleecy blue-white clouds, handing me a sickle-shaped peacock feather. He told me that what He was giving me was very important and that I should always keep it with me. This dream and the gorgeous peacock feather had always lived with me for many years but, strange to say, it was farthest from my thoughts till I entered the Samadhi to take Baba's *darshan*.

I was the last as we all waited in line after evening aarti. As I stepped into the Samadhi, my eyes fell on the painting of Baba in the tomb area. He was all in white, surrounded by fleecy white clouds and waiting as if to welcome me. A certain familiarity in the aura struck me very forcibly and I was impressed to ask Him just one question: 'Baba, if it was You that came to me in my dream six years ago, please show me now that it was You. Show me the sign of a peacock, in some way.'

I was the last to come out of the Samadhi and join the group as they stood just outside near Mehera's tomb. Nan was just explaining to everyone all that she knew – what was what and who was who. I arrived just in time to hear her say, "This is the resting place of the personal effects of Baba's mother and father and of some of His close followers. These are the little tombs of Baba's favourite dogs, and also of His peacock!"

My hand flew to my heart as it began to thud violently. "What did you just say, Nan?" I asked in awed tones. It did not take them long to realise that something really momentous had taken place. I was as white as a sheet as they helped me to the bench, where it took me a while to settle and explain to them what had just occurred.

Much later, I made my way to 'Moti' – the peacock's grave. I sat there a long while in silence and gave my thanks to Baba: Dear Baba, this was more than just an exhilarating experience for me which will be printed in my mind forever. I am so grateful to You for having made all this possible, for I know this is only the start of much, much more.

After reading this chapter, you may think that Baba spends His time just in giving signs to all those that come to Him. But signs are not always everything. They are just one of the many loving ways He finds to make us take our first steps on the path. While some travellers come to Baba and Meherabad looking for answers, there are also some who come with no clue of what to expect and go back home finding a love and contentment unparalleled to anything they have ever known or felt before.

Rishi Vohra was one of them. Before leaving, he was in a confused and disturbed state of mind due to the current state of affairs in his personal life. He really came without much expectation and quite sure that he would go back in the same frame of mind that he left with. But once in Meherabad, nothing seemed to matter anymore and each time his forehead touched the cool stone in Baba's Samadhi, he felt an instant soothing sensation that calmed his senses and lightened the heaviness that he was carrying.

Rishi confesses: Though there is a lot about Baba that I have yet to learn, I know that His love is unconditional and endless.

I am grateful that circumstances brought me in contact with Him, for He took me along to that divine new world which itself is a sign that He considers me as one of His loved ones. At first, I kept asking for many things and to clear all the obstacles in my life. But as time passed by in Meherabad, I found myself thanking Him for everything that I have. Now I feel the strong urge to have a deeper connection with Him and make Him a part of my life completely. I wish to extend my journey further.

CHAPTER 7

Like Master – Like Pupil

I am deeply grateful to Baba for all the signs that He has so often given me in my own journey to Him. They act as signposts for me and I am forever beholden to Him for this. Baba signs speak so clearly to me about the wonder of His love and compassion. They open the windows of my soul and make me love Him more and more every day.

When I first went to Meherabad and to the Samadhi, I must admit that I went more to 'see' Karl than for Baba but through the years things have changed and the urgency to 'find' Karl there does not seem so important anymore. I am now just so happy to be there, near to Baba, and secure in the knowledge that my son is in Baba's care that I do not ask or expect Karl's 'appearance' anymore. Besides, I remember clearly what the famous medium Ivy Northage once told me. She said, "You do not know what you are asking, my dear, I do not think you really understand just how difficult it is for Karl to do this every time you go and how hard he has to work to accomplish what he has set out to do." After she told me that, I do not ask for more proof of spirit presence for myself, but Karl never stops trying, and Baba never stops allowing for these little incidents that help so much to heal the heart.

While I am totally aware that the ultimate goal is Baba, the use of any spirit representation is just a signpost to put us on the road leading to Him. Baba fulfils spiritual needs. If signs are needed, that becomes the order of the day for that particular person. If intellectual stimulation such as meditation, surrender, renunciation and other disciplines of service to God is needed – that is also provided. Each spiritual experience is unique to the individual, implying Baba's special attention to detailing one's path and growth towards Him. So, to me it just seems so beautiful that all this is possible, and here I would like to tell you more about some of the heartwarming episodes that have taken place in my own life.

I often wonder if it was just plain coincidence that way back in 1986, the very first book I read on the subject of life after death was *Out on a Limb* by Shirley MacLaine. Seven or eight years after Karl's accident and demise, Jimmy and I, with great difficulty, finally persuaded ourselves to take a holiday abroad. We boarded the plane with many sad thoughts, thoughts about how our bags had been packed and ready for Karl's first trip abroad, of his excitement at having been given a chance to match his skills against some of the best jockeys in the world – his heroes Lester Pigott and Steve Cauthen. We remembered vividly how Karl had spent days fantasising how his plane would circle over in the mist and eventually land at London airport. But it never happened.

As I sat in my seat, all these terrible scenes came before me to haunt me and the tears started pouring down. Oh, why had we come? I wanted to turn back and go home again. Looking at Jimmy, I could see that he was quiet, in his own thoughts, and looking more than just depressed. "Baba, please help me, help me in some way not to feel so sad," I begged.

The worst part arrived. We were landing at London airport. The plane touched down, taxied and finally came to a standstill. We unbuckled our seatbelts and were about to rise when over the speaker system there was an announcement. "Attention please, there is a message for a passenger on board our aircraft. A Mr. Maclane is waiting to welcome you at the airport!" Sadness flew out of the window; the very name of Maclane brought back strong memories of that wonderful day when we first made contact with the spirit of Karl at Baba's Samadhi, the day he made his appearance as a fair, good-looking foreigner, wearing a red shirt, brown pants and no shoes on his feet. His name – Hamma Maclane.

I am convinced that this name of Maclane appeared here so prominently, as it had often done before, only to prove to us that even though Karl's physical presence was not there, he was indeed with us at London airport with all the excitement he had ever dreamed of when in his physical form.

However, this connection with Baba, and the name, only became much clearer to us a few months later. I was sitting in

Meherabad one day when someone came and gave me an unexpected big hug. It was Kristine Maclane Carlson. Yes, the very same Kristine I had met at Mansari's home that first memorable day at the Samadhi. After exchanging I-love-you's and pleasantries, her eyes suddenly lit up as if she had just remembered something and she said, "You know Nan, I have something to tell you. You remember long ago, you wrote to ask me if I could throw any light on the name of Hamma Maclane? Well, I have solved the mystery for you. I have concluded that what Karl actually wrote was 'Huma'. It sounds so similar to 'Hamma'. Didn't you know that Huma was Baba's pen name? That whenever Baba wrote something and wanted to remain anonymous, He used to sign Himself as Huma!"

I was amazed! My heartbeats quickened, for the more I thought about it the more I understood the connection. Baba was behind it all along. We were all connected somewhere, somehow. And to think that all these years I tried so hard to find out who was that all-important Hamma, and this never struck me as a likely answer. I never really guessed!

I never really guessed, when in 1996, I stepped into my auditor's office to acquaint him of the fact that I had written a book and needed his advice on how to go about publishing it. "A book," he shouted incredulously, "You have written a book! What about?" He was an old, orthodox Parsee gentleman and I did not want to give him any more shocks, so I just mumbled something under my breath. He reluctantly explained the logistics of how to open new accounts and told me that the publication had to be given a name. He closed his eyes and with fingers on forehead, sat quietly for a few moments as if in deep thought. Then all of a sudden his eyes flew open and he said, "Why don't you call it Huma Enterprises?" I got the start of my life! Why in God's name did he say the name 'Huma'? "Just a name," he said nonchalantly with a shrug.

But for me it was not just a name. It was Baba's way of giving His approval. That actually it was Baba who had been the thinker, the writer, and the perpetrator of the contents. It was His way of telling me that *Sounds of Silence* and the story of Karl would go out into the world with His blessings and under His umbrella. I went home floating on air!

So, like Master, like pupil. With the intense love that Karl has for Baba, I am sure that he must long to follow in his Master's footsteps and to do a few unexpected things on his own also.

The Royal Western India Turf Club has nominated a race and presented a cup in remembrance of Karl, and I travel to Mumbai each year to present it. In 2001, the Turf Club had changed its ruling and also allowed children to attend the race meetings (how Karl must be wishing it had been a rule in his time!). So, all my children, grandchildren, cousins, nieces and nephews were present at the racecourse that day. Pesi Shroff, my son-in-law, who is also a jockey, had a mount in Karl's race that had a good chance to win. Everyone in the family was over-excited about it.

Before the actual race started, a few announcements were made about prizes for the right tanala combinations; to win a Chopard watch, or a ticket to Goa, or two tickets to Dubai for the shopping festival. Normally I would not let anything deviate my attention from the actual race but this time somehow I encouraged my daughter Tina. "Let us try our luck, let's go to Goa, Tina," I said, but she passed it off by saying, "You buy whatever you think Mum and it is fine by me." So I toddled off to the window to buy the necessary tickets. As I expected, when the winning numbers of the Goa trip were announced, they were not mine.

The next event being Karl's race, I soon forgot all about it especially when the race was actually won by Pesi, much to the delight of the family present. And to add to the excitement, the owner of the winning horse was Karl's very good school-friend Zaheer Lalkaka. So, actually, when the time came to present the cup, there were many hugs, kisses and emotional moments instead of the customary handshakes.

As I was walking out of the paddock, a voice over the mike said: "If the winner does not come forward to claim the two tickets to Dubai, they will be given away to the next one. Last call, ticket number... ." Something clicked in my mind and I opened my wallet to have a closer look. Yes, there it was. It was my ticket. I had actually won a prize and that too on the day of Karl's Cup!

There was the usual announcement, and I walked up to the podium amidst cheers from the family to claim the prize. A gentleman came forward to present me with a envelope and his card. I thanked him and walked away. As I was about to join the family, I looked at the envelope in my hand and almost fainted. It not only contained the ticket to Dubai but it read, 'With Best Wishes from Karl (Weiss)'. It was a ticket from heaven!

It was the 28th of December 2002, and I was depressed. Christmas was just over, and New Year was around the corner. I could not help letting my mind drift away, remembering all the happy days together; the Christmas parties, the tinsel, the beautifully wrapped presents, the tuxedos, the gowns, the dances, and the circle of friends joining hands at midnight singing the New Year in. I missed Karl so much. I called out to him. I called out to my son, my 'Colly', for that was what I sometimes used to affectionately call Karl. I had not used that name for a very long time!

I tried hard to shake away this cloud of depression and longing that had, for no real reason, suddenly settled on me. I tried to concentrate my attention on my morning chores, and to the whole pile of letters and greeting cards that were lying before me. At random, I picked up the card closest to me. The picture showed a young boy holding a single, long-stemmed red rose. The flower was partially hidden behind his back and there was a mischievous expression on his face, as if to say, "Shall I give it to you or not?" I smiled to myself as I carelessly flipped the card open. I was not prepared for the words that jumped out at me. On the first blank page was written, "This is Karl saying he loves you, with a rose."

Picture of boy with red rose.

Depression flew out of the window and though my mind was still in a whirl, I slowly allowed my eyes to drift to the next page. The printed words said, "I am wishing you joy, prosperity and contentment to last throughout the year. Have a great new year 2003. Love to you, Colly."

I almost died!

How could this card with this inscription, and this name, come to me on this day? Baba, this was Baba, and for me it was one of the sweetest and kindest gestures in the world. Baba could not have thought of anything better. It took a while for me to pull myself together and wondered who this was, this Colly, whom Baba had selected to help fill the void in my heart? I eventually decided that I knew of only one other in the whole world bearing that name. It must be the dear lady who lived on, depending only on the messages she got from her late beloved husband, through Karl, keeping them under her pillow and looking at them when "loneliness overwhelms me." It must be her.

I took the pen and wrote her a letter telling her just what her card, the inscription, and the signature meant to me. As a token of my gratitude, I asked Karl for another message from her husband and enclosed it with my letter. A few days later I received a reply from her telling me how happy she was that she had been instrumental in bringing me so much joy, and added, "But you do not know what you did for me. Your letter and my beloved husband's message came to me on the 5th of January 2003, which is my husband's death anniversary!"

Whenever I plan to go to Meherabad, somehow Baba snowballs it into a nice big group. This time, in July 2005, I was joined by Chuck from New Zealand, a family from Ghana, and a group of five ladies from Mangalore. Besides that, we had a mother and daughter from Mumbai, as well as a mixture of old and new friends from Pune. That made about twenty-four in all.

As always, there were messages of love and hope from Baba through Karl and the day before we left, I was transcribing them all for the persons concerned. So on the morning before I finally boarded the bus, I was pleasantly surprised when Karl said, *"Hi Mum, don't think that I won't be present just because you have so many to deal with. I will be the postman who will be delivering letters to you and taking all the answers back. That is my job even here, so watch out for me, Mum!"*

A postman in Meherabad! In all these years, I had never seen one coming to the door. However, as always, I shared this with my friends and soon forgot about it. The day was rushed with so many people having to be shown around and made comfortable, and the only relaxing time was after dinner when we all sat chatting on the verandah outside. There was a slight drizzle, the lights were dim and the atmosphere peaceful. My conversation was interrupted by the sweet voice of a stranger that said, "Aunty, I have something to give you," and with that she put a white envelope in my hand. I was about to put it away to be seen later, when one of the group shouted, "Nan, the postman!" With the letter clutched in my hand and my heart racing, my first reaction was to jump up and give my darling postman the biggest hug possible. Then I calmed down enough to open the envelope and what did I find? A big sheet of white paper. There was a heart drawn on it, with the rays of the sun surrounding it. 'Love U' was written in scrawly writing at the bottom.

The sounds from the silence are truly amazing!

Picture of Postman's letter.

I later asked Karl, one day, why he thought it necessary to continually give us these beautiful little signs and reminders of his presence? Didn't he know that we were totally convinced and that it was not necessary for him to work so hard in order to prove himself anymore? This is what he said:

"But of course I love you Mum and I need to get that through to you every now and then. When human beings love each other don't they frequently say, 'I love you'? A person needs that verbal assurance and so we also like to give it to you oft and on. That is the main reason and nothing else, Mum. To add to that you may also say that it is to keep the battery charged, to keep the fizz from getting flat, to keep you happy, and to make you know that Baba is with you in every possible way. In other words to keep your interest alive, so that you can continue to tell people all about the new and wonderful things that happen. So that you do not have to repeat the same old stories over and over again. Even Amie gets bored with them, don't you see that Mum? Baba loves to play mischief and so do I. We love to see the eyes flash open, the sudden intake of breath and that 'Huh' look freezing on your face. Then we smile at one another, give ourselves a 'high five' and shout, 'We've done it!' Now what more can I tell you? Love Karl."

Karl really does deserve a 'High Five' for what he did next.

The family was all gathered together to celebrate my son Neville's birthday at the farmhouse of my sister-in-law at Kamshet, near Pune. It was raining heavily and so outdoor activities became limited. Sitting around with windows closed and curtains drawn, we suddenly thought of Karl; we missed him so much. So we decided to skip the normal routine for once and call him to be with us. In the process of our conversation with him, one of us asked, "Karl, are you really here? If so, show us something to prove it."

"Open the curtain," he wrote, *"do you see the musical note on the window pane?"* Zara sprinted to the window, tore the curtains aside, and there large and clear, was the most beautiful treble cleft you can ever hope to see. It was etched on a clear space on the window, all surrounded by dripping rain.

A runaround for a camera produced a blank. Maybe it was just not meant to be photographed.

CHAPTER 8

Building Bridges

You have already read a few stories of how people have found Baba and learned to love Him, but I am sure that after you read the next few, they will help to convince you that there is a life after we pass away. I also started off by thinking that after you die there is no tomorrow. That after your heart stops beating, it is the end of your journey on earth. But now I have learned otherwise. It took a while for me to accept all this as real and true, but with time I became convinced that when our eyes close forever and we pass into spirit, we still remain the same persons we were on earth. If the person has been strong enough to face life's problems with courage and come to terms with it all during his lifetime, it is easier to move on. But young or old, if it is a sudden death, then normally the first thought of the one who has passed on is usually to try and get back to give some assurance to their loved ones left behind. The search for a way to do so goes on.

I find it so fascinating to be a witness to how Baba finds ways to reach the heart, and to build the bridges that connect the other world and ours. God visits us every day. So can your loved ones.

This chapter is all about such visits. Each story is beautiful in its own way and so I have decided to give it to you exactly the way it came. First is Smruti Mirani's story.

Baba's promise is that, whether we remember Him or not, He will always be with us, guiding and taking care of us, bestowing His blessings on us, making us so happy. His words and His smile help us to deal with all obstacles, and help us to live life to the fullest. He has helped each one of us to become a better human being. It is hard to believe that in our search for our Dad, we have eventually found Baba.

Everyone's father has to eventually pass away, and the only father we are left with is our Father in heaven. I know that, and yet when my father Narendra Parekh's physical life came to an end suddenly one day, my mother Hari, my sister Chaya, and I, Smruti Mirani, were left totally forlorn and distraught, and our life came to a total standstill.

Why, oh why, did it have to happen this way?

He was the most wonderful human being in the whole world. He loved life, he loved his children, and he adored and pampered his most precious wife. He did everything for us; without him we were, and could do, nothing. He always said, "Heaven will not tempt me or keep me away from you all."

So, when a friend gave us *Sounds of Silence* to read, in our distraught state it was like a light in the wilderness. The book was as enchanting as its title. It gave us a glimmer of hope and helped to make us believe what we desperately wanted to believe – that our father had not totally left us, that his spirit was still there helping us and protecting us, and that it was possible to actually be in touch and ask for his continued care from the spirit world. With this hope in our hearts, we made an appointment and had our first meeting with the author, Nan Umrigar.

It was I who did most of the talking, while my sister Chaya, sensitive, soft, fair and quite lovely to look at, added in her little bits. My mother, her slightly greying hair tied back in a little pigtail, had a sad and lost expression on her pale face and sat like a robot through it all, just listening to all that was said and never uttered a single word through the evening. We had all read the book quite thoroughly for we remembered every chapter, person and incident, and told Nan in no uncertain words that at present we definitely wanted to make contact with our father and then learn to continue it ourselves.

"Who will be doing the writing then?" asked Nan, and that is when we heard my mother's voice for the first time. "I will," she said.

So, the first message from our Dad found its way to us through Karl, and it touched us deeply for it was so 'him' and we found no difficulty at all in believing its authenticity. After that, with Nan's help, it was easy to start off and learn how to do automatic writing and get our own messages.

About six months later, we met up with Nan once more. I am sure that she must have been more than just surprised to see a totally different family – the biggest change being in my mother. She was a transformed person. Gone were the dowdy clothes and the hair tied back in a tight pigtail. She was now dressed in a lovely *kurta-pyjama,* her hair loose over her shoulders. There was a spring in her step and a smile on her face. The change was so amazing that I am sure that Nan could hardly believe she was looking at the same little mousy lady she had met just six months ago. "What happened?" she asked in surprise and wonder.

Aunty, we explained, Mummy began her writing with the usual scribbles, lines and loops, and it went on for some time till the day of her birthday, when suddenly the whole page was filled with 'Happy Birthday, Happy Birthday'. Mummy was so delighted for she really felt Papa's presence that day. In the evening, the whole family decided to go out to Papa's favourite place for dinner, but we did not have a reservation and looking at the long line we did not have much hope for a table. We suddenly heard the steward come forward and announce, "Mr. Parekh's table for twelve is ready," but we were only eleven. We just knew that Papa was there with us to celebrate Mummy's birthday. He just couldn't have kept away. Since that day, our lives have changed.

That was only the beginning, and instances like this kept on occurring. Chaya, who is a successful young artist, took the longest to recover. Just before father passed away, we had arranged for a showing of her paintings at Harrods in London and had been excitedly preparing for it. Now the time was drawing near and the paintings were far from complete, but Chaya seemed to have lost all interest and had neither the will nor the inclination to carry on without our beloved father. I did my best to encourage her to make an effort to finish the task but somehow she could produce nothing of note. Her heart was just not in it.

So, with just a few paintings, the three of us took off for London. We checked into our hotel room, lonely and afraid, only to be confronted by a huge picture of three big and beautiful galloping racehorses. It instantly gave us the desired confidence to go ahead for we felt sure that it was a sign that Karl was there with us.

Chaya's mood changed, and she sat down then and there to do a painting of the picture. After that, inspiration seemed to flow like magic and she finished all the other portraits well before the day of the exhibition.

In the meantime my mother, Hari, guided by Nan's experiences went off to the Spiritual Centre, at 33 Belgrave Square, to see what she could discover and the results were more than fascinating.

Needless to say, our exhibition was a roaring success and almost all the paintings were sold out, but more than this, diffidence changed to confidence, and we continued our visits to the Spiritual Centre to get more and more proof of our father's presence.

Now, nothing could hold Mummy back. She was uncontrollable in her desire to get more knowledge about the spirit world. She even prevailed upon us to enroll into Stanstead Hall, the college of psychic studies in Essex. We stayed there for three whole weeks, imbibing all the knowledge that the mediums had to impart. We learned all about aura-reading, psychometry, clairvoyance and clairaudience. It may be hard for you to believe that it was actually my mother who went on stage many a time to partake in all the different demonstrations that took place!

But, the best experience we had was when one of the mediums saw Papa taking a walk in the clouds with a Saint dressed in long white robes, and we knew that it had to be Meher Baba. At last, He had shown Himself to give us His assurance that it was through His grace that our dear father had come back to us. We were so happy.

After that, we made many visits to the Baba Centre in London where the air was always so heavy with Baba's presence. He walked along with us as we strolled peacefully among the lakes and gardens and smelt the heady fragrance of jasmine flowers. We met lovely people, all followers of Baba, who showed us His films and videotapes. We sat at the Centre, under the shadow of His picture, basking in the sunshine of His warm face and lovely smile, and passed many long hours listening to His favourite songs.

Finally, after all these wonderful experiences, it was almost time to go home to Bombay. The last stop was the highlands of Scotland. As we walked through the streets one day, we were attracted by a beautiful church and on a whim we walked in, only to find that it was a Spiritualistic church and there was a meeting in progress. We sat at the back quietly, watching and listening to the medium, who was giving much evidence of survival and many lovely messages to those present. We were a little disappointed when it all came to an end and there was nothing for us. We were just about to turn away when the medium pointed to us, and in her strong Scottish accent said, "Wait, wait, there is a gentleman here who will not take no for an answer. He is pushing everyone aside and wants to say something to you but I cannot really pronounce it correctly. It seems to be a name and it sounds something like Naren – Naren – Naren."

We left with tears in our eyes. Our beloved father had indeed pushed his way through all barriers that divided our two dimensions and had even given evidence of his name, Narendra. How could we expect anything more?

So it goes on. My mother, Hari, continues to thank Baba everyday and is taking a keen interest in life once again. Baba's prayer is on her mind, on her lips and in her heart. It is etched there to remain forever. I am happy with my family and my children, while Chaya continues to paint and hold many successful exhibitions. We have written our story because we all want to do our utmost to help all those who, like us, are shattered and torn apart, by telling them of our experiences.

With the help of Baba and Karl, we have started to live again. We know we will have to live out our karmas before we are united with Dad once again. We have realised and accepted that his physical presence is not here, but it is not the end, in fact it is a new beginning to a relationship that continues beyond; beyond to another world and another life... forever.

Haldwani is a small town at the foothills of Nainital. This is in the Kumaon region, surrounded by the snow peaks of the Himalayas. Amidst the natural beauty of this valley, I, Poonam Joshi, began my married life with Alok.

He loved this small hamlet we lived in. But it was all too short-lived, for at just thirty-two years of age, Alok suddenly passed away, leaving me with a six-year-old son. The beauty of the place meant nothing to me and life itself became full of pain. I lived on because I had to – that's all.

Till one day, in loneliness, I flipped through the pages of a *Society* magazine, which was bought by Alok when he was in physical body, and my eyes suddenly got riveted to an article about a book *Sounds of Silence* by Nan Umrigar. I was more than just amazed by what I read, and I sent a letter to the editor immediately asking for the author's whereabouts. I know now that I must have definitely been guided by someone.

Living so far away from civilisation, there was no way I could easily get a copy of the book except with help from the author herself, and that is exactly what happened. Nan Umrigar sent me a copy accompanied by a loving letter. That was the beginning of a new source of life for me, for she taught me how to connect and talk to Alok in Baba's world.

It was on the 26th of November 1997, my eighth wedding anniversary, when with Meher Baba's permission and Karl's help, I began to auto write with my beloved husband and my life changed once more from the depths of pain to at least some semblance of normalcy.

A whole year went by as I struggled with words and sentences, always being encouraged with loving messages from Karl and Nan. I knew also that the Grace and loving presence of Beloved Meher Baba was with me and I yearned to go to Meherabad to the Samadhi if only just once, so that I could put my head on Baba's feet and thank Him for His love and care. I constantly begged Baba to make it somehow possible for me to be there for my next wedding anniversary on the 26th November, and will you believe me if I tell you that this really came to pass. One day, I was actually ready to leave and make the long trip to Pune and then go with Nan to Meherabad.

I asked Alok if he would come to be with me and how he would present himself. He answered, "By Baba's light shining on you." Not having so much confidence in my own ability to get the right answers, I requested Nan for a message and this is what Karl told his mother:

"We will be with you – plenty of boys, and with these boys will be a person who cannot see very well and will be helped by me. The person is really Alok hiding behind a facade of being blind but actually he can see Poonam very clearly. He wants to tell her that he is very, very happy that she is here and will have her desired wishes fulfilled. We shall be with you."

We all went up to the Samadhi and we did meet a whole lot of little boys, but no blind man. However, the energy and the comfort level was just so lovely that actually there was not much time to feel sad, and I was happy just to be there with Baba.

Our two-day stay was coming to an end and the only thing remaining was to go to Meherazad to meet the mandali and see Baba's home. Just before leaving, we stood under the trees outside the Pilgrim Centre to take pictures of our whole group and then piled into the bus and were soon on our way. As we passed Ahmednagar town, one among the group expressed a desire to stop off at a boutique in order to do a little local shopping. The others all agreed, so we branched off into a little side lane and soon arrived at a quaint little bungalow hidden under a huge Banyan tree.

It happened to be the boutique of Amrit Irani, one of Baba's close followers. Her husband Dara was standing at the doorway as if waiting to welcome us.

There suddenly seemed to be a great deal of confusion in our private bus and I couldn't really understand why. The truth is that those who had been to Baba before were all aware that Dara was Baba's nephew, and he was blind!

No one seemed to know what to do next, so we trooped out of the bus in silence and, as we walked in, Nan introduced each one to Dara. When it came to my turn, he held my hand in his for a long time as if getting the feel of it; he turned his face upward, sniffing the air like an animal when it senses something, and said, "Poonam, Poonam, why do I have this distinct feeling that I have met you before." There was a hush from the group and I felt a great emotion well-up inside me. Nan, sensing that I was in danger of breaking down, quickly took over and ushered us all in. Yet, he did not let go of my hand but requested me to sit with him on the settee and to tell him all about myself. I do not really know when the actual fact really hit me that here I was sitting close to him, telling him everything, and that he really couldn't see a thing.

Slowly I picked up courage and also began to ask him about his life. He explained how his blindness had come upon him gradually, but continued to stress that it was only at the age of thirty-two that it had become total. I did not realise the significance of this till it suddenly hit me – Alok had also passed away exactly at the age of thirty-two.

Karl's message had come true. Everything else seemed to fade away, and time stood still.

The others soon emerged from the boutique and enthusiastically began showing us their purchases. We all shared a cup of tea and soon it was time to leave. Amrit and Dara, totally unaware of what had transpired, came to the bus to say goodbye. As we were about to board, someone called my name. It was Dara. "Will you come again, I will wait for you," he said.

Tears welled up and spilt over as I shyly put my arms around him and hugged him. "I will come for sure," I answered.

It is now over a year since that momentous day. I still have not been able to make the trip back but I do often get a letter from him to say, 'Hello Poonam, just to let you know you are in my thoughts and I hope to see you again very soon – Jai Baba, Love Dara.' You know, when Baba is there, wonders never cease.

Poonam with the light shining on her.

When I came back to Haldwani and had the Meherabad photographs developed, there was indeed a surprise waiting for me. There is a picture of Nan and me, standing with our arms around each other, and there is the most beautiful shaft of light coming through the trees right on to us, enveloping us with its beauty.

I had asked, "How will I know you Alok?" He had answered, "By Baba's light shining on you, Poonam."

Now Baba, God, is my guide. I want to pass on this love to others. I want very much to work for Him and spread His love and His name. Someday I will also go back to the Samadhi and put my head on Baba's feet with all my love.

CHAPTER 9

The Young Ones

Of the many challenges provided by life on earth, the death of a child is perhaps the most difficult. Some say that we all choose our challenges before birth. If that is so, I often wonder how and why I could have chosen something that not only broke my heart, but that of my family too. But, as Baba brings new people my way, I see that there are so many like me who have suffered the same heartbreak.

Most of those who have read *Sounds of Silence*, and made a contact with Karl, have somehow come to Meherabad to bow down to Baba and, in the process, been blessed by receiving some proof from Him. It is His way of lighting the lamp of love in the hearts of those who have lost their faith, and to help those who are devastated to find a place in the world for themselves again.

Only Baba's love can let this happen. He may allow it out of compassion for a suffering mortal, so that he come to terms with death, or just so that he knows and understands that even though the physical presence is not visible, life still goes on. He may also just simply use it as a stepping-stone to further spiritual knowledge. Whoever He chooses to help and whatever way He chooses, the way He reaches out is like a benediction, like the splendid sunshine of a new day, always carrying a message of hope and love.

Here is Naved Hassan's story.

The typical boy next door! No, that is not the way you could describe our son Azhar. He was this extraordinary soul that touched any and everyone who came in contact with him.

He was fond of all games and outdoor activities. His passion for cricket, however, had him completely immersed in the game. His cricket kit always included a few pumps, as he was asthmatic. Apart from that, he was a healthy and active boy who loved life and lived it to the fullest. On that fateful 17th November 1997, we lost our beloved Azhar to asthma, which led to cardiac arrest.

We were devastated.

A visiting friend, Suraiya Masters, told us about Nan and her contact with Karl. And sure, I was interested, but my wife Lubna was not. She was convinced that this would disturb her son, and so she hid the copy of *Sounds of Silence* that Suraiya had so kindly sent to us.

But Azhar's persistence in making contact with us carried on. Now, he seemed to have got an ally from somewhere, for soon another copy of *Sounds of Silence* appeared out of nowhere and this time it was given to Lubna in my presence. Needless to say, I could not wait to start the book and on reading the contents, all the signs we had got so far from Azhar suddenly started making more sense to me. We asked for a message from Karl through Nan, but were told we had to wait three months.

I do not know if it was Baba's love or Azhar's persistent desire to communicate with us that eventually made it all possible, but today I definitely feel that it was a combination of both. On 17th of February 1998, I asked Lubna to make the call and see if there was any message for us, but she was still unsure and kept avoiding to make that call on one pretext or another. But it was Suraiya who eventually made the call for us.

The shrill ring of the telephone woke us up. It was Suraiya (God bless her) with a beautiful message from Karl. Surprises do not end from the spirit world, for just a couple of hours later, another friend who communicates with her father, called us with another message from Azhar. It was very clear now that Azhar wanted to establish contact with us – but how?

We decided to visit Lubna's family in America, and Nan was kind enough to see us in Bombay, at short notice. She tried hard to explain this phenomenon to a totally devastated family, who really wanted to believe every word she said but did not have any clue how all this could be possible.

I had in fact, by then, secretly made up my mind that I would like very much to learn how to personally do the communication, but Lubna was still not in favour of it. As we sat together, Nan spent much time explaining to us that the communication would not work very well if there were any negative vibes around. This might just confuse Azhar in the spirit world and so, she advised us to proceed to the USA, give it some serious thought and then decide one way or another.

She tried and tried, she did her best to explain, and then seeing the blank expression on our faces, a sudden thought seemed to strike her. Out of the blue she asked, "Have you seen the movie *Ghost*?"

"No," was our reply. Then she insisted that we try to get a copy while in the States. However, she took care to explain that the movie was an old one and the videocassettes may not be available now.

So, expressing our sincere thanks and saying our goodbyes we left for the airport, still heavy hearted. We had gone to Nan in the hope that we might be able to talk directly to Azhar and, to be honest, we were very confused.

Still arguing the issue, we boarded the plane for America. Seated in the aircraft, ready to take off, I could hardly hear the safety instructions given by the crew. Lubna was still sulking with me, not willing to give in. She even turned her back on me in defiance and stared out of the aircraft window. All of a sudden, my ears grew hot! Had I heard correctly? The safety instructions were announced, followed by the commercials, and then the movie of the day, *Ghost*!

A hard pinch from me drew Lubna's attention. Tears streamed down as the movie progressed. No words were spoken as the reality of eternal life unfolded itself. Deep, deep down, all that Nan had explained started to make sense. Your loved ones never leave you, they are right beside you, telling you: 'Here I am; open your hearts to me, see me, hear me, feel me!'

I started to communicate with Azhar in April 1998 and, after a very disappointing month, finally formed the first legible word – 'Love'.

Ever since then, love has been the essence of all Azhar's messages. Love is the only reality and all other emotions are because of love. By mid-May, clearer messages began to flow. And let me say that the experience was most rewarding. Six months later, however, Baba thought that at last we were ready to visit His Samadhi. We made a trip there accompanied by Suraiya, Nan, and some others. It was an experience that was overwhelming and reassuring, and so very peaceful.

Karl's message said, "*Azhar and I will be together. You will see the shape of elephants. In front of them will be marching people and animals with long horns and protruding teeth; that will be us.*"

My reaction was 'Christ Almighty'! What kind of a message was that? Where on earth would we be able to find elephants in Meherabad?

Although to be with Baba, to know Him, to love Him, and to thank Him was the main purpose of our visit to Meherabad, nevertheless we spent two nights and two days in anticipation of some kind of 'a shape of elephants'.

Nothing happened. Nothing was seen, not a hint, not a sound, or even a picture of an elephant – nothing! In spite of all our resolve, I could feel that there was a lurking sorrow in the hearts of my little family. We had travelled all the way from Bangalore to get some assurance from Baba that our dear son was in His tender care but, of course, we did not say anything.

The time came for us to leave. Reluctantly, we said our goodbyes and Jai Babas. The bus took off, rolled on for a few miles, turned off the crossroads, and over the bridge. The passengers all began to relax, some even to nod and take a quick nap, when all of a sudden we heard a shout from Leila who was sitting in the front seat of the bus. "Oh My God! Elephants! Elephants!"

There, by the side of the road, we saw the shape of two large, ungainly, black elephants. Their backsides were swinging from side to side, their little tails wiggling wildly to keep off the flies. As the bus sped by, we saw a procession of men dressed in long white robes, walking slowly in front. Each of them had a garland of bright orange flowers around his neck and a large dark-red *tikka* on the forehead. In front of the procession, majestically walked two white bulls with silver paper entwined on their beautiful horns. The bulls carried a howdah which housed a *Ganesh* with a trunk and long protruding teeth.

It was an absolutely unbelievable sight! Unbelievable, heart-breaking, and breathtaking! There was bedlam in our bus. Some stood up to get a closer look, some waved their arms wildly and shouted, "*Roko, roko*" (stop, stop), some screamed in delight while others gaped in awe. No one knew where the procession had come from or where it was going, but I knew one thing for sure – Baba had proved His point! Baba's love had proved too strong to let a bereaved family go home without their wishes being fulfilled.

Now it has been ten years since we went on that memorable trip. A lot of time has passed. We still communicate with Azhar and, like Karl, he still continues from there to help many. We too love Baba with our whole heart and thank Him for the blessings He has bestowed on us.

'Love is the law of God. You live that you may learn to love. You love that you may learn to live. No other lesson is required of man.'[1]

"Life is a journey," Azhar had said when asked to define life. His physical journey has ended, but his spiritual journey continues.

It was St. Valentine's Day, February 1999, when Raghav, my beloved son, met with an accident on the way home from a party and went away to the world of Meher Baba. I, Poonam Mehra and my family were left numbed, shocked and helpless in the face of the terrible tragedy, with a whole lot of unanswered questions.

How is it possible that someone you love so much is simply not there anymore? Is there really life after death? If there is a soul, where does it suddenly go? Was there any way to know how, where and with whom Raghav was, or did we just have to sit back and allow him to fade into nothingness?

Amidst all this grief and chaos, something suddenly came to mind. A book, a youthful face on a cover, and the title – *Sounds of Silence*.

My mind raced back to the day that I had read a review in the *Femina* magazine, about a book that had just been published. It had held my attention so strongly that I had searched all bookshelves in Punjab for a copy. Then finally, as though prompted by God, I had entered a small nondescript little bookshop to find one copy tucked away, as if especially just for me.

I read through it with tears in my eyes and was so touched with the contents, that I shared the story and all the unusual experiences with my own children Varun, Raghav and Sakshi. I told them about Karl who loved his mother so much that he had broken all barriers to come and give her a message of Avatar Meher Baba.

All this and more now came back to mind as though through a mist. I knew one thing for certain. I had to contact the author in some way – any way.

Through the publishers, I searched frantically for her telephone number, called her and sobbingly told her of my tragedy, begging her to please ask Karl to find Raghav, if only just to tell me how he was. She told me that she would do her level best and let me know something as soon as possible.

In a few days, we got the news through Karl, that Raghav had reached and that Meher Baba and Karl had gone to greet him, that he had recognised Meher Baba and, surprisingly, already knew of Him. I am sure that Nan must have wondered how, for little did she know that Raghav's only knowledge of Baba was through her own book, the chapters of which I had read out to him just two years ago.

For the moment, the thought of my son being in the blessed hands of Meher Baba comforted me greatly. But it was not enough for me. My acute desperation to hear about Raghav drove me insane.

At last, after three and a half months, Karl said, "*Now Raghav is free to speak to you,*" and the next day I got my first message from my son, through Karl. He said, "Mummy, you have told Karl to look after me, and I am being looked after so much that, at times, I feel I was a baby again and that you and Papa are standing by my bedside. Baba has shown me what I was, and helped me now to be what I should be, so I am going to work towards being the same son I was to you. I love you all more than anything, but have come to realise that now our lives have to be separate, though linked in another way. I feel so happy that I can talk to you and be with you, so start to learn how to communicate with me. We shall then be able to continue our relationship and our love. All of you must start to feel happy again, for without that I will not be able to go forward. I need your help and your strength to help me on my way here. Baba says you must try, mummy, so that in return, I can do the same and more for you. I have left my penknife at my home; keep it safely for me mum. Love Raghav."

You can well imagine what our reaction was! When we read this message, we simply looked at one another and wondered about the penknife. We had never seen it with Raghav before. Varun dashed up to his room and we all sat downstairs with bated breath. Varun searched frantically through his cupboards and drawers, and we sat silently praying to Baba. Suddenly, we heard Varun racing down and in his hand he held aloft a small little penknife. We put our arms around each other and just wept joyfully. There were no words, simply no words, to express our common thoughts. Yes, Raghav had somehow reached out to his family.

Thus, slowly but surely, the days went by. I gradually regained my lost composure and after a few more messages of reassurance, the way opened up for Raghav and me to actively start our communication with one another. With Nan's help I began to auto write with my son. Soon the usual dots and wavy lines began to progress into hills and valleys, then move on into the usual circles and patterns and eventually into the first beautiful words, 'LOVE YOU MUM'. I thought my heart would burst.

Time went by, with more and more words and sentences, which filled me with a new warmth, till finally one day Raghav asked us to make the trip to Meherabad and Baba's Samadhi. A date was set and we, as a family, travelled from our home in Ludhiana to Pune. There we finally saw Nan and, although we met for the first time, it seemed as if we had known her for years.

In the meantime, my writing had improved by leaps and bounds, and I had received my own message from Raghav as to how he was going to present himself. He said, "Mummy, Meher Baba will come to bless you. You will know I am there when you see a girl of the West in the dress of your own country."

It was morning aarti time. We were told that something quite unusual was going to take place. Baba's mandali was scheduled to come to Meherabad, which I believe was a rather rare occurrence. Very anxiously and eagerly we went up to the Samadhi, and all of us lined up to meet them. Nan, who was standing nearest to where they were climbing, suddenly started making frantic signs to us, for there, walking up the slope with Baba's mandali was a lovely western girl in an eastern dress! The sun was just rising and the pale rosy glow highlighted her fair skin and golden-brown hair. She looked like a vision from another world, beautiful in her lovely, pink *salwar-kameez*. As they came up to us, they greeted us with folded hands and a soft 'Jai Baba'. We stood rooted to the spot for there was no mistaking it. Helped by Baba's Divine Energy, Raghav had come to meet his family.

After that trip, Raghav and I soon settled down and seemed to be more at peace – he in the spirit world and I in the physical world. My faith grew stronger by the day for I became convinced of the fact that by Baba's Grace I had actually found a way to reach my son. Life began to have a meaning for me again, business started picking up and things seemed once more to return to normal. I would get messages from Raghav every day, sometimes checking with Nan without disclosing the contents, and many a time my messages would prove to be correct. The fact that they were validated did more than thrill me.

Shortly afterwards, my other son Varun declared his intentions of marriage with a young girl, Honey. I loved her as soon as I set eyes on her and very soon a day was fixed for the engagement.

Of course we all wanted Raghav to be present for the ceremony and had hopes of him indicating his presence to us in some way, via some photographs and pictures – maybe a face, a word, a sound, anything!

On the 1st of July 2001, Karl gave us a message. *"Raghav is very happy that his brother is getting his heart's desire and that his mummy has been persuaded to go along with this. It is all Raghav's doing and he wants to wish Varun and his intended wife much happiness. Baba says birds will always be there in Varun's life, and whenever he hears the sound of birds, they will be memories of games played with Raghav. But apart from this, birds are pals of Raghav here also, and he helps them to get on with their lives and proceed onwards. He is with the peacocks at the moment and, with all good wishes, wants to send his brother a peacock feather for good luck. Wait and watch."*

Was it at all possible? Ludhiana was just a tiny town having a small population and a noisy little market place, so I am sure that to Nan's limited knowledge, Karl's message must have seemed rather bizarre and inappropriate. Little did she know that there are actually many birds in Ludhiana and that it was quite a normal ritual with me to feed them on my terrace at least once a day, especially the beautiful peacocks!

The engagement was over. I desperately told the photographer to develop the pictures as fast as possible.

On the very next day, the engagement photographs were delivered to us. No gold threads, no faces, no hints of Raghav's presence as we had so longingly expected. The family was more than just sad and dejected.

But a couple of hours later, a videotape of the ceremony arrived. The first shot showed a picture of our home. The second showed Honey arriving with her family. In the third scene, the cameraman, for no apparent reason, seemed to focus his lenses on the roof and suddenly the camera zoomed on to the most beautiful peacock you ever saw! It was sitting there, gazing downwards, its gorgeous tail feathers hanging just above the doorway, and just as Honey was poised to enter, unbelievably, the peacock cried out as if in ecstasy. It was Raghav welcoming the new bride into our home.

Karl had said, *"Wait and watch."* We were watching and there were no dry eyes in the room.

A couple of days after the engagement ceremony of Varun, there was an article in the newspaper saying that eighty peacocks had died. It took us back to Karl's message, which said, *"Birds are pals of Raghav here. He helps them to get on with their lives and proceed onwards. He is with the peacocks at this moment."*

Love holds us together through time and space, for love is timeless. We, as souls, have been and always will be together. Through death, we only lose the power of seeing, hearing and touching our loved ones, but really we can never be parted. Our physical bonds are nothing compared to our spiritual bonds. Meher Baba's love for us connects us to each other forever, merging the two worlds together, and it is this love that will help us never to part.

Though I still miss my son very much, I have stopped grieving for him, for I know that he is not only my beloved son, but also Meher Baba's son. This is what I want to share with you and with all those who have come with me to this school called 'Earth'. For those who believe, there is no need for miracles, for those who doubt, no miracle is enough.

The peacock on the roof of the bridal home.

CHAPTER 10

More Tests for Me

August 2000. I was awakened one morning by excited shouts. "Mummy, come down quickly and look – look at what is in our garden!"

I ran down into the hall. My daughter-in–law, Sabita, took me by the hand, led me out on to the patio, pushed me into a chair and said, "Just sit down mummy and fix your eyes on these stones. Look under those bright green leaves in the garden. Do you see anything?"

Although I could not see anything straight away, I focused where her finger pointed and was startled to see the faint outline of a face. I stared at it in wonder, and after a while I could actually see an image of Baba imprinted on a rock under the bright green leaves of a bush. Seeing the expression on my face, Sabita said, "Oh, it is so clear mummy, how can anyone fail to see it?" and she ran into her room and returned with a camera. She zoomed in on the rock and clicked a few times till all of a sudden the camera jammed and, to her disappointment, she could take no more pictures. Then, being scolded by Neville for getting carried away, she returned to her room, and that was the end of the morning.

A few days later the photographs arrived and, lo and behold, there it was – an absolute likeness of Baba, clear and beautiful, the eyes, the prominent nose and the wide smile. It was so apparent that there could remain no doubt even in my mind that somehow Baba had actually made His appearance in my garden! It was just too good to be true, and Sabita was thrilled.

My thoughts went back to the message Karl had once written a long time ago which said, *"Baba is like an Almighty Rock. Hang on to Him. He will not give way to anything. He stands in the middle of storms.*

Baba's face on a small rock in my garden.

In the middle of heaven and great big hell. He stands firm and strong. He can never break or fail, and so if you hang on to Him, you go with Him everywhere. Tell everyone He has made them all part of His love, and that Love will never fail. So hang on to Him. He will take you through any pain or sadness. Happiness and joy are waiting for you all. Just Be With Him, that's all I have to say."

Again much later, I remembered reading an article entitled *Remembering Mansari*, in *The Glow* (a quarterly Baba magazine), and was struck by the comparison. It said that Meher Baba once asked Mansari, a member of the mandali, ***"What is Love?"*** and then went on to answer the question Himself. He said, ***"You have seen how a rock in the ocean is repeatedly hit hard, very hard and very often. In fact the waves strike the rock with such great intensity that it wears the sides down. But the rock always stands firm. Your love should be rock-like — love that never falters or wavers."***[1]

But in the middle of my joy I began to wonder why Baba had chosen this time to show Himself? I was to find out just a few months later.

For the last four years, my husband Jimmy's health had been deteriorating. He had been plagued by kidney stones from a young age and, when Karl was in the hospital, Jimmy had suffered agonising pains, not only mentally but also physically, due to the stress and the tragedy of it all. With the passage of time his kidney functions deteriorated further and, after we shifted to Pune, he was eventually put on a programme of two sessions of dialysis a week. As days went by, this was increased to three times a week. He went through all this bravely, never complaining, for four years.

Now he was getting weaker and weaker by the day. His kidneys were hardly functioning. He was finding it difficult to drive himself to the dialysis sessions, or to sit through his beloved race meetings, or watch the horses as keenly as he used to. Yet his courage and determination to be independent and self-sufficient were more than just admirable.

During this time, I held on tight to Baba's *daaman* – I just did not let go. I drew on my love for Baba to help me through this difficult time. I pulled His love and His light around us, and constantly covered Jimmy with it. The two of us sat together and discussed almost everything including my strong attachments to my family, my fear of being left alone, and my continuous dependence on his presence. I promised him that if ever it came to a stage where he could not be mobile or do his own things anymore, I would go along with any decision he made regarding the continuation of his dialysis. I also promised that I would not call him or disturb him in the other world, unless I really needed him. Outwardly, I tried to be brave, but inwardly, I held on desperately to Baba, for I was more than just afraid. I dreaded the day when I would have to face life without my dear husband. Sometimes, sensing my anxiety he would asssure me, "Baba is there and I know you will be fine – I know that you will be looked after." I gave him my word. I never really thought the day would come so soon, but it did.

By the middle of December 2000, he had become weaker and weaker and found it very difficult to get up from his bed. I cried out to Baba for help. A few days later, Karl asked me to keep repeating Baba's name and to keep putting Baba's 'Undhi' (dhuni ash) on Jimmy. *"By Sunday, things will become clearer mum,"* he said.

Monday came, and Jimmy could not get up anymore. He missed his dialysis that day, and again on Wednesday. His toxins were rising. We took him to the hospital on Thursday. On Friday, although the dialysis centre was just across the road from his room and he could have easily gone by stretcher, Jim held the doctor's hand, looked into my eyes, and shook his head in denial. He had had enough – he had decided!

Jim's eyes closed forever a couple of days before the year ended, and the one I loved most in all the world, went to Baba.

The four-day prayers we held for him in our own home and garden were gentle and soothing, full of positive vibrations and beautiful memories. I sat through the hours staring into the glowing embers of the fire, listening to the sounds. All I could hear were happy ones – sounds of the many years we had spent together. Through the smoke and the lovely smell of sandalwood, I heard the joyful voices of the three children we had raised, and remembered the way we had stood together through all the vicissitudes of fortune that had come later. I looked out at the beautiful bougainvillea plant that climbed high up to the roof of my little bungalow and then came cascading down in trails of pink and white blossoms – it seemed somehow to represent all the highs and the lows of our life. Through the prayers, all I did was to ask Baba to help Jim to get through his transition period and to reach Him safely. I also prayed earnestly for help to be able to live the rest of my life, the way Baba would want me to. I heard the birds singing and began to feel a certain peace.

Although, in all these years, Baba has appeared in my active communication only on rare occasions, this was one time I knew He would definitely come to talk to me. Baba knew how much I needed Him and, sure enough, the very next day, He was there for me to give me a very beautiful message that really warmed my heart.

Talk about Baba's love!

Karl took over from there and said, *"Mum, you have no idea how much Baba cares. He has been here every minute of the time. He is sitting and talking to Daddy, and laughing with him about all the things Daddy had to say about him in his lifetime. Dad is now thinking hard and regretting some of the negative thoughts he had about Baba, but feeling very happy about the loving and positive ones. Now Dad knows only too well, that he is dealing with a very human God and not a godly God, who only made miracles in order to prove His existence and His love.*

"Most of all, Daddy says to be sure to send his thanks to you all for helping him to release himself, for actually, this is what he wanted more than anything else. Now he is here mum and he is fine – so you do not worry anymore. Love Karl."

My husband Jim was my life; my everything. I certainly do miss his physical presence, but here also Baba has shown me so beautifully that he still lives on with his beloved son Karl, and with dearest Baba. And yes, in spite of all that was said between us about not communicating with him as a routine, I do talk to him at times and, one day, just like old times, he even reminded me not to forget to lock my cupboard!

I could never have imagined accepting with so much equilibrium, what was such a major upheaval in my life. I had always dreaded being alone, and now suddenly Jimmy was not here to share life with me – but Baba was. Time passed. I stopped being afraid. I became confident that if I needed Baba, all I had to do is call. Baba, in His compassion, had at last freed me from the fear of being alone, and the burden of the strong attachments to my family that I had carried ever since I can remember.

I understood now that loving does not mean that you have to be constantly near and attached to someone all the time. Loving also means letting go – loving means being free.

CHAPTER 11

A Channel to the Other Side

"There are more things in heaven and earth,
Horatio, than are dreamt of in your philosophy."

– William Shakespeare

The last few chapters you just read have been all about building bridges; the bridge between life and death. I agree with Linda Williamson when she says, "Perhaps the last bridge that we have to build is between each other, here on earth, so that we can bring about the peace that comes only when we realise that we are all spirit and come from the same Source." [1]

Long, long ago, most people thought of mediums as little old ladies with frilly blouses and long, beaded necklaces, sitting in darkened rooms, gazing into crystal balls and conjuring up the dead. At that time spiritualists were subjected to a degree of persecution, sometimes arrested and, like Joan of Arc, even burnt at the stake. Mediums had to be brave and dedicated souls to be able to hold their own against a hostile and sceptical public.

Gradually the image changed. In the West, mediums like Doris Stokes (*Voices in My Ear*) and Doris Collins (*Woman of Spirit*), reached out to the people of the world. Here in India, just to mention a few that I know, we had the likes of Mr. and Mrs. Rishi, and Mr. and Mrs. Kapadia. The proofs they gave were indisputable. They managed to show that the spirit world is all around us; that death is not an end but a beginning; that they were not motivated by any desire for personal glorification, but only to be of service to humanity.

They were followed by mediums like Stephen O'Brian (*Visions of Another World*), Coral Polge (*Living Images*), Ursula Roberts

(*Living in Two Worlds*), Mrs. Bhavnagri (*The Laws of the Spirit World*), and many others. The books they wrote reached out to many and succeeded in making some people believe that it was possible to go further into another dimension.

Mediums are now more recognised, respected and sought after. They are not thought of as something 'strange', but as psychics who come forward to help in times of trouble. Because of their concentrated efforts, people have now come to a stage where they do believe that it is possible to bridge the great divide; to understand that death is not the end but really the gateway to a new existence.

Today we have Brian Weiss, who delves into past lives and talks so openly on the subject of reincarnation. His book *Many Lives, Many Masters* has become a bestseller. We also have Neale Donald Walsch who has had his own *Conversations with God*. These books are not only very popular but some of them are now being made into films and will soon reach out to millions. There are many other movies being made on the subject of life after death, as well as TV serials such as *Ghost Whisperer* and *Mano Ya Na Mano* (Believe It Or Not) in Hindi, that have been very popular. There are also organised cruises where you can enjoy seeing the world, as well as meet celebrated mediums in person.

It is said that all of us have the potential to be a medium, that we all have the ability to raise our consciousness and link with the unseen world, but most of us are not aware of it. We all come into this world from the spirit sphere, from God, which is our true home. But once in this world, our everyday life crowds out the memory. As Wordsworth, in one of his famous poems, once said:

"Our birth is but a sleep and a forgetting,
The soul that rises with us, our life's star
Hath had elsewhere its setting
And cometh from afar...
Heaven lies around us in our infancy."

Actually, mediums are not delicate, sensitive creatures belonging to another world but practical and down-to-earth people like you and me. A few take the platform at large meetings in theatres and halls and work publicly, some give private sittings. There are some who are born into this world with the psychic gifts of seeing, hearing, healing and channelling, and others who need to go into a development circle to enhance their gifts. And then, there are some like me, who reach out and develop only because of a desperate need.

My visit to the college at Stanstead Hall in Essex, where I had the privilege to go in my early years of searching for the truth (chronicled in *Sounds of Silence*) was responsible for my development in many ways. Gordon Higginson taught us that "personal messages from loved ones should not be an end in themselves. They should be just the first steps along a pathway of spiritual knowledge." I may not have thought so at that time but, on hindsight, this definitely helped me to know that though I had far to go, I was on the right track. In the college we were also taught that there is a subtle difference between a psychic and a medium; that psychics use their own psychic powers, whereas mediums rely on the assistance of their guides. They try hard to make their minds passive so that a clear channel of communication between the two worlds is provided. Mostly, they do not predict the future but help counsel and just send love.

Slowly but surely, this is how it became for me. I definitely started out by going into my auto writing only to be with and talk to Karl. Baba was only there for me because He loved Karl and was looking after him. But many moments of grace from Baba came my way to show and prove to me that it was always Baba who was the Source and the soul behind it all. It just took a little bit of time for me to realise it.

Even now, much as I would like to, I cannot 'see', 'hear' or 'do' anything. There is no way I can foretell the future or play the game of lost and found. My work now is not only to contact those who have passed on, but also to help, guide and lead people to find their happiness by contact with Meher Baba. As far as I am concerned, everything is Baba's. There is a saying that 'you can lead a horse to water, but you cannot make him drink'. So, I can take you there but then the rest depends on you. You come from Him and go back to Him. Karl and I are only the channels in between.

Here is one story of a naturally gifted medium, Mehroo Gandhi, and another about Saraswathi Nandkumar who developed into a medium.

Mehroo is one of the oldest and most powerful natural-born mediums that I know in India today. She is one who has the intuitive ability to see and hear spirit people and does not have to raise her consciousness to do so. She has also developed further under the tutelage of Mr. and Mrs. Rishi, and has had sessions with Mr. and Mrs. Kapadia, all mediums of international status and repute. Here is her story...

I have been sensitive to the spirit world for as long as I can remember. I have been born with the gift of seeing and hearing, but it took a while before I realised just how much Baba meant to me.

I came to know about someone called Meher Baba when I was about nine or ten years old. I lived in Grant Road and heard many controversial stories about a Zoroastrian called Meher Baba, who was supposedly observing silence for a period of time. There was much conjecture as to whether he could really be keeping this silence like everyone said, or whether he could be talking on the sly.

In 1994-95, I was coming back from Shirdi and spent the night with some of my friends, Amy and Jangoo, in Nasik. As soon as I stepped into their dining room, I felt a very strong presence there. Not only could I sense the vibrations but also felt someone continuously patting my head and shoulders. I looked back – there was nobody!

Amy asked me what I felt about her house – whether I could feel good vibes – and I said, "Yes, vibes are definitely good but there is something much more powerful in your dining room." She laughed and said, "This is the room where Meher Baba did His meditation." Her husband Jangoo was closely connected with Baba.

This was my first formal introduction to Meher Baba.

After a few years, I came across Nan's book *Sounds of Silence* and was thus re-introduced to Baba. In the intervening years, I had been drawn to spiritualism in a big way and was learning to develop myself as a medium in the Saturday group, with the then famous mediums, Mr. and Mrs. Kapadia. So, I did have my own guides and my own group where we held sessions and did a great deal to help people as much as possible with their problems. But until I read Nan's book, Baba really did not have much meaning for me. Suddenly, after that, He came into focus.

Have I been ever able to 'see Baba'? Oh yes, a number of times!

One Saturday, Nan was invited by my group to give a talk about her recently published book. Being new to this, I am sure she was a little nervous and as she was talking and being questioned and somewhat grilled by some members of the group, I clearly saw two figures walking up and down the room, very concerned for her. It was Baba; but there were two of them – one a younger Baba, and the other an older Baba.

Being highly impressed by the book and with all that Nan had to tell us, one day my whole group decided to set off for Meherabad to see for ourselves what all this was about. We were picked up from the station by a devout couple, Dolly and Jal Dastoor, and driven in a Sumo to their house just below Meherabad hill. As we were going along, I saw someone sitting on the bonnet of the car. Who is this? A young fellow sitting happily on the top of the car, his hair flying in the breeze!

I entered Dolly and Jal's house and saw a hundred photographs of the same person at different stages of his life. Then I realised that the person I had seen sitting on the car was none other than the younger version of Meher Baba.

Have I ever 'heard Baba'? Oh yes, several times, but only in my mind and heart and it is always the Voice of Love.

One day, my friend Anita Lawyer informed me that she was going to Meherabad for dhuni day. I felt I would like to go along with her. Just before leaving the house, I was praying at my altar and I heard Baba say, "Will you put my photo here?" and I answered, "I will put it if I get one, but I will not go looking for it."

At the dhuni, there was an old Maharashtrian gentleman giving *prasad,* and together with that he was handing out some photos of Baba, but it was a big photograph of the older version of Baba. I did not like big pictures nor did I fancy the older Baba, so I rolled the big picture and put it away saying, "I don't like this Baba, I like your younger photo much more."

The words were hardly out of my mouth when I saw Anita come towards me holding out a few pictures of Baba. "Choose one," she said. I did, and it was the younger version of Baba that I had always loved and admired.

'Hmmm, Baba, it seems you are determined to capture me. You are not letting me go. Now I will have to put you on my altar,' I thought. So, I put Him there and promised that I would light a *diya* every day. Thus, I began to talk to Him more and more and understand all that He told me, in my heart.

On 10th of July, Silence Day (the day that Baba went into Silence in 1925), even though I knew that it would be overcrowded, I was still drawn to go to Meherabad. I am physically a heavy person who suffers from severe arthritis, so it was not easy for me to manoeuvre myself in a crowd, and I sat there just listening to the silence.

It was so beautiful, because it was a day when nature was talking and the people were silent. Birds were chirping, trains were whistling and the wind was blowing. There was a long serpentine line. I found it difficult to stand for long, and had given up the idea of going into the Samadhi. I sat down on one of the benches to pray and said to Baba, "I have taken the trouble to come so far, please see that You give me a proper darshan."

He said, "Close your eyes." I did. In my inner vision, I saw the tree near His home where His face had appeared and saw some flowers around it. I said, "No, I will not accept this Baba, this I can even see when I am in Bombay; what I want is a darshan in Your Samadhi. This is what I have come for."

Everyone was silent; but determined to get my way, I was preparing to find a paper and pen to write a request to the person in charge, when I heard Baba's voice say, "Come into the Samadhi after the lady in the blue *sari*."

"How can I come?" I argued, "there is still such a long line!" Just then, the lady in charge looked at me sitting desolately on the bench and gestured for me to get up. She asked me to follow the lady in the blue sari and to go into the Samadhi!

Once inside, I was so touched by Baba's consideration that the tears just came pouring down. I knew for sure that I did really link with Him and He did answer me. Without a thought I knelt down.

Years have gone by. Now, everything I do, every word I say, and every person I help is with Baba's help and guidance. It is motivated with love in my heart for Beloved Baba. He is a very important part of my life and my work. Everything is possible because of His grace and because of the power of His love.

Saraswathi Nandkumar stays at Rasta Peth, very close to Baba's Centre in Pune. From 1993, she was in the habit of going to her terrace every morning for a walk. She used to stop for a few minutes daily to admire the beautiful garden of roses in front of the Centre, but not once did she stop to wonder or try, or want to know about the person whose Centre it was.

Till October 1997, she was just an ordinary down-to-earth working mother of two lovely children, trying to strike a balance between a full-time job at the bank and her family. A strong desire to heal came into her life at this time and with that there was a most beautiful shift. She began to try and help people get relief from various physical and mental ailments.

On 12th of July 1998, her husband came home in the night, quite excited. He had met their *Reiki* Master, Karun, on his way back from office at M. G. Road. Karun, who made it a rule to refuse invitations to any student's house, had suddenly invited himself to their house for dinner. The excitement was highly infectious. Saraswathi called a few of her Reiki friends and shared the news with them, making them all a little jealous in the process. Little did she know that the purpose of Karun's visit was not really related to healing at all!

Saraswathi continues: Karun came home at the appointed time and unexpectedly asked me to show him around the house. As soon as he entered the bedroom, his eyes fell on a batch of books I had borrowed from the Pune Club library a few days earlier. He took out the book called *Sounds of Silence* from the pile and exclaimed, "Oh, I have been wanting to read this book for a long time and here it is." I had picked this book, attracted by its title, but had no idea of its contents. Karun told me that Meher Baba was his Guru and that he regularly visited Baba's Centre in Pune, situated so near our house.

Karun's introduction to the book made me read it with lots of love and respect. I identified with the mother, Nan Umrigar, in her sorrow at losing a precious child and in her joy in regaining him, so happy under Baba's care. Thus, it is through *Sounds of Silence* that Baba finally entered my life – soft as a breeze and yet powerful as a hurricane.

A few days after I had finished reading the book, in the middle of my sleep at around 4 am, I was awakened by the lovely fragrance of flowers around me. I sat up, puzzled. There was nothing in the room. After a few minutes, the fragrance faded and I went back to sleep.

That weekend, I was telling the story of Karl to my children Anusha (thirteen years) and Yogesh (nine years), when Anusha suddenly jumped up saying, "Mummy, I am getting a lovely fragrance of flowers." Both Yogesh and I also got it. It was the very same smell that I had experienced in the middle of the night a few days ago. We rushed to the window but found nothing inside, and nothing outside.

Anu, Yogesh and I started getting the fragrance quite frequently but for the life of us we could not identify the flower it belonged to. My husband was the odd one out, looking suspiciously at us whenever we discussed it. He thought it was my imagination and the children, innocent as they were, just agreed with me. But my sincere devotion to Meher Baba made him take the trouble of finding out Baba's residence in Camp and one day, very kindly, he took me there. Baba's 7-shaped room was situated at the backyard of the house and I was busy looking at the photographs, moving from picture to picture, when suddenly a familiar fragrance wafted on the air. I was overwhelmed. "Can you smell it?" I said excitedly. I expected him to refute it as usual but he did not. Instead, he pointed with shining eyes to a big photograph of Baba's, which was garlanded with masses of beautiful white flowers. We were told that it was the *Gulchedi*, Baba's favourite flower.

By now, other than just being sensitive, I had already started to do a little healing. I soon began to feel Baba's presence very frequently, whenever I stilled my mind. I often wondered how all this had come about and one day, while I was reading *Hands of Light* by Barbara Brennan, I got my answer by the grace of Baba. She says: 'When a healer, with heart and soul, makes attempts at healing people, he is always supported by a holy spirit, a guide, who makes his presence felt through the fragrance of flowers.' From an ordinary, monotonous existence, my life had taken a beautiful turn.

After planning for a long time, we finally went to Meherabad on the 26th of February 1999. Once there, I was totally lost and, as I bowed down and lowered my head on the Samadhi, I clearly heard a voice, "I am with you, I am in you."

One evening, after giving healing to my friend Veena, I left the room. After about twenty minutes, she came out extremely happy and thanked me profusely, telling me how great she felt. I said that it was Baba who did it. Then she shared this with me. She said, "Saraswathi, I heard your footsteps going out of the room and I opened my eyes. I saw a beautiful golden form sitting near me, with hands on me. I immediately closed my eyes and enjoyed the state of bliss. Now I understand why the energy feels so special. I know now that Baba has done it through you, and I have been lucky enough to have seen Him." Needless to say, psoriasis, which had been troubling her for more than a decade, has now almost vanished.

Life was becoming more and more beautiful with Baba guiding and protecting me every minute. In April 1999, a colleague of my husband lost his young son, Pushkar, under extremely tragic circumstances when the family had gone for a holiday to Darjeeling. A week after this, when I was meditating, I heard a voice telling me, "Please tell my parents that I am under Baba's care and I am very happy. Please help them come out of their grief." I knew instinctively that it was Pushkar's voice. As I had not met Pushkar's parents before, I was a bit confused and reluctant to pass on the message. But whenever I was meditating, the pleading voice very softly kept requesting me to do so. Still I could not muster up the courage. Pushkar, however, was not one to accept defeat and the day after his father joined the office, Pushkar seemingly worked a miracle. He made his father approach my husband with a very peculiar request: 'I know that you and your wife both have a special gift. Please, please, can you help us to come out of our grief?' My husband could hold himself no longer, for they were the very same words that Pushkar had spoken to me! Pushkar's mother, who had been totally shattered and could not walk properly after his death, with Baba's grace and help, slowly but surely regained the lost light in her eyes and, since then, the couple has become great devotees of Meher Baba. Now, Pushkar, along with Baba, readily appears whenever I want protection and help for anybody. The impossible is getting done effortlessly.

Enlarged view of Baba's profile seen in the crystal.

Baba is working wonders in my life and in the lives of all those who come in contact with me. Everything is happening with Baba's grace, for He has made the impossible, easily possible. I have even started healing with crystals now and many cures have been achieved. People have escaped surgery, severe cases of depression have been cured in just one sitting, failure of the elimination system – which had no treatment even in the USA – got cured in a month. My mother could avoid surgery for carotid block and my father's heart problem simply vanished. My sister in Detroit, in spite of severe pregnancy problems, eventually delivered a 9½ lb baby without any trouble.

Baba's gifts to me are very, very special, but for me the greatest gift of all is His love.

A special proof of His love happens to be his beautiful face, which one day appeared in one of my crystals. A totally clear crystal suddenly started showing some formations and I was curiously following it, till one day I discovered it was Baba's face – irrefutably etched in. The very next day I got this message from the book *Crystal Enlightenment* by Katrina Raphael... "when a guardian angel is supporting you in your healings, very frequently he appears as a form in one of your healing crystals." Needless to say – my joy knew absolutely no bounds.

Well, the day came at last when my meeting with Nan Umrigar took place. It was a special time for me – a time when I could tell her how my life has changed and what a difference her book has made for me.

But most important of all was the day – 26th January 2001. It was the day at Meherabad, while I was praying at His Samadhi, and I told Baba of my deep love for Him.

I bowed down before Baba and thanked Him from my heart and soul for making me a channel, through which His love, His goodness and kindness flows to those in misery.

I know that the best is still to come and although I am proceeding in many ways along the path of spirituality, I just cannot thank Baba enough for giving my life on earth a meaning, a very beautiful meaning.

CHAPTER 12

Rays of Angels

Healing is also a medium's gift. There are many methods of healing and different types of healing therapies available today. However, I write this chapter on spirit healing with the firm conviction that it was Baba who led me to the finest healer that I know. I write it not because I want to displease anyone or make them go against what they firmly believe, but only in the hope that it might help all those who are stricken and without relief, despite the care of doctors and nurses.

I wish to convey to you the idea that it is possible for the spirit body to receive treatment which in turn gets passed on and helps the physical body to heal. I believe that this is called spirit healing.

Spirit healers claim that, "The healing powers used in spiritual healing are of divine Source. The healing comes direct from God. It forms part of the natural laws of the universe and must be used accordingly. For this reason, it is available for the use of all mankind irrespective of colour or creed. It is then directed by guides in the spirit world who use the healer as a vehicle, through which they channel the healing energy. Again it is the healer who is the bridge for his spirit helpers."[1]

But the person I am now going to talk about is a little different from the ordinary. He came into my life in the most unusual way and I sincerely feel that it is with Baba's grace that this happened. I am talking about George Chapman, a 'spirit surgeon' who lived in Wales. Over the years, not only did I develop great faith and trust in him but he and his wife, Eliane, became my close friends as well.

It is many years since I first made contact with George and even though he always advocated that he could only help if your karma allowed it, to my limited knowledge he has been instrumental in effecting a great number of cures.

It began for me the day my grandson Zahan, just a year old, began developing bruises all over his little body. A visit to the doctor, and the tests carried out, showed a sudden drop in his platelet count. The doctor had diagnosed I.T.P. (Idiopathic Thrombocytopenic Purpura) and warned us that a further drop could be dangerous as there was no known cure for this. His mother Sabita came home and wept. Not knowing much about it, we imagined the worst and once more I rushed to Meherabad and begged of Baba not to put us through another ordeal.

After my return, that very night, a book came to my door; its title was *Healing Hands* by Joseph Bernard Hutton. After dinner I settled down and read the first two pages. It began, "I might have gone blind, I might have died. That neither happened..."

The book went on to tell of a channelling trance medium, George Chapman, whose healing exploits have now become world famous. A former Aylesbury fireman, Chapman claims to be controlled by the spirit of Dr. William Lang, an ophthalmic surgeon who died in 1937. The book also tells how when Hutton actually visited Chapman and encountered the spirit doctor, an unexpected miracle happened. His sight was restored.

I read far into the night.

Could a doctor really come back from the other side to carry on his work, I wondered? As I read on, somehow, a strong conviction was born. I knew that Meher Baba had 'found' this book for me. I had asked Baba for help and He had answered me.

So, we continued to correspond with George Chapman, who in turn continued with what he called 'Absent Healing'. Days went by, and although Zahan still suffered from nosebleed, he steadily improved until finally after just two months, one day, Karl said, *"Now he is well and you need not worry anymore."* A visit to the doctor confirmed this. Zahan's count had touched normal once more. You can imagine how happy we were.

I was so impressed with this 'George Chapman – Dr. Lang' phenomenon that I became determined to visit him. I was sure that

Meher Baba had sent him to me and I could not rest until I had seen him for myself and thanked him in person for all his help.

At this time in London, I caught up with a friend from Switzerland who agreed to accompany me to the remote village of Machynlleth, in Mid Wales, where George Chapman lived and healed.

We boarded a train from London's Euston station and we were soon chugging our way across rugged country till we reached the hilly slopes of Pant Glas. The beautiful dark green hills were dotted with woolly sheep and fat little Welsh ponies and there, snuggled in between a valley surrounded by trees with a spectacular view of Cardigan Bay, lay the most beautiful sanctuary you could ever find. The peaceful feeling was very similar to that of Meherabad.

We were a little early and so had time to enjoy the early morning freshness as we sat and waited for him to come. A man came striding up the pathway from the house into the sanctuary, and I met George Chapman for the first time.

I was introduced to him by his wife, Eliane, and he spoke to me briefly. He was a man of medium height with slightly greying hair, a smooth face and lovely, kind, blue eyes. His voice was firm and strong, and his figure straight and erect. He went through a door into a small room and, since mine was the first appointment, I was soon ushered in.

The healing room had an ambience and energy all its own. A table and chair, a stool, a healing couch, a small red light and a bowl of water was all that was visible at first glance. George Chapman was seated at the table and welcomed me with a smile. He asked me to sit down and bear with him for a while till Dr. Lang made a connection with him. At this point, I did not know or realise what a privilege it was to be able to actually see George Chapman going into the trance state. I believe not many had the chance to witness this unusual phenomenon.

He sat absolutely still, closed his eyes and they seemed to close tighter and tighter, till his face kind of puckered up and a remarkable change came over his features. He became older, wiser, and bent over. His voice took on a strongly southern accent and became weaker and highly pitched in the manner of the aged. I was faced with the same man, but not the same at all.

He got up and extended his hand in greeting. "What can I do for you, young one?" he said. Was I young compared to his wise years? Charmed by his manner, I told him that I had come to thank him personally for helping my little grandson Zahan, and that his love, his dedication, and his care and concern had touched my heart. His responses were silent as he indicated that I too should lie on the couch, as there were a few areas of my body that also needed his attention.

He held his hands a little above my forehead and I felt a strange tranquillity. He held his hands over my arthritic knees and I felt a quickening of my blood flow. He clicked his fingers as 'unseen helpers' passed him 'instruments' and he proceeded to perform surgery on the cartilages.

"There now," he concluded, "I am sure you will be fine." My visit soon ended and I found myself making my way back down the hill, but with one difference. I was walking, but I felt as if I was floating on air. I felt like a bird that wanted to spread its wings and fly away into paradise. I felt no more pain, only happiness.

After this, my connection with George Chapman continued over the years and I referred many sick and ailing patients to him.

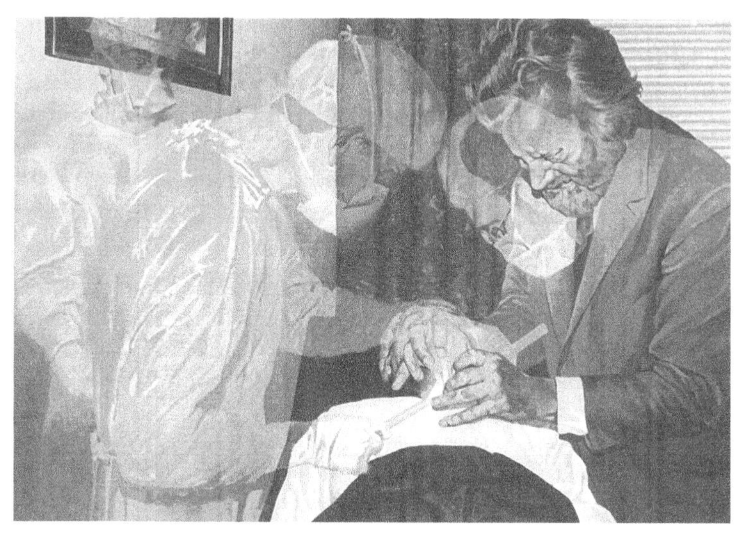

An artist's impression of George Chapman being assisted by Dr. Lang and healers from the spirit world.

He never failed to reply to anyone and most of them seemed to be helped in some way by the contact.

One day in 1989, Karl surprised me by saying, *"Dr. Lang says he wants to come to Bombay. You will see."* I did not pay much attention to this as I considered it a rather remote possibility. George Chapman had clinics in France, Switzerland and Germany, and I felt sure that with his advancing age he would find it difficult to travel all the way to India. But, a letter soon arrived stating his willingness and enthusiasm to come, requesting me to set up the arrangements for his visit.

Panic! Karl reassured me. *"Baba says you do not have any choice. He has made up His mind. Baba promises you everything will be looked after by Him."* And so it was.

George Chapman arrived. Accompanying him, as always, was Eliane who trebled as helper, protector and translator, arranging his appointments and was always beside him in the healing room. She had met George Chapman many years ago when Dr. Lang treated and looked after her little girl, Isabelle, till the day she passed away peacefully. She subsequently dedicated her whole life to him and his work.

George Chapman and Eliane arrived in Bombay. We met them at the airport, housed them at the Sheraton, looked after them, and tried our best to treat them with the love and respect they deserved. Many helpers rallied around. Some offered to get a hotel discount, others offered a car, so many came forward to help with the daily arrangements. Incidentally, the Chairman of the Royal Western India Turf Club, where Karl had been such a prominent figure, kindly offered me a place to have the healing. As Baba had promised, everything just fell into place.

Dr. Lang treated more than three hundred people in six days. Young, old, rich and poor, the sick and the suffering, all flocked for appointments. As usual, I spent the entire six days a nervous wreck, despite Karl's assurances from Baba that everything would be alright.

Jimmy, my husband, had by that time frightened the daylights out of me. "If someone dies, you will be responsible; if someone has a seizure or a heart attack, you will be taken to court" and so on. By the time the last day came, I was a bundle of nerves. I begged of Karl to ask Baba to be there, to protect and guide. Karl said,

"Mum, Baba will help you in whatever way He can, and today I will be present, I will be there."

I was sitting outside at the booking table, surrounded by people clamouring for a chance hope of seeing the spirit doctor. Suddenly, Eliane came out of the healing room and beckoned to me. "Nan," she said in her French-English, "Dr. Lang say to tell you, Karl is eeenside."

Such a beautiful happiness welled up inside me and overflowed in tears. No one except Baba and Jimmy had known of my morning message. I walked into the quiet of the healing room with its soft red glow and peaceful stillness. I stood quietly at the side. Although I could not actually 'see' Karl or 'hear' him, I knew he had come, as promised, to show himself to me, to help his beloved family and all those that believed in him. I had to thank only one person for that – Baba.

I have to add one more thing. Only one person out of the so many that came, cancelled his appointment. His daughter phoned me a few days after George Chapman had left for his home in Wales. She regretted the fact that he had been unable to keep the appointment and that he had passed away a few days later. I guess Jimmy's fears were unfounded, and mine too, when I was told that spirit healing sometimes may not help, if that is your karma, but it is never known to really harm anyone.

Michael Chapman (right) carries on the work of his father George Chapman.

It is now over twenty-three years since the day I first met George Chapman, but I used to keep in touch with him regularly by phone or by mail. As far as I am concerned, it is with Baba's grace that there have been many miraculous healings done by him in the intervening years.

The Dr. Lang and George Chapman partnership goes on, but not from this world anymore. George has passed away, but his son Michael, himself a successful healer (but not a trance healer yet), now carries on his father's work in partnership with Dr. Lang's son, Basil Lang, who is also on the other side.

The fact of there being a father and son healing team in both worlds is a remarkable phenomenon. It is also remarkable how Baba brought him into my life.

There now follow stories of two unbelievable healings that have taken place.

Hormuzd Narielwalla says: I was lucky to have crossed paths with Meher Baba when I was just sixteen, though at that time I didn't realise the significance of having such a strong spiritual force guiding me. I am just twenty-five now, and I feel these last years have probably been the toughest for me. I'm fortunate to have met Meher Baba, my eternal friend, and though I never had the opportunity of meeting physically, the love I have for Him is deeper than I can describe.

My life so far hadn't been spectacular, or lived to its fullest. To be honest, I didn't really know what I wanted to achieve in life. I was trying to explore the possibilities of becoming a fashion designer. All these confused thoughts came to an abrupt end when I became bed-ridden and was diagnosed with a slipped disc. I went through the process of meeting every doctor in Pune, Bombay, and even a German doctor; I knew of every physiotherapist, over-enthusiastic sports doctors, as well as ayurvedic and homeopathic doctors; I practiced yoga and was given numerous back exercises. I regularly had X-rays taken and even had to go through a CT Scan, but what really scared me was that, during this whole ordeal, I was on five painkillers a day and was putting on weight drastically. My situation worsened. I was fed up of being surrounded by walls, and ironically my bed had now become my sanctuary. Six months had passed and I vividly remember when I was finally advised that I needed surgery. All this time I thought this was just a bad backache which would go. I didn't realise what a problem I was in. How could I not? I couldn't lift my legs up, I was losing sensitivity in the side of my right foot, I could only bend ten degrees and, of course, there was the shooting pain. More than the pain, I was losing hope and my self-esteem was at its lowest.

I remember the day my mum's relative, Silla Aunty, spoke about her experiences with a spirit doctor in Wales and how he helped her recover through some sort of healing powers. How magical and how unrealistic it sounded. Was this going to be another foolish attempt to get me out of this? But she eagerly called her sister Nanny and she came to meet us the following week.

We talked for over an hour and she spoke about her experiences with her son Karl, Meher Baba and finally Dr. Lang. All I did was quietly listen. It sounded like a story straight from a movie. For a minute I thought the painkillers had got the better of me and that I was chatting with this lady who had suddenly become my imaginary friend. However, the plan was to write a detailed report and send my medical history to George Chapman, and Nanny Aunty was going to connect with Karl and ask for help. Was this also going to be another waste of time?

I had now finished eight months in bed and a part of me had wanted to believe that things would improve. A week passed. I was feeling marginally better but there wasn't a fantastic change and, realistically, I didn't expect one.

One night, during one of my peak pain periods, I suddenly rolled off my very high bed, only to fall straight on my back. Surprisingly, I awoke midway and felt something or someone cushioning me. It felt like I fell on a bed of feathers! However my mum, who never gets up from her sleep, heard a loud thud, came running down, and was shocked to see me lying speechless on the floor. This was it, I thought, I'm going to die! I said a small prayer and then for the first time, I used Meher Baba's name and asked for help. "Please Baba, help me to get up and go back to sleep," I begged, and shockingly that's exactly what happened. I slowly got on my feet, in absolutely no pain and went back to bed. I got up the next morning thinking this experience was just a dream, but it wasn't. In retrospect, when I think about that night, I think of how the slightest touch would send spasms of pain up my spine and in my sciatica nerve, and how such a fall didn't hurt me the slightest bit. How could it be? Was it Baba, Dr. Lang, help from Karl, just coincidence, or a combination of all?

My faith in Baba and the existence of another world, slowly began to increase. I was then advised by Karl to seek physiotherapy and to start swimming. That is when I began to lose some weight and the painkillers began to slowly recede. Ten months had passed with letters going up and down to George Chapman, and many messages from Karl to keep me centred on Baba. We finally made a plan to visit Meherabad with a couple of friends who are Baba devotees, and arranged also to meet Nanny Aunty there.

My first visit to the Samadhi was in the evening. It was an enchanting night, people had gathered around and everyone was singing and reciting Baba's prayers. Then came the moment of bending down and paying respects. I panicked! "It's never going to happen, I can't," I said to myself, but as I steadily approached all I could see was a big painting of Baba smiling down at me, and I just knew He would understand. However, as I walked closer, I thought maybe what I could do was somehow get on my knees and just touch the stone. But something made me go one step more. I bent over to kiss the floor. I did it, and effortlessly too. You cannot imagine what it meant to me. It was exactly ten months since I had bent down. All this time I had to have someone else tie my shoelaces, I could never pick up anything from the floor, bending down to get into the car was a challenge by itself, and here I was actually kneeling to pay my homage to Meher Baba. It was a miracle by itself. Love poured from my heart and tears from my eyes. With Baba's help, I had overcome the biggest challenge so far in my life.

That night I made my choice. I chose to pursue fashion and there was no looking back. But I wasn't totally satisfied with what I had done and felt restricted in Pune. I was getting nowhere, and I wasn't interested in doing it in India. So, I applied in Paris as well as a few other centres, and guess what? Of all the places in the world, I got accepted at Wales! A personal visit to George Chapman for a personal healing was then definitely on my agenda.

I write this now in an IT suite at the University of Wales, Newport, in the United Kingdom. I have successfully finished the first year of my degree and look forward to the next two years. I know that completing this is going to be a challenge in itself. But I know I need not worry. I have learned to believe in my capabilities and I have Baba looking after me. I love Him dearly.

The process of meeting Beloved Baba was through pain, but I know now that it was the best thing that could have happened to me. So, open your hearts and believe in Him, love Him like you love your life, and love your life like you love Him.

Zarina Messman says:

If you have a staunch and unswerving faith in Baba, He can do anything for you, even give you a new lease of life, as He did for me. I would like to narrate, in short, what Meher Baba did for me, and why I have no doubt that He is God.

In 1992 I had a hysterectomy. As soon as the effect of the anaesthesia wore off, I started complaining of a pain in my throat. The doctor put it down to soreness, but it was not. Leave alone solid food, I was not able to swallow drinking water or to retain it. Then started my rounds from one hospital to another, and from one specialist to another. Endoscopies revealed multiple strictures and a complete closure of the oesophagus. Then started the painful and distressing dilations. But even after twenty-eight such oesophageal dilations, and being in the hospital for one-and-a-half months, I was feeling no better. After six years of surviving on a clear liquid diet, I had lost twenty-two kilos.

The doctors gave up hope for my survival.

In spite of meeting with wonderfully devoted mediums and healers, my trials continued. Now it was decided that I should undergo surgery for removal of the food pipe. The specialist we consulted said I had a 70% chance of success. Through my friend Vira Keshwala, a renowned medium who works with the *ouija board,* Meher Baba said, "No operation."

I did not listen. By hook or by crook I wanted to get well and be normal like everyone else.

I was wheeled into the theatre. Three big circles were attached to my back. Wires were clipped to my fingers and the gas mask put on my face. My doctor entered. He examined the X-rays, suddenly turned to me, and said, "Are you scared?" When I said, "No, I was not," he said, "I am. It is a ten hour operation but you know what, when I see your stomach, your hands and face, they seem to be quite filled out and, in spite of everything, I feel that there is someone taking care of you." He stopped, closed his eyes and seemed to ponder for a while. Suddenly he turned to me saying, "There is a voice in my head, strongly telling me not to cut you up. I cannot ignore it." With that, the surgery was cancelled and the next day I went home.

Deep in my heart, I just knew that Meher Baba had something to do with all this. But I was disappointed with Him because He had stopped my operation; my only chance of getting well was gone. The thought of having only liquids for the rest of my life, and such a fervent longing to eat bread and butter, was such a heartache for me. Why could I not be like everyone else? Why, Baba?

However, it seems that Meher Baba had other plans for me. A fortnight after returning from the hospital, I had laid out some buttered bread for my son when I heard a distinct voice say, "Pick it up and eat." It kept on urging me, till finally I picked up a small piece and put it in my mouth. I could swallow it! I could actually swallow it! I tried more and more, till I greedily finished two whole slices of bread and butter. From that day, I started eating food. What the doctors were unable to do in six years, Meher Baba did in a matter of seconds. Who can give you back your life except God?

Many times in those six years, I have experienced Meher Baba's love and compassion. He was my constant companion. Now looking back beyond those years, when I did not know about Baba, I wonder how I lived without His presence in my life. A life that was meaningless and worthless without Him.

In 1997, Baba sent me *Sounds of Silence,* the most wonderful book that I have ever read. It was a source of great inspiration to me and showed me the way to proceed. It worked like a magnet and kept pulling me towards Meherabad and Baba's Samadhi. Now, whenever I am feeling low, depressed or sad, I pick up this book and turn the pages, and it never fails to lift up my spirits and put me on the right path. I keep the book by my side and it has become almost like my Bible to me. I derive immense comfort from talking to Karl, and his lovely messages give me the necessary strength to fight the battles of life.

So far I was under the impression that Meherabad must be some ordinary place like the *dargahs* that we see around, but Nan's description of the Samadhi, the Pilgrim Centre, and of the love and energy there, fired my imagination so much that the urge to go there and see it with my own eyes grew more and more with each passing day. Could there really be a place like this on earth? It sounded so heavenly! Oh, how I longed to go.

Baba must have heard me for, that very night, Vira Aunty rang up to say that her family had planned a trip to Meherabad and that she had made arrangements for me to go along with them. I jumped with joy.

There are no words to describe my first sight of the Samadhi; the beauty, the peace, the love and energy of the place seeped into my very soul. Tears began pouring out of my eyes and I sobbed for a very long time. The hill, the stones, the little shrubs and the colour of the flowers; everything was just so beautiful. I felt as if the very trees were spreading out their branches to welcome me with open arms and everything looked alive and vibrant with life. The whole area had a fragrance all its own and I had a wonderful sense of belonging. I felt that after years of wandering, I had at last come home.

Now my life is influenced completely by Baba's all-pervading presence. I feel that all those years of starvation, physical pain and suffering were worth it, as it brought me in close contact with Baba. He has given me a second chance to live for which I am eternally grateful. And now the only thing that matters is my love for Him. For me, Baba is Everything and Everybody and my entire life revolves around Him.

Meher Baba takes care of those who really leave their lives completely in His benevolent hands. This is His amazing grace.

CHAPTER 13

Guidelines

"In the performance of His universal work, the Man-God has infinite adaptability. He is not attached to any one method of helping others, He does not follow any rules or precedents, but He is a law unto Himself. He can rise to any occasion and play any role that is necessary under the circumstances without being bound by it."[1]

Auto writing came to me as a moment of grace from God, to heal my heart and to draw me towards the light. It changed the course of my life. I became that "little pencil in the hand of a writing God who is sending a love letter to the world." – Mother Teresa

Even before I showed up in Meherabad for the second time, I was already mired in controversy. News of the story I had told on my first visit, of my communication with Karl via the auto writing, had already reached the Baba community. This seemed to go against the grain of Meher Baba's instructions; that His followers should not meddle with the occult. I believe that in His lifetime, Meher Baba had deemed it to be a spiritual trap and pitfall, and had warned His followers that more harm than good would come from their involvement with it.

However, being totally and blissfully ignorant of all this, I continued my loving journey towards Baba, and I was always welcomed in Meherabad with a lot of love and affection. Mehera, Baba's beloved, and Mani, Baba's sister, and the mandali simply followed their Master's example of unconditional love and allowed me my space to grow towards Baba the way He wanted. Baba had called me and that was enough for them. How and why did not really matter. In all honesty, as Mansari once told me, they thought that the writing would stop once the mission was completed.

But instead of stopping, it has grown so much over the years and has been instrumental in drawing so many to Baba. It has become such a strong new branch on the Baba Tree, that one day I myself could not help asking Karl for an explanation. This is what he said.

"It really must be understood by you that when Baba laid down these precepts, the world was without so much knowledge of tapping the occult medium to find a way towards the light. This has now gathered momentum and has become a way to reach God. So as times change, thoughts change, and Baba who rules the world makes His own additions and selections the way He chooses.

"So Mum, do not dwell on this. Have the trust you always had, that what you are doing is right, and that you have Baba to look after you. Have the strength and the will, the faith and the love for Baba, to be able to put all this aside so that when we communicate, we do so with a love we share and project to those who have no one to sustain them. Baba wants you to feel free and not fettered by any ties. Love Karl."

So what then is auto writing?

When I went to the Arthur Findlay College at Stanstead Hall in Essex, and spent a week there in order to gain more experience, I learnt a great deal more than what I already knew from reading books by well known authors on the subject in question. In the words of Edain McCoy, "auto writing is the art of contacting other intelligences, through the use of pen and paper, while in an altered or meditative state of consciousness." It is not difficult and most people have some degree of success fairly quickly. It is very necessary for you to follow the ground rules and try to understand the 'whats and hows' surrounding it.

Many gifts lie within us and our minds have many marvellous powers, but we do not know how to tap them. By using these gifts the right way, by merging ourselves with a universal mental energy, our superconscious mind can open many doors and gain access to a great deal of information hitherto unknown to us.

Auto writing then is mostly a fusion, when two minds join together, and the answers flow from the spirit mind to the human mind. The thought first passes through the brain and then out through the hand and, if you spend a little time and effort, it is really not that difficult or dramatic. However, many a time, especially in the initial stages, words and sentences tend to repeat themselves over and over again, till you wonder if anything else is ever going to come, and then suddenly a new word flashes on the paper, and you feel overjoyed. Then, most important of all is concentrated practice.

When you are auto writing, the best thing to do is to shut off all distractions and noises from the outside world. Sit in a quiet familiar place, still the mind, and try and place yourself in a medium-level state of consciousness. Edain McCoy says, "there is never any danger in this, because you do not at any time sever your connection with the outside world. Though you will be intently focused in your efforts, you will not be completely aware of what you are doing and saying. Your eyes are open, your ears can hear... you do not lose contact with any bodily functions. You are simply harnessing Psychic Energy... and making it work for you."[2] You should then use it, definitely not to foretell the future, but for ideas, advice, and to draw help from the spirit world. Most importantly, you should never let all this overpower or overtake you, but use it with a greater purpose in mind.

At the college, we were also told that there are three types of contacts or connections that you can make. You can contact your Higher Self, other loving entities, or your own spirit guides.

Who then are the spirit guides that you can communicate with; what is their role in our earthly lives; and how can we know them?

We all have what might be called our own 'guardian angel' – a spirit who watches over us throughout our life. These guardian angels stand patiently by, loving and helping us to get through our chosen life in the best possible way. Many of them have lived life on an earthly plane centuries ago, and have reached a high level of spiritual development. They are the trusted and valued friends who have great wisdom and courage, whom you have made a contract with to watch over you while you are living your life.

Guides are not really there to teach or to interfere with your free will. Divine guidance never makes choices for you. This is because of the fact that every one of us has to deal with the consequences of our own choices. Guides are truly the messengers of God, only there to show you the way and to ensure that the plan you have charted out for yourself is followed through. Their guidance normally follows the laws of the spirit world; it does not usually predict the future but helps you to discover your life's purpose and mission. They can be male or female, sometimes have past-life connections with you, or have been family in days gone by. They can auto write with us, appear to us in dreams, or give us signs. They will rarely reveal who they have been in their earthly lives, but try their best to be of service and use any means available to get their messages across to us.

How do you know if what you are receiving is really from the Source?

Everything that flows from the other side is always supportive, strong, powerful, mostly direct and to the point. It never tears down your confidence but gives you strength to carry on, and assures that you can do it. It fills you with a warm and loving positive energy, gives you hope for the future, and assures you that God loves you and all will be well.

Harry Edwards, a great healer and psychic, advises that there is one very important point to remember. You are receiving information from another dimension and just because someone is in the spirit world, it does not make him God! He is still what he was in life, so listen to what he says but also use your own intuition and powers of reasoning. Do not blindly follow any commands, except those that your own heart dictates. The best way to judge the accuracy of what you have written is to see how much of it comes true.

Because of love, many links are made. Some continue on the periphery, just content to talk to their loved ones, while some develop further to begin helping others and continue along the spiritual field. The same goes for those on the other side. They also have their own roles to play. Some continue just to give their loved ones hope and peace of mind, and some guide, help and lead people on to the spiritual path, and some do not want to be disturbed at all.

I remember Karl's first message to me, through Mrs. Bhavnagri, which said, *"Mummy, I have worked very hard for these past few years to reach a high level and want to guide you on earth, but only few can do so."* At that time they were just words to me, words that made no sense at all because for the life of me, I could never imagine Karl on a spiritual mission! I remember also that just after my friend Amie had begun to communicate with her daughter Nicol, Baba had substituted Nicol with another spirit soul because Nicol was put into training for a while by Baba. Amie herself was told that she had to read, study and find out everything about the five key religions.

With so many beautiful experiences and stories you have read so far, you may get the impression that all the messages that come through in the auto writing are totally correct. It is Karl's faith in Meher Baba that enables him to give messages of hope to all that come to him. At times, his messages have been astounding in their truth and clarity, and sometimes there have been doubts. At other times they have made no immediate sense, but proved themselves at a later stage. Although Karl has always persisted in producing indisputable proof in order to validate the communication, the ultimate contact with Meher Baba has given each person a bond of love and, above all, a trust in His non-physical presence.

There was a time when I was approached by a lady who desperately wanted Baba's help to get her oven working again. I was aghast – what a thing to ask? But then I was mortified about my thoughts when I found out that she was running a cake shop and a bakery, and the proceeds helped pay for her medical treatment. She was a patient with a very serious handicap. Now even in her shop, it has come to a stage that whenever there is a major breakdown of any of the appliances, even the workers say, "Baba koo bolna" (why don't you tell Baba).

It was a lesson learned; that what may seem to be trivial to one may not necessarily be so for another.

Very soon after that, a young lady called Sonali (name changed) called me from Canada to tell me that her close relatives had been murdered in cold blood in their own home. Their only son came home one night to find the bodies of his parents lying in a pool of blood. Distraught and unable to make any sense of the tragedy, Sonali wondered if Karl could throw some light on the matter.

I am aware that my writing does not really help solve murder mysteries, nor should it be used in order to punish anyone. At the same time, after my experience with the lady and her oven, I felt that though I should use my discretion, it is not for me to decide what questions to ask and what to avoid. So, I left the decision to Karl to answer in whichever way he thought fit. And I received the strangest message.

"They do not wish anything to be done at all. From the family left behind, no one is to go to the police except to report the incident, and not to pursue it any further. They feel love and sorrow for the son but not for themselves, for they are settled and already with Baba and so do not wish

to change things. They have nothing lacking except the child they left behind, and have asked that the investigations be left absolutely alone. He will be told by the police that they do not have a clue, but they do, and he will be led up the garden path – so, best not to ask anymore. The truth will be revealed to him in the most unexpected way. They send deep feelings of love."

What would you make of this message? Before reading any further, go over the message again and try to find the answer, because we tried and failed. Why did the parents not wish the investigations to be pursued?

The police searched along 'the garden path' and that is where the murder weapon was found. It was the son who was suspected of the deed! Suddenly, Karl's message made perfect sense to us, for the parents were ready to forgive the boy who they loved, and still love, so dearly.

Baba once conveyed, ***"The Powerhouse will never fail, provided the wires take care of their connection with It."***[3]

So keeping in mind everything that Baba has said, we have to understand that all that is received by us, is transmitted from across 'the great divide'. That on this side, we are still human beings, with human minds and thoughts of our own, only deriving our energy from that other dimension. So, just as in telephonic conversations, it is possible for lines to go out of order. There can be disturbances, emotional and atmospheric, sunny days and rainy days. There never is a total shutdown, but you do have to make allowances for communication gaps or even a wire failure.

I have now been communicating with Karl every single day for twenty-five years, except when I am in Meherabad. As far as I am concerned, my connection is only with my son and I do not have access to any other means of communication. I just plug into his energy, connect up with him and then let the writing flow. I do get signals, my thumb throbs and mostly the hand moves as if it has a life of its own. It sometimes even tingles and feels a little heavy.

Through the years, I have learned so much and sometimes also the hard way. Due to my own lack of self-confidence I still feel hesitant to give messages to people, for though I do not doubt the veracity of the messages, I do often doubt my own ability to receive them correctly. What if I have received it wrong?

What if it has been coloured by my own thinking? What if I have been too judgemental in my attitude?

Normally, Karl keeps me grounded by telling me that *"Everything is Baba's"* and that I am not responsible for who comes and who receives what. I try to follow this but I still lack the self-confidence for I have no real psychic qualifications or aspirations to speak of, except a real and deep love for Baba. So, each message that comes and goes is still followed by a few thumping heartbeats.

I remember when I first mentioned to Baba's sister, Mani, that I had put down my experiences in *Sounds of Silence*, she said to me, "Dear Dhun (Mani always called me by this name), this is your own private and personal story, why not keep it as such? Most people may not understand about auto writing and how it has all come about, and it might cause some controversy. Why not avoid it." Then seeing the disappointment on my face, she kindly said, "But I myself would love to read it, so why don't you just leave it here and I will go through it at some future date." I was disheartened! I had spent so many hours, days, and years in the making of this book. So much work had been put in not only by me, but also by my friend Amie. I had been helped and encouraged by so many other close Baba friends that this reaction from someone who really mattered to me, blew my mind! However, I did not have the inclination or the heart to go through with it without Mani's permission and blessings. Contrary to all expectations, my husband Jimmy, who usually always poured cold water on anything to do with my Baba activities, piped up in my defence. He pumped his hands on his hips and said, "Why? Why did Mani say no?" I shrugged my shoulders and shook my head. I was close to tears and could not say anymore. I had decided that I did not want to offend the sensibilities of my dearest Baba's mandali for I loved and respected them too much. So, I left the manuscript for Mani to read in her own time and was fully prepared for a long wait, and maybe a refusal.

However, two days later, I got a call from her asking me to come and see her. She hugged me tight and said, "On reading your manuscript, I do feel that I have no right to stop you from publishing your story for it is your own personal journey to Baba, no matter which way it is. I leave it to Baba's wish and Baba's will. I do, however, have one request to make. If new people are brought to Baba through your communication, it is fine, but please do not give any older Baba lovers any messages. Please explain to them that since they are already connected with Baba, they might just lose their intuitive ability to connect with Him. So though the temptation maybe there for them, unless you feel that they really need it for some reason, please do not encourage them to get answers through the communication."

I told her that I understood and, that unless it was a directive from Baba, or I felt deeply that it was necessary, I would not indulge or encourage this. I have kept my word to Mani. I never communicate with Karl when I am in Meherabad. For me it is not necessary, for I know that it is Baba who is the Source and who is the Goal.

I am aware that in many cases, Baba's grace, Karl's role of helper, and maybe mine as counselor, does help towards a successful conclusion, but this should not be considered as the ideal solution to everyone's problems. I have to keep in mind that very often things do not work out that easily, and problems can arise because of karmic debts, or when there are lessons to be learned, and sometimes there are no real conclusions in sight. There have been

Baba's sister Mani.

many ups and downs, and many more lessons to learn. But in the process of this journey, with every successive trip to Meherabad, and with every day that passes, I have come still closer and closer to Baba.

In the beginning, if you had told me that Karl's messages to me would stop, I would have been devastated but not anymore. Sure I will miss speaking to Karl, for he is my son, but it will not be the end of the world because now I know that everything is Baba's. When Baba is there, there is no beginning and no ending, there is only forever!

CHAPTER 14

Shopping Around

"Once you open your wings to fly, you must fly straight like the swan. Do not flit from tree to tree like the sparrow or many things will distract you on the way, and the journey is long."[1]

Sounds of Silence was written more than ten years ago. Today, a large section of the world's population has begun to show interest in the occult and life after death. But at that time, those around me, my husband included, were not only sceptical but some of them were downright derisive and critical of it. So, I was initially very wary about sharing the communication and afraid of writing about something that was so close to my heart.

The experience of the writing was everything to me and, therefore, my reality. I am not making excuses for myself, but I was so new to it, that to have doubts was only natural. Most people depend on their vision of the world as they experience it – that is each one's reality, sometimes dependable and sometimes not. So they shop around. The universe provides you with what you have asked for, and so each one's reality is unique in experience. Each one's reality is judged and questioned by the other. The question is, who is right and who is wrong? Who is weak and who is strong? Who is ahead of the game or lagging behind, intellectually and spiritually? The rich and famous are in the limelight; the poor are ignored and forgotten. One wonders, is all this for real? If so, then the universe leads you on and your growth depends on your own style of thinking. It is set and it is perfect, till a Master steps into your life. Then begins a journey of discovery, not of the universe and all its wonderful attractions, but of the Self.

Sounds of Silence therefore became a different kind of story, written simply and with heart. It became the topic of conversation, because not only did spiritualists consider it as something unusual but marked it as being one of its kind. It warranted a read, it merited grace and required no justification, just because it was sourced in occult beginnings.

However, to have self-doubts was only natural for messages can come in different ways, colours and sizes, and can be delivered by different people in different ways. We have to decide what suits us best, what we feel happy with and then, most importantly, we must learn to stop at that. But we do not. More often than not the temptation is too great, we tend to go off the deep end and continue on and on – shopping around.

Though the centre of my world is definitely Baba, I have often taken off in different directions hoping I am not deluding myself, and looking for more answers and proofs as I go along. The spirit world then has its own ways of stopping me and, oft and on, giving me a sharp wrap on the knuckles, and Baba teaches me my lessons in His own charming way. Sad to say, this has happened to me more than once.

The first time was when I had just started communicating with Karl. I was in the throes of so much excitement, trying to find more ways and means of connecting with my son. At this time, I had developed great faith and respect for Ernavaz and Phiroz Kapadia, both mediums of many years' standing, who were also closely connected with Mrs. Prabhavati Rishi, the medium I had met on an earlier occasion.

Phiroz and I had long discussions on my experiences and doubts and, although he had his own interpretation of spirit phenomena, he could find no explanation in the ambit of spiritualism for Karl's representations in different forms and shapes. However, he held no doubts about the reality of my experiences and strongly urged that I trust the guidance, as it was being controlled by a Spiritual Master. Not many people, to his knowledge, had this advantage. Besides, the person I was in direct contact with was none other than my own son.

He asked me if I would like to attend one of his Saturday meetings in order to get more experience of spirit phenomena, and I readily agreed. But when asked, Karl was not so happy about it. *"Why do you have to go anywhere to learn more, when we are here to teach and guide you; is there any need to go elsewhere Mum?"* he said. But I was ready for the session and off I went.

I was ushered into a large hall. There was an inner circle comprising those who were actively going to take part, and an outer circle of mostly those not so closely connected, as well as the newcomers. I was told to sit on a chair in this outer circle and to maintain absolute silence.

I was more than excited. My initial contact had been with Mrs. Khorshed Bhavnagri who had got the first message from her sons at a similar meeting held at this very place, with the very same people. I was really hoping that Karl would come forward with a startling message for me.

The whole congregation went "Auuummmm." I joined in. They were giving spiritual energy to their leader, Phiroz, to connect with his guide. I was most intrigued. His voice changed – became gruff and loud – and it really did not sound like Phiroz at all. Very soon, his guide came through and proceeded to give us a talk on the benefits of spiritualism. I was impressed for it really was most enlightening. How could another entity speak from another world and tell you so many beautiful truths?

This session ended and it was the turn of Ernavaz to go into a trance. I was fascinated! The spirit of a nun came into her. Her voice and the intonations of her spoken words changed. "My child," she said, as she proceeded to walk around the room and give meaningful messages to all in the outer circle. She was approaching me. I closed my eyes; I was so sure that Karl would come through and give me a soul-shaking message. She stopped one step away from me, she wavered, she rocked and swayed from side to side and seemed to be losing some of her power. "Mmm...," she mumbled. The whole congregation gave her additional spiritual support by saying "Auuummmm!" She pointed in my direction, "Something, something is coming from there, and I cannot progress beyond this point." With that she turned and went back.

I shrank into my chair terrified! What was happening? I wanted to run away. Phiroz smiled a benevolent smile. He indicated by gestures that I should not worry. He was used to this and knew very well that it was probably Karl who was disrupting this whole meeting because he wanted to prove a point. He wanted to show his mother that it was Meher Baba who should be the most important issue in her life, whom I should learn to know, to trust, and to believe.

Another incident like this occurred when I went to the Arthur Findlay College at Stanstead Hall. I have already related this at length in *Sounds of Silence* but feel the need to talk a little about it here, because it had a great effect on me.

The world-famous psychic, Coral Polge, recommended the Arthur Findlay College to me. It is a college that dates back to 1096 AD, one that people from all over the world come to visit. Ivy Northage, also a famous medium, had warned me, "I would not go if I were you," she said, "for it is difficult for the mediums there to understand the natural guidance of a Spiritual Master such as Meher Baba. In fact, you may not even stay the whole week out." In spite of the warning, my friend Amie Rabadi and I checked in there for a seven-day visit and, as usual, we had to live and learn. After having kept quiet for the whole visit so far, we reluctantly decided to share our story about Karl and Meher Baba with everyone. I was unprepared for the reaction. As predicted, the mediums there could not understand an experience such as ours. They tore holes in our story, denigrated automatic writing, and expressed serious doubts about our guides. Hurt and disappointed, we left the college a full day ahead of schedule.

Another such time, and the last I hope, was when I had just shifted to Pune, and awoke to find my house burgled. When I came out of my room in the morning, it was only to find everything in complete disarray; clothes were strewn around, cupboards wrenched open, and all electrical goods missing. The arrival of the police with their sniffer dogs did nothing to solve the problem and, although we waited for days, there was no news of the robbers or any hope of recovery of the stolen goods. Asking Karl in the writing produced only a pointer to say it was an inside job and, that Baba was not there to punish. It seemed pointless to ask for further clarification as the question was purely materialistic and, I thought, maybe too trivial for those in the spirit world to spend their time and energy on. So, there the matter rested.

One day, in all good faith, a neighbour told me of a local lady who had the gift of clairvoyance or farseeing and who could perhaps give me some leading clues as to who the robbers could be. As she lived quite far from my area, somewhere close to the airport, I did not want to go alone, so off I went with my neighbour without informing Jimmy. We had to pass through some uninhabited areas, uncultivated fields and wide-open spaces, before we finally reached a winding road that led to a small village. There, in a tiny hut as big as a thimble, was the lady soothsayer. She listened to my story and then, after mumbling some prayers, she gave me a talisman wrapped in cloth. She asked me to keep it for ten days and then to return for the answer.

When the stipulated time was over, I called up my neighbour but he was unable to come, so of course, brave me, I decided to go it alone. It had been raining quite heavily but that did not stop me, and I found my way quite easily through the open spaces. I drove my little Maruti car fearlessly over the rocky places, straight into the fields and into the slush. Before I knew it, I was stuck! The car had sunk half-way in! I pushed the door with all my might and just managed to squeeze myself out with the greatest difficulty. I looked helplessly around, there was not a soul in sight. My heart began to hammer as I saw my car sinking, slowly but surely, further and further into the mud. I began to wonder at my foolishness. Why had I come? Why did I do these things? Was it that important?

I waited in desperation. Suddenly I spotted two cyclists in the distance. I stuck four fingers into my mouth and let out the loudest whistle I could muster. I jumped up and down and waved frantically to attract their attention, but they just waved back and continued on their way. Fortunately, they must have noticed that I was in some sort of trouble and somehow, after a while, they changed course and came my way. Imagine their reaction when they saw that my car was about to disappear into the mud!

I really don't know how but I am sure Baba must have helped for, between us, we somehow managed to bodily lift my little car out of the slush and put it on the path again. But guess what? To my horror, I found that instead of putting it on to the side where I could go home again, we had dumped it on the wrong side! You can imagine just how scared I was for now I had no option but to move forward and find the lady's hut. I do not recall how I got there, only to be told that it was her *upvas* (fast) day and that she was not seeing anyone at all.

Now, how was I to get home? I sat in that car and tried hard to still my thumping heart. I tried to remember all the things that I had read and been exposed to that stated positive thinking is a way of helping God to make you use His power to help yourself.

I kept telling myself, "Don't panic Nan, Baba is on your side. He is always with you." Then, calling His name, I started the car and just blindly drove along the pathway before me.

It worked – it actually worked! For suddenly, as if from nowhere, another car came into vision and, believe it or not, it was actually going my way. The driver, obviously seeing my distraught state, was kind enough to give me a lead and so waved me on to the main roadway.

I reached home after five hours to a furious Jimmy who demanded to know just where I had been and why. You can imagine the scene, especially when he saw what the poor car looked like.

Since that day, and the lesson learned, I have not strayed and no amount of temptation has taken me away to 'shop around'. Maybe those who read this will also think twice before embarking on such a journey, and learn to depend solely on the One who has come into our lives and looks after us with so much affection.

CHAPTER 15

Laughing with Baba

"Before I met my Beloved in Union, I lost everything – ego, mind, lower consciousness. But, thank God I did not lose my sense of humour!"[1]

Baba's humour is so very evident in everything connected with Him. It is so prominent even in all the messages that come my way. They surprise me, fascinate me, and convince me that the spirit world is a happy place to be in. A fun place, where we can leave all our earthly worries behind, enjoy ourselves with Him, and progress in His loving care.

Whenever you see a film of Baba, He is mostly smiling or making gestures that make you laugh. In some of the movies, you see the loving way in which He plays the game of throw and catch sweets with the youngsters around Him, and then claps His own hands in delight. There are also many stories told about Baba's ways of amusing His followers when He was in the physical world.

I believe that there was a time during the war when Baba and a few of His mandali had to travel in a small third-class bogie from one place to another. As trains were always crowded and overflowing with passengers, Baba, for His own work, did not want any outsider to board the bogie at this or at any of the stations en route. But the members of the mandali could not think of any possible way to manage this, nor did they think that it would be advisable, for mob fury could sometimes be dangerous. Ultimately, Baba Himself hit upon a plan. He asked for a white bed-sheet from one of the mandali. He covered Himself completely and lay down at the entrance – absolutely motionless. He also asked the mandali to look grave and sombre, and not to talk or reply to anyone who may ask questions.

The plan worked. As soon as the train rolled into any station, Baba and the mandali took their positions. Passengers would see the 'corpse' lying right at the door, pay their respects, and pass on to another bogie. Once the train rolled out, Baba would sit up. In this way Baba travelled the distance without any intrusion, as desired by Him for His own reasons.

Karl tells us that *"Baba says always try to face life with a smile. Always try to see the funny side of life, for everything treated with laughter will work a hundred percent more than if it is frowned upon. God made life so that it could be enjoyed, so go ahead now. Just think of Baba, picture His face and know that He is always there to laugh with you."* Knowing Karl, I am sure that he must be the first one to be joining Baba there in all His humorous activities and thoroughly enjoying them too.

I wonder who planned this one?

It was on one of my trips to Meherabad that a very strange incident took place. Mealtime is a friendly time at the Pilgrim Centre in Meherabad, when people from different countries and different walks of life all sit together in one room, not only to share meals but also to get to know one another. On this particular afternoon, we had just finished lunch and soon began to relax, open up to each other, to share experiences and exchange stories of the little miracles of Baba's love.

When it was my turn, I do not know what prompted me to tell the following story.

I smiled at the recollection as I began: As you may know, my daughter Tina had a very special, light-hearted relationship with Karl. She was his younger sister and, like all children, there were many altercations between the two that continue even now.

Tina has always been very fond of her food. Her brother Karl had always been a little jealous of her capacity to put it all down. Being a jockey, he had to really watch his weight, and so could never eat the way he would have liked to. Sometimes just to tease him, Tina would dangle delectable morsels of his favourite foods, tantalising him till he literally drooled, and then would quickly pop them into her own mouth. This always produced a major showdown.

Karl passed away. Years passed by.

Tina was expecting her second baby and the time of delivery was approaching fast. She was definitely not looking forward to her few days in hospital and grumbled to me, "What am I going to do about the food, mummy? What the hell do you think I am going to eat there for so many days? Ugh! Hospital food!" she grimaced.

"Come on Tina, don't fuss," I chided. "I am sure that you can manage it. It will only be for a few days."

Soon the time came. She checked into her hospital room, still grumbling about her food but carrying, as always, Baba and Karl's picture with her. As she unpacked, she gave them pride of place on the dresser next to her bed.

After the preliminaries were over, the hospital dietician walked in. I watched Tina's face fall as she proceeded to read out and allocate the dull and bland diet according to the rules. Then a miracle happened. All of a sudden her eyes fell on Baba's picture on the dresser. Her official attitude suddenly vanished and her face broke out into a smile almost as big as Baba's. "Oh, you are a Meher Baba follower, how lovely! So am I," she said. "I tell you what, you just

Baba in a happy and playful mood.

tell me what you would like to eat and I will do my best to pop in those few extras for you."

You can imagine the lift in Tina's spirits. She could not believe her good luck.

She took up Baba's picture, smiled, and thanked Him over and over again for his kind consideration. She screwed up her face, stuck her thumb out at Karl, as if to say, "There, you see, I got it after all!"

As I came to the end of my story, there were many oohs and aahs of appreciation from those sitting at the table, except for one particular lady who I noticed seemed decidedly uncomfortable. I was embarrassed at her reaction and I looked at her and said, "Excuse me please, have I said something to disturb you?"

She lowered her eyes, then smiled a little smile and said rather sheepishly, "No Ma'am, but I am that same dietician." I wonder what, or rather who, made me choose this day and this particular moment to share this story.

Here is Adil Gandhy to tell you one of his hilarious experiences connected with Baba.

I was depressed. My marriage had just fallen through and I was looking for something to interest me. So, when a little ICQ flag kept flashing on the net one evening, out of interest I tuned in and found that it was a Nimi from Jamaica. I casually started chatting with her and soon discovered that she seemed to be a rather interesting and intelligent person.

To my surprise, this net acquaintance developed rapidly and I found myself getting more than really interested. One day she said she would like to send me her photograph. She warned me that she was really quite old and hoped that I did not mind having an elderly net friend. Although I was taken unawares, I assured her very gallantly that age was no barrier to friendship and waited impatiently for the picture to arrive.

The picture that appeared really took my breath away. I gave a gasp! I stared at her and then burst out into uncontrolled laughter! A hundred-year-old wrinkled face looked out at me from the computer screen!

Nimi, the online friend of Adil.

This unusual correspondence continued for a while, till finally she admitted that she was only joking and then she sent me her real picture. It was quite stunning. I appreciated her rare sense of humour and soon the two of us became good friends – good enough to share experiences about our lives. That is when I told her about the separation from my wife after twenty-five years of marriage and how it had eventually led me to greener pastures and to spirituality. Instead of going into lengthy explanations about everything, I wrote and sent her my full story.

You won't believe what happened! She turned out to be a Baba lover herself! She was charmed with the whole incident as much as I was and is looking forward to reading *Sounds of Silence* and going to Meherabad with me. She agrees that there are no coincidences where Baba is concerned – for everything is meant to be.

All I can say is, can you imagine that out of millions and millions of net users, one message flashes, we get friendly, and it turns out to be a Baba lover!

Now if this was not specially arranged by Baba – what is?

And last of all, here is Anita Lawyer to tell you about one of her own humorous experiences with Baba.

March 7, 1997. The beautiful green lawns of the racecourse were lit up with a million bulbs, music was playing, and couples were gracefully gliding along the dance floor. Little did I imagine that those same million bulbs would very soon bring so much of their brightness into my existence, and that the dance of my own life was about to begin.

I spotted Nan in the distance. Seeing her there against the backdrop of the racecourse brought back memories of her graceful form on a horse.

I walked up to her where she was sitting with family and friends. Her book, *Sounds of Silence,* had just been released. I had heard so much about it, but as yet not been able to get hold of a copy. After exchanging pleasantries, I left Nan, assuring her that no matter what happened, I was going to lay my hands on it the very next day.

But the next day brought something totally unexpected. My dearest friend, Cawas, suddenly passed away of a heart attack in Pune and I rushed to be there for his funeral.

In Pune, I happened to be staying with my close friends, Feroza and Faisal Moloobhoy, and during that sad and harrowing day, I casually mentioned that it would have been so wonderful had Nan's book been with me at this time. Before I could say another word, the book was placed before me. Feroza had the book!

Needless to say, the book was wonderful and once I started reading it, I could not put it down. Till then, I had no real idea about the actual contents except that it was about Karl and his communication with his mother Nan.

So this is the first time I was really introduced to a Master, Meher Baba, and then of course all I could think of was, making my way to Meherabad.

The first time I went turned out to be the most exciting for me. Yes it was definitely Baba who drew me there but, it was also all the things that I had read about, the manifestations that took place which intrigued and excited me. What kind of a wonderful place was this where God's love and compassion shone through, where Baba's energy was so powerful, where He could make His presence felt so strongly? How could there be a place like this where people forgot their problems, found help and consolation, where tears dried up, and where loved ones could be united?

So, before I left my home, I knelt at my altar, said a small prayer of thanks, and begged of Baba to oblige me by sending me some message or proof. It came to me in the most remarkable way.

We were all sitting on the porch at the Centre, when, amidst the trees, I thought I saw a little horse. My love for animals, especially horses, pulled me in its direction. I ran the last few steps, for there indeed was a horse but he was a pitiable sight. His little legs were bent and misshapen – in fact he had almost no hooves. He was almost a cripple! Tears ran down my cheeks as I went instinctively forward to stroke and touch him lovingly.

A little later, Nan took us on a tour of the grounds and the surrounding areas and suddenly, there he was, that same small horse standing in a corner, a little away from us. We stopped in our tracks. I put out my hand and slowly, very slowly, the little fellow hobbled towards me. We looked at each other, he was so sweet and I stroked him tenderly. But we had to move on, so very regretfully I left him behind but though I walked away, my heart and thoughts somehow remained constantly with him. I could not talk of anything else and the first opportunity I got, I asked Janet, one of the residents, to tell me his name. His name was Donald.

Poor little Donald.

Apart from the wonderful contact with Baba at the Samadhi, our stay was dotted with many interesting episodes like listening to a talk by Bhauji, one of Baba's mandali and a trip to Baba's home at Meherazad. But it was the visit to Mohammed, Baba's *mast* (a God-intoxicated soul stuck between the planes) that really intrigued us, and we spent a good half hour in his company. He is now nearly a hundred years old and bent almost double with age. There are many interesting stories of Baba connected with the mast, too long to tell you just now, but we were really fascinated by him.

The hours passed all too soon and it was time to leave. Nan and I were packing when all of a sudden she shyly said, "Anita, I want you to know that in Meherabad it is always Baba who is most important. It is Baba whom we must concentrate on and strive to get closer to, but this Karl, he always puzzles me. I am really finding it difficult to understand and pinpoint his message to me this time. I wonder what, or rather who, he is today." And she smilingly confided the message Karl had sent to her earlier.

The message said, *"I shall be without anyone – all alone. There will be nobody with me, no one belonging to me, and no one who has come to Baba because of me. I have hands that have no fingers and toes that are peculiar."*

Oh my God, so there was a message after all. Baba may have really heard me and my prayer had been answered. Only problem, who was Karl?

But the day was over, and we were already piling into the bus for the two-and-a-half hour journey to Pune. On the way back, we all had plenty of time to put our heads together and mull over the intriguing message from Karl. We thought, we argued, we compared notes and opinions. Most of us came to the conclusion that it had to be the mast, who had so impressed us. He was the only one who was alone with no one really belonging to him, and he did have hands and feet all bent with age. We were, however, interrupted in our thinking by one of our companions, Roxanne, who said that she did not agree at all. Her gut feeling told her that it was the little crippled horse that we had been so drawn to. "He had such human eyes," she said.

But to be honest, I thought that this Roxanne Marker sounded nuts! So then who, who was it?

Still wondering, and not having reached a conclusion, we stopped for lunch, at Dorabjee, a restaurant renowned for its delicious Parsee food in Pune. Still arguing, we seated ourselves at the only table available and then all of a sudden our attention got diverted. There, on the wall, staring at us across the table was a huge poster of a mischievous chimp. He was grinning from ear to ear. His expression said, 'Made a monkey out of you!' The caption underneath said, 'HI – I AM DONALD!'

The whole group looked at one another and broke into uncontrolled laughter. Baba had answered our question – and in the most amazingly funny way!

To end this chapter, I would like to tell you something about a personal experience which I did not find half-so-amusing, at least not at the time.

Long ago, in the year 1959, my husband Jimmy and I were invited to Pune to stay a few days at Guru Prasad, then also known as the Baroda Palace. This kind offer was made to us by a friend who happened to be a relative of the Maharani of Baroda.

The thought of having a rollicking holiday with young friends in a Palace was more than just exciting, and we all looked forward to it with great anticipation. However, the joy was short-lived for in the middle of our holiday we were told that a Guru, a certain Meher Baba, had chosen this very time to come. Our holiday was to be cut short because of this!

You can well imagine our reaction. I can assure you that the spoken and unspoken thoughts we had were not very pleasant. 'Just who does He think He is? Why the hell should we get out because He has decided He wants to come? Let Him wait or go somewhere else.' But, of course, we had to leave.

These distant memories remained like shadows somewhere in the background, till a few years later, I was sitting with Mehera, Mani, and the mandali, on the porch in Meherazad, where stories of Baba in Guru Prasad happened to be related. Then suddenly a bell sounded, loud and clear. Realisation dawned and I thought, 'My goodness, that was Him! It was this same Meher Baba who had shunted us out and spoilt our holiday!'

I guess Baba had the last laugh there!

Meher Baba on the lawns of Guru Prasad Palace.

CHAPTER 16

Howzzat!

Baba loved playing games, and spent much time with His followers doing simple things like playing with marbles and flying kites. He was also a good runner and a strong walker. I believe that once or twice Baba also had His beloved Mehera's favourite horse, Sheeba, running in the Gymkhana races and that He loved the animal.

Talking about horses and racing takes me back to a time way back in 1985, when I had asked Baba why He had come forward to help my son, and all of us, when we never had any previous connection with Him or, for that matter, even known His name. Through Karl's written message, Baba had answered:

> *"Racing, I love it Myself. I used to come and watch from the outside, and I have seen Karl many times riding a horse. I have watched him and admired him as a small boy, and I knew that I would look after him forever if anything happened to him. I always knew that he was destined for greater things, but his career was cut short. I was as sad as all of you. I was crying from here. I took him immediately."*

Much later, Baba's beloved Mehera had confirmed this to be true. His reasons are not known but Baba used to go and stand outside the racecourse and watch the horses go by – and even buy a race book sometimes! But it was not horses and racing that really held Baba's attention, it was the game of cricket that was really His passion. The story that now follows is a vivid example of the same. It not only goes to show that Baba loved all sports, but that He also admired and went out of His way to help those that played the game.

Shireen Lala came to Baba in a very simple and natural way. Actually there was no dramatic incident or miracle, but Baba very slowly and gradually gathered her whole family into His fold through her father, the famous Indian cricketer, Polly Umrigar. Therefore, it was her parents who brought her to Baba when she was just three years old. They did not know then that it was the greatest parental gift of love they could have ever given their child. Here, Shireen would very much like to tell you all about it herself.

Actually my story began in 1959, when the Indian cricket team was to go to England. Prior to their departure they spent a few days in Pune. Some high official with the cricket board suggested the whole team should go and take Meher Baba's darshan before embarking on the tour. He wanted them to have Baba's blessings. That is when my father first came in contact with Baba. What a blessing this was, he was to know only later. Nothing much really happened then. The next day as the team was leaving Pune, one of Baba's closest mandali, Nariman Dadachanji, came to the station and handed over to my father Polly, a beautiful written message from Baba Himself. My mother has kept this letter safely at home for all these years and I very much want to share this beautiful message with you.

Meher Baba with Polly Umrigar and the Indian Cricket Team – April 1959.

To

The All-India Cricket Team

In going to England to represent India in the field of sport you have also the unique opportunity of yourselves practising, and of conveying to the people there, the great spiritual lessons of concentration and love. When you take the field, if you play as 11 men with one heart, each enjoying excellence of performance in another player as he would in himself, whether that player is on your side or on the side of the opposing team, and so eliminating feelings of jealousy, anger and pride which so often mar sport, you will not only be entertaining the spectators, but demonstrating the real spirit of sportsmanship. True sportsmanship is concentrated ability enlivened with appreciation of the performance of others. And when this is manifested, every one, both players and spectators receives spiritual upliftment as well as good entertainment.

Some of you are " all-rounders ". I am the greatest spiritual " all-rounder " of all times, because I feel equally at home with saints, yogis, philosophers and cricketers as well as with so called sinners and scoundrels. I give you my blessing that in all your actions you show forth the spirit of love.

- Meher Baba

" Guruprasad "
24- Bund Road,
Poona - 1.

2nd April 1959.

0000000000000

My father also remembers the verbal message sent to him by Baba at the station.

He said, "Don't worry that you have not been made the captain this time, but you will perform very well on this tour."

After that, my father left for England with the Indian cricket team. Whilst playing, he kept wondering why Baba had chosen him to receive the special message. He read it out and shared it with his team members. At that time he was not even captain. On that tour he did incredibly well and there was a lot of thrill and excitement over his playing. It was almost as if Baba was playing through him, for he built up really dramatic scores. He scored an incredible three double centuries and two normal centuries, and was quite overwhelmed with his own performance. There was a total upheaval in his emotions as to whether all this was some sign from Baba. He remembered Baba's message and realised that it had all come true. It was like Baba had kept His word to him. On the one hand he was reluctant to go to this Baba again, thinking his parents and wife would surely disapprove. Yet, he felt a sort of longing and deep pull towards Baba. When he returned from England, his close friend Dada explained to him that rarely does Baba choose someone like this and even send his mandali to give them a message. He guided and encouraged my father to go to Him. Once he went again to Baba, there was no turning back for him this time. He was hooked for life.

Since that day, my father started coming closer and closer to Baba. He first took my mother Dinoo, and then my two brothers and myself. Like other parents take their children to the fire temple or their own holy place, I was taken to Baba's by my parents. What do I remember of meeting Baba? I was only three, too young to remember any exact details. I remember the Guru Prasad days. I loved going there. To me it meant fun and friends and the close family's joy in Baba's love. My main childhood memory of Baba himself was His beautiful feet. I still get this picture in my mind of how they used to shimmer; there was this silvery white skin, very soft and downy. I used to get a big thrill by pressing my head down on them. The thought that must have come to my child-like mind then was that no human could have feet like these, they belong to the world of fairies and angels... and these were no ordinary human's feet... they were God's feet and this was so because Baba is God.

My mother says I would run around collecting flowers and place them on Baba's lap, and then run away thinking it was a great game. I cannot recall that. But what I do remember is that there were always huge crowds, flowers, and garlands, a lot of loving friendly grownups around, and lots of children to play with. It was a very special place and a very special someone my parents were bringing me to.

Years passed, and after the Guru Prasad days came the Meherabad days. They made a deep impression on me. On one side we were this big Baba family and it was always a lot of fun and games. On the more serious side, I was understanding and learning what Baba was all about, what spirituality meant to me and how to follow Baba's teachings in everyday life. Baba's most meaningful words to me, and I use them now for everyday living:

> ***"Attend faithfully to your worldly duties, but keep always at the back of your mind that all this is Baba's.***
>
> ***When you feel happy, think – "Baba wants me to be happy." When you suffer, think "Baba wants me to suffer."***
>
> ***Be resigned to every situation and think honestly and sincerely: "Baba has placed me in this situation."***[1]

My thoughts, as a young girl, of Baba's mandali – I loved them and still do. We all shared such closeness. They showered us children and teenagers with so much love and affection. I loved the Meherabad of those days and get quite nostalgic, even though the Meherabad of today is as special to me.

Today I realise that it was through love, togetherness and fun times that Baba was actually teaching me His lessons to prepare me for what I would have to face later in my adult life. He was helping me to learn to deal with or to cope with all that He wanted me to go through, with what was to happen later on, be it with my children or any other hurdles in life. What was deeply imbued in me by then was His particular message: ***"I want you to keep happy and cheerful and stop worrying over anything. You are steadfast in your love for Me and this suffices to face all and all things."***[2]

CHAPTER 17

The Compassionate Father

"The aim of life is to love God, and the goal of life is to become one with God."[1]

Baba's life and teachings help us tune our own values, perspectives, and priorities in life in accordance with a fresh understanding of the true goal. His life of unconditional love and absolutely selfless service is the best example of His compassion. In fact, His very being in the body is His compassion; that is, His descent on earth was to make His presence more real, to make His love more tangible, and to be a gauge against which we can measure ourselves, as to where we are and where we ought to be.

Baba's compassion flows to us in many different ways. There are times when Baba thinks it fit to come forward to solve for us our mundane problems, giving us what we need and, in doing so, helping us to get closer to Him. And there are times when He feels it is more beneficial for us to struggle while all the time having His loving *nazar* (gaze) on us, helping us to learn our lessons and to grow, giving us a direction in our life, and intuiting us in following His wish.

There are many instances to prove this point but the one closest to my heart is the story of my dearest friend and neighbour, Freny Dadachanji. She was an ardent and faithful follower of Meher Baba, no, not from the beginning of her life but only after she was married. How she realised Baba is also a fascinating tale, but let it suffice here to say that He must have had a very good reason to send her to be my neighbour in Pune. Baba knew I had so much to learn from her.

As time went by, we became extremely close and I shared all my little episodes and experiences daily with her. She really kind of kept her eye on me and always gently guided me when she thought I was getting carried away by my emotions. Today, I send her my deepest gratitude and blessings for being there for me.

A few years ago, Freny developed cancer. She had innumerable operations, went through tremendous pain and chemotherapy, but always with a smile on her face and Baba in her heart. Through her illness, there was always a certain grace about her and her concern was always for others before herself.

You could never make out that she was suffering so much because she took such great care to look good. She kept her skin looking soft and smooth and was always immaculately dressed. Never once did she complain or ask to be cured. And although our homes are just separated by a fence, never once did she waver in her faith or ask me for a message of help. There was no need. She had surrendered herself totally to Baba and her love and trust in Him was so absolute, that she knew everything was happening according to His wish. Towards the end, it was I who could not bear to see her suffer and in desperation one day I asked Karl, "Why Karl, why when she loves Baba so much and has dedicated her whole life to Him, why does He let her suffer so much?"

And Karl said, *"Because He is taking her closer to her goal – God-realisation."*

"Oh," I thought, "how wonderful for her."

I understood then that God-realisation is the goal of all in Creation. Suffering is one of the means to eradicate the sanskaras, in order to reach the goal. Hence, the need for it.

Freny passed away soon after. Today she must be really where her heart is – with her Beloved Baba. I love you Freny.

Another lovely story from the Baba world is about the Satha family, in Ahmednagar, who have been closely connected to Baba.

One of the family, Dhun, lovingly called 'Dhunu', had been a patient of muscular dystrophy. She was short and thin, and the disease affected her entire body. She had to be lifted and carried from place to place. In one of Baba's films she can be seen having His darshan, her eyes gazing on her Beloved Baba and, Baba, in turn, looking tenderly into her eyes.

Dhunu had a keen mind and a witty sense of humour. She would constantly write humorous notes and 'news bulletins' to Baba from Akbar Press in Ahmednagar, where she lived, which would create a cheerful atmosphere at Meherazad and make Baba smile and sometimes even laugh. Dhunu elaborately decorated birthday and other cards for Baba and Mehera, tediously gripping the brush or pen in her fist and mouth. But she never asked Baba to cure her. She was completely resigned to His will.

Someone or the other would beseech Baba to cure her of her illness and suffering, and Baba, in His infinite compassion once said to her, that it was better to finish the suffering now and not save it for the next time.

"Love can change your life – I believe that now," says Villoo Irani as she sits in her wheel chair surrounded by all those who have come to share a cup of tea with her.

"And how is that?" we ask.

"I will tell you how," she says.

Viloo continues: I was married to Sarosh Irani in 1927. I came to Ahmednagar as a young and radiant bride of sixteen. One day my husband said to me, "I have a Guru, Meher Baba, and I think that He is God."

Oh, God is upstairs, I scoffed. How can he come down? No, I am not going to believe in this God of yours.

I loved life. I was looking for fun and frolic and did not want to be tied down to any Gurus or Babas, nor did I want to spend my precious time listening to all this hocus pocus about being spiritual, honest, and true. I would much rather go for high tea and a game of cards with my new-found friends and leave Sarosh to adore his Meher Baba the way he wanted to. Yes, I used to go and visit Him at times just out of respect for my husband, but when Sarosh overdid it, I used to put my foot down in no uncertain way. I even objected to him keeping Baba's photographs in the house and laid down the law, keeping Baba out of my life in more ways than one. I didn't like it, and Baba knew that I did not like it, but He always said, "Let her be, Sarosh – when her time comes, she will come to Me."

Not likely, I mused. However, I did go to Him once and that was when I wanted a diamond necklace and Sarosh refused to give it to me. That was the time I went to ask His intercession on my behalf and was thrilled when Baba took my side and told Sarosh that he should always try his best to please me in all ways.

"What do you think of Him now?" asked my husband.

He is ok, I said, but I will only believe in Him if he makes miracles for me. Then my sister died and I was shattered. Poor Baba came and sat with me for hours explaining to me about life and death and that I should not feel so sad, but I was adamant. I wanted that miracle from Him now, and now was His chance to prove it to me. I wanted my sister alive again! Of course that was not possible – and I knew it!

Many years went by and I was still waiting to see that miracle happen!

In 1962, Baba was asked to go to Hamirpur, a district in Uttar Pradesh. Since Baba could not make it, He asked Sarosh to go instead. He also extended this invitation to me, promising He would arrange all the comforts I was used to like a clean bed and hot water for my bath. So with that in mind, and as I was feeling rather bored with life at that moment, I thought it might be exciting to go along. Maybe I could meet up with some young officers and their wives, and snatch a few games of cards with them.

But, because Baba was not there, I found myself placed in the front row, faced by the thousands who had come to take Baba's darshan. Oh, what had I got myself into?

And then, suddenly, I saw their gaze resting on me. My reaction was 'Oh my God, they are coming this way, what shall I do?' I was a very finicky person. I hated to be touched, so at first I was terribly repelled, but then God only knows what happened to me. To my surprise, when faced with this barrage of humanity, I recalled how Baba always hugged each and every one, regardless of rank, age, sex, caste, creed or religion. With my own eyes I have seen Him hugging each one that came to Him as if they were someone special. He held them in a warm and loving embrace, which had some simply ecstatic, and some weeping with the very joy of being loved. This was my turning point.

I realised the Majesty of Baba, that when He said, *"You and*

I are not we but One,"[2] it was not only a verbal assurance to the world, but He lived it too. I realised that the loving hugs from Baba were always something that was carried home, that this love He gave everyone from His heart, would be treasured for lifetimes by those like me, who had the good fortune of having come into contact with Him. I found myself slowly following Baba's example, and trying my level best to reach out in love to all those that came.

Much later, when my Sarosh died, Baba came to visit me in a vision. With His loving gestures He pointed to His two eyes and then at me, assuring me that He would always look after me and my family. Baba has kept His word to this date.

Villoo has now passed on at the ripe old age of ninety-six years. To the end, she still loved life, she still loved to play cards and only one thing changed; she did not need a miracle to prove that Baba is God.

Leila Captain's story shows that Baba's love is unwavering and totally unconditional. She says:

Bhau Kalchuri, Chairman, Avatar Meher Baba Trust.

I was visiting the N. H. Wadia Institute of Cardiology, as usual one morning, and was informed that a patient from Meherabad had been admitted. He had undergone by-pass surgery a few days ago and it would be great if I visited him on the second floor. So, off I went. I knocked and opened the door. Who do you think I saw in the bed? Bhauji, the head of the Baba Trust in Meherabad! I had no idea he was scheduled for surgery in this hospital. He was on my turf, in my hospital, and he was looking so tired and sad that I was compelled to take his hand in mine and stroke his head with the other. What could I do to help?

After some questioning, I found that Bhauji's companion needed an e-mail connection. I spoke to the administration manager, got necessary permission for them, informed them of the arrangement, and left.

Some days later, I wanted to visit Bhauji again but was informed by the very same 'Floor-Sister' I had met earlier, that he had been discharged. But as she was speaking to me, I saw her eyes look repeatedly, in a very puzzled way, at the pendant I was wearing.

"Whose picture is this?" she asked.

"Why?" I said.

"Oh, because this same picture used to be on the patient's side table and I thought it must be his father. You see, this gentleman in the picture used to come each night to ask about the patient's progress, then sit by his bedside on this chair and so lovingly hold his hand!"

I was amazed! The picture was of Meher Baba, and this nurse had actually seen Him every night when she was on duty!

CHAPTER 18

A Hug to Remember

Yes, a hug can change your life, but if there are distances and dimensions between us, how can love overcome this, and where then does God fit in?

This is what happened to Faten in Kuwait. It is about the hugs that came from Heaven.

This story starts on a morning when Faten woke up to see her husband Abdulla bending over her. She looked into his eyes and asked, "Tariq?"

He quietly nodded his head. Their son Tariq had met with an accident and passed away. Tariq was just twenty-three years old, the younger of her two sons, and was studying abroad. He was the joy and sunshine in her life, a bundle of happiness and energy, spreading it everywhere he went. He was gone, and her life lay shattered around her.

Faten says: I shuffled about my house in Kuwait in a daze. I was numb to everything. I did not want to see or to talk to anyone, wanting to shut myself out in order to cope with my grief. I wanted to be by myself. My husband, kind and gentle as ever, silently understood my every need and helped me as best he could.

A year-and-a-half rolled by and during this time the feeling that Tariq was still close to me had become more and more distinct. I somehow just knew that he could not simply go away like that – we loved each other too much. I had to pursue this feeling. Although I went about my normal duties, I shut myself up almost like a recluse and devoured over a hundred books on the topic of life after death and the after-life. I had to learn to understand everything there was to this. Where was Tariq? I had to find him. It was at this time that I heard of a cruise organised by Dr. Brian Weiss, the celebrated psychoanalyst and writer on past-life therapy, and the renowned medium, James Van Praagh. Abdulla and I joined up for the cruise.

The weeklong cruise was a rewarding experience. With every passing day, I received many answers. I was convinced more than ever that there was life after death. I was becoming more and more aware.

Towards the end of the cruise, I was approached by an Indian lady from Bangalore, Nilima Rovshen. We somehow felt drawn to each other and soon got talking. Among other things, she asked me if I had heard of auto writing. When I said that I was unaware of it, Nilima told me about a book that she had read which had given her much hope and solace. She promised to send it to me.

Much to my scepticism and surprise, Nilima kept her promise. The book arrived and it was *Sounds of Silence* by Nan Umrigar. And strangely, the date she had signed it on also happened to be my birthday.

As I flipped through the pages, it seemed as if the author had taken the words right out of my heart. I related instantaneously with every little thought and feeling that she expressed and cried with her through her pain because it was mine too. When I was halfway through the book, I realised that I had to see this lady. The feeling was overbearing. I rang up Nilima in Bangalore. "I want to speak to the mother," I said, "please contact her for me. I feel a strong calling. I have to go to this place – this Meherabad."

Nilima kindly arranged for me to meet with Nan Umrigar. After finalising the time and date, I flew down from Kuwait to Pune where Nan picked me up from my hotel. Soon, we were on our way to Meherabad.

It was the 19th of November 2001. Although I had not really expected it, Karl had a message for me. It said, *"You will see us together in two places not one. Tariq has asked a special favour of Baba – to be able to hug his mother, and that is why you will get special hugs, once in the morning and once in the evening. The hugs will of course come at the normal place and with all the usual ceremony, and will give you all the usual feelings of love that you get. One will be from Tariq and one from Baba. It is Baba who has brought you to us, and us to you. There is no need for further clarification of who or what. You will know as soon as you feel this hug that it is your son who waits for you, and who is jumping up and down in his excitement because the time has come so close. Baba Himself waits to welcome you and wishes to give you a bear hug to show you just how much you mean to Him. Tariq says, 'Mum, your love is my salvation and my lamp post.' Love Karl."*

Although I have stayed in ashrams before, I had to adapt myself to the sparse living conditions. But what was definitely not scarce was the love that was in abundance all around. It just stole my heart away. Everyone around had so much love to give and share that I cannot tell you how happy and peaceful I felt just being there.

The whole day I was busy looking at everything, searching frantically for 'the hugs'. Although they seemed to be present everywhere, as everyone was so loving and kind, nothing happened to convince me that it was my son Tariq or that it was Baba welcoming me. I could feel that Nan was also tense although I'm sure she has been through it a hundred times before. I knew that in her heart she really wanted me to find my son Tariq, just the way that she had found Karl, but I guess she knew for sure that Baba had something in mind that only He understood and, therefore, we just had to go with it.

The next morning at 7 am during aarti time, as is customary after the prayers, songs in praise of Baba were being sung. The air was filled with beautiful music. All of a sudden I felt something stir inside of me. "Something is happening," I said to Nan who was standing quietly beside me. There was a huge surge within me and before I knew it tears were streaming down my face. I could not contain them; they just seemed to keep pouring down. At that moment, I felt it right in my heart, that this was my first connection with Baba.

After breakfast, there was a rush for the baths and a great hurry to get ready for a visit to the mandali and to Meherazad. On the way there, the bus full of pilgrims stopped off at the Trust Office to allow us to pay our dues and to hurriedly buy books and pictures of Baba to take home to family and friends. The stop was only for ten minutes, so Nan was rushing me through when we were approached by our roommate Susan, to say that Bhauji, the head of the Trust and one of Baba's most loved and trusted followers, wanted to meet with me. Of all the people in the bus, why had he picked on me? I was surprised and more so when Bhauji came out of his office followed by a few young helpers. He asked the bus driver to wait and led us into a little room. "Bhauji wants you to put this garland on Baba's picture," explained Susan.

Baba's picture was at a height so I had to climb up a small stairway to reach Him. Soon I was standing alone on the dais looking straight into His eyes, eyes that told me many stories, eyes that looked directly into my bleeding heart, eyes that said, "Call Me, and I will be there for you." I reached out, slowly put the garland over the frame, folded my hands and stood there for a long while thanking Baba in my own special way. The rest stood behind with joined hands and I could hear them say a small prayer.

As I came down from that dais, Bhauji came up to me and enfolded me in a strong and tight embrace. My heart stood still. I instantly knew that this was 'Baba's bear hug'. I was overwhelmed.

We turned away and were about to leave when there was a tap on my shoulder. I heard a small voice say "Maha Salamat," and wheeled around to look into the shining face of a young boy with curling blond hair and a smile as big as a half-moon.

My head whirled, and the world spun around. The words meant 'goodbye' in Arabic!

"My God, where did you get that from?" was my instant reaction.

He paused, looked around confused, as if wondering at himself and grinned, "I don't know," he replied.

"Where do you come from?" was my next question.

"America," he replied.

My heartbeat quickened at an alarming rate and my eyes clung to his.

"How old are you?" I asked, not daring to hope.

"Twenty-three," he answered.

I broke down and cried. He stepped forward and hugged me lovingly and I clung on to him, not ever wanting to let go.

Yes, it was Tariq. His body felt exactly like him – twenty-three, bony, thin and tall. I lost all count of time as the tears came pouring down. I did not know what I was saying or doing. "Give me another hug," I begged. We were all so charged with the emotion of the moment that I cried, Nan cried, he cried, and even Bhauji was close to tears, without really knowing what was happening.

The bus was waiting and we had to leave. With Nan's help, I tried my best to take control of myself as I walked to the bus and travelled all the way to Meherazad. Once there, however, I managed to get hold of my senses only to discover that in all the hurry and confusion, I had left my reading glasses on the table under Baba's picture. One of the kind ladies offered to stop the bus on the way back, and I ran in to retrieve the missing spectacles.

What do you think! Sitting on the sofa were two lone figures, one was Bhauji and the other the same young boy, with my errant glasses in between. No words were spoken but I got my second set of hugs! One was in the morning, and one in the evening!

As far as I was concerned, Baba had achieved a miracle and Karl's message had come true.

Two years have passed. My life goes on. I have now occupied myself in organising an Ayurvedic Healing Centre in Kuwait, with expertise from Kerala. I make regular trips to India for the same. Time after time, I have also been to Meherabad, not only because of Tariq but because Baba has drawn me there with His love. I feel Him in my heart.

I do not ask for a message too often now, but the depression does return and in those times I turn to Baba. Then, through Karl, Tariq never fails to send me messages that warm my heart, not only because they are beautiful but also because they always turn out to be so true.

One day I asked Tariq if in some way I could know what Baba thought of the work I had taken up – that of running the Ayurvedic Healing Centre in Kuwait. Did He approve? Was there any help or guidance He wished to give me?

The message said, "Mummy, you always were a wonderful mother and a good friend, but in the last few months you have also become a good human being. A good human being means having a care for others outside of your own family. Baba is also soooo happy to see this change in you, and wants to tell you that the hard work you are putting into your project is really fabulous. And Baba says 'Quo Vadis'. Love Tariq."

Nan did not know how to interpret the message. 'Quo Vadis' – what did it mean? What on earth was Baba trying to say? So she sent an SOS to her support group for help. She had not long to wait for before the next fifteen minutes were up, there was a very excited call from one of them called Jayaa. "Nanneee," she screamed, "you will not believe what happened. After your call, I ran hither and thither looking for answers for you – no luck there. I did not want to give up, so as a last resort I decided to call up a scholar friend. I dialled his number, just one ring, and it was immediately answered by a strange voice that said, 'St. Paul's Cathedral, this is the pastor speaking.' I was taken aback. I didn't know what to say! I stuttered and stammered and then blurted out, 'Excuse me, but would it be at all possible for you to tell me the meaning of 'Quo Vadis'?'"

"Of course I can," he replied. Then he gave me a long story about a time of terror and horror, when Nero was persecuting the Christians, a time when St. Peter was running away for his life and was confronted by a clear vision of Jesus, who asked him to go back and complete his mission saying, "I go with you." St. Peter was eventually crucified there. The Reverend Pastor concluded his amazing story by saying, "This then is the legend but, as I see it, the biblical and actual interpretation of the term 'Quo Vadis' is 'Wither thou goest – there goest I'."

Jayaa and Nan were not the only ones who were stunned!

There is just one more thing I have to add here. Last year, my husband Abdulla and I were in Germany and he fell seriously ill. I had to put him into hospital and leave him there. I was terrified. I remembered everything that I had gone through with Tariq, but then I also remembered Baba's message and His promise that He would always take care of me and mine.

I walked out of the hospital door and the huge neon sign of a restaurant across the road stared me straight in the face. It read – 'QUO VADIS'.

Faten's amazing story does not end here. I have to tell you one more really wonderful and mind-blowing incident that took place, as greater proof of Baba's love and of Tariq's continued presence in her life. This was told to me by my son Neville and my daughter-in-law Sabita, who were actually present at the time and saw it all.

The year was 2005. Saad, her elder son, decided to get married to a lovely girl from Turkey. She took this opportunity to invite all her near and dear ones, which included my family and I, who had all by now become so close to her. I was unable to make it, but my children went from Pune carrying the all-important messages for her.

Yes, Tariq would be there with them throughout the festivities and make his presence felt, as usual by the hugs, and Baba too would in some way be present to give them His blessings.

It was a week of warm and colourful celebrations. The air was filled with music and dancing, and the mood continued for days. Throughout the wedding, Faten and her daughter Abir kept feeling Tariq's presence close by, so much so that at times Abir would feel herself being hugged and turn round to find no one there.

After the wedding was over, and some of the guests had flown back home from Turkey, Faten took the remaining party for dinner to the famous old fish market in Istanbul. As always, it was noisy, lively, and the young at heart were really having fun. In the midst of this, Sabita's attention got focused on a man sitting with another party about two tables away. He looked like a slightly handicapped person, dancing and drinking, but had other youngsters around all poking fun and laughing at him.

To her surprise, he soon made his way towards their table and out of all the people gathered there went straight to Sabita and kissed her hand. Now why would he do that? Then he went to the other side of the table, rested his head on Neville's shoulder and put his hand on Neville's heart. How could he possibly know they were related? Lastly he turned to Faten, gently took her hand, put it on his chest, and looked at her as if searching for the love of a mother. It was only then that she noticed that he had a white hat on his head on which was written in bold red letters, the words: KRAL BABA.

She was dumbstruck. She could not believe what she was seeing. She could not believe that something so wonderful, so warm, so human, so true was happening to her and that too in the middle of a Turkish fish market!

For Faten, it actually felt as if Tariq had come to enjoy his brother's wedding day. He remained with them throughout the evening, till it was time to go. Then he came to her again, took her hand and looked at her with eyes that pleaded, 'Don't leave'.

That did it. She was beside herself and could bear it no longer.

She said to him "I know who you are."

He nodded "Yes."

She lost her cool and shouted, "I told you not to drink and smoke, and you didn't listen."

The tears rolled down his eyes, he looked down and said in a small voice, "I am sorry, so sorry."

He was the only figure who stood on the sidewalk, hand raised in a goodbye, till their bus rolled away.

A couple of years have passed by since that wonderful day. Faten and her husband Abdulla still make regular trips to India and to Meherabad. My family has become her family now and we share a closeness I cannot explain. Faten's love for Baba keeps her going. She knows that everywhere she goes, and in everything she does, she is getting Divine help from Him. Her love for Baba, and her continuous connection with her beloved son, are the two mainstays of her life.

The man wearing the 'Kral Baba' hat in the fish market of Istanbul.

CHAPTER 19

"God, Why Me?"

Everyone seeks happiness, yet most people go through some kind of suffering. Pain and pleasure are always entwined in our lives. Happiness comes to us fleetingly, like a shining rainbow; stays with us for a while and then is gone just as fast, leaving us very often staring at darkened clouds in a sky where the light has disappeared.

The question is, why do we suffer? And who is to decide who suffers what, and how? Why are some born rich, and some poor? Why are some taken away in the prime of life, and some live to a ripe old age? Why do some live their lives bound to a wheelchair and some enjoy freedom of movement and expression? Does God choose what happens to us, and why?

> Baba says, ***"Before karma is created, the individual has a sort of freedom to choose what it shall be... The pleasure and pain experienced in life on earth, the successes or failures that attend it, the attainments and obstacles with which it is strewn, the friends and foes who appear in it, are all determined by the karma of past lives... The actions of past lives determine the conditions and circumstances of the present life, and the actions of the present life have their share in determining the conditions and circumstances of future lives... Karmic determination is popularly designated as fate."***[1]

This means that you normally interact with those whom you have been connected with not only in this lifetime, but other lifetimes as well. Love is continued, hate is tempered down, enemies become friends, and friends continue to be helpful in the working out of karma. Good overtakes evil and, if you are lucky, life takes on a new meaning to make you realise what you have missed before. Through your own choices and actions you become what you are.

Now read Lisa Lawyer's story of what happened to her and what she learned from it.

When I look back at my past, I wonder how I ever managed to get by. But then the answer always comes loud and clear – 'Meher Baba'!

I have had so many experiences that brought me to where I am today. I could not have done it without Beloved Baba, and help from Karl. I have always been a believer in all religions and had a lot of faith, but I realise that my faith now is unquestionable in comparison to how I used to feel before.

I got to know about Karl and Baba eleven years ago, when I was just about eighteen years old. My mother brought home *Sounds of Silence* and requested me to read it. I had an interest in the occult from a very young age, so the content of Nan Umrigar's book was not new for me. However, Baba was.

Taking my own time to go to Meherabad and then reading more about Meher Baba, I began to figure out my own understanding and relationship with Him. I found myself more and more in awe of Baba's love, and His service to the people whose lives He touched and changed. I never realised that very soon my own life was never to be without its own surprises.

It happened this way. Although growing up in Bombay, my dream was always to go to the US to study drama and music. I knew that it would be difficult for someone like me to work and live there, considering I had never completed my education nor did I have any desire or qualification to get a nine to five job to help me live there and work. But I applied. In spite of my weak work resume, miraculously the approval for a green card to the US came to me the day before my birthday in 1998. It was truly a dream come true in every sense of the word. Soon I was on my way to discover myself and know what life really was all about.

However, if I had known all the things that were going to take place over the next six years, I am very sure that I would have reconsidered my trip to the US, for I could never have imagined my timid self having to deal with what was to come. America turned out to be very lonely, and a lot of hard work. There were days and nights when I would sit alone and cry for hours, wondering what my life was all about. I had various part-time jobs to help me survive. I tried hard to stay focused on achieving my goals to be an actress, but somehow I was always side-tracked by the necessity of having to survive and the struggle to keep my head above water. I ran out of money, fell ill, and started to really question why I had been given a chance to live in America. Why had Baba let me come here if I was going to suffer so much?

In sheer desperation, I begged Karl for some message to help me and give me the courage to do whatever Baba wanted me to. I got a reply that made all the difference to my life. It said, *"Soon two angels will be sent to you, and it will be Baba's work you will be helping with."* That very same week, in a crowded local bar, a tall good-looking man caught my eye. Weeks later I was introduced to him.

So, the first angel came into my life and became my greatest support and confidante! His name was Kevin, the son of a preacher, and really my saviour! He helped me through the worst times and looked after me, and fed me when I could hardly afford a decent meal. Later that month, I started working at a hotel and met another boy there. He was really the funniest. He and I worked together over the next few months and soon he became my second angel! Though ridiculed for being gay by most of the people at work, we had each other for support, and he felt he needed no one else. His name was Andres.

It was not very much later that we discovered that he was HIV positive and that he would not have more than a few months to live. Shattered by this, again I questioned Baba. Andres was such a sweet and wonderful person, why had he been given such a heavy cross to bear?

I called Bombay and asked for a message from Karl to help Andres through this terrible time. My wonderful mother responded immediately and Karl's message and a copy of *Sounds of Silence* were on their way by the next Air India plane.

The weekend passed. But early Monday morning I got a call from Andres and was astounded by what he had to say. He said that night he had experienced something that was not easy to explain or even rationalise with. In his dream, he was floating over a small hill with very peaceful surroundings. So when he came to the top, he went into 'a temple-looking place' where there was a tall man dressed in white, with a beautiful glow around His entire body. The man beckoned him in slow motion to come closer. As he approached, he could not help notice a large beaming smile overlapped by a long flowing moustache. The Man then nodded as He touched Andres's face, almost as though He was telling him 'Andres, it's alright!' The next thing Andres remembered was that he was wide awake in his bed, with the calmest and happiest feeling.

The next day, I was given Nanny Aunty's book and Karl's message for Andres which had come so quickly – half-way across the world. He glanced through the book and came across the page with the Samadhi photograph. His eyes widened, as from his back pocket he took out a small drawing he had made of the place in his dream. We compared both of them. To his amazement, and mine, they were the same! Even more amazing was the message to tell Andres that he *"should allow Baba to enter his life and allow himself to be touched by His love."* It was unbelievable!

Andres is now a Baba lover and has learned to surrender to whatever is to be. He is healthier than ever and amazes the doctors every time he goes for a check-up. It has now been six years, and Andres shows no sign of leaving our world. He says he owes it all to Baba and Karl!

There are many people across the world who have probably received Baba's Grace such as Andres has, but for this I will be eternally grateful. I conclude from this experience that sufferings are the rungs of the ladder which we climb in order to get to Him. That total surrender is acceptance of all situations, not willing or controlling a change of life's circumstances nor wanting any change for one's self. Therefore, whatever the outcome maybe, or how difficult the experience, I have learned not to resent or question the sufferings and to try my best to surrender to Baba.

I honestly have no words to describe how my life has changed since I have known Baba. He has given me strength, the ability and the willingness to surrender to His will. I have developed a greater understanding of purpose of my life and of why we have to suffer. It is because of Baba that I am consciously aware of what it really is to experience the beauty of His Everlasting, Non-judgemental, Universal and Unconditional Love that is… Life!

My prayers have changed from saying, "Baba, I want..." to saying, "Baba, I thank..."

Now it is Meher Castelino's turn to tell you how she has learned to cope with her life:

My life has had as many lows as it has had its highs. But it was only since 1996 that I have been able to handle them in a restrained manner. Thirteen years ago, when I lost my husband Bruno suddenly one evening, life came to a standstill for my children and for me. He was my friend, guide and my darling life partner and, for my children, a very loving father. I was angry with God because he had taken away our most precious possession.

As always, life carried on for both my children and me but at the back of my mind the question 'Why me?' always reared its ugly head. 'Why me, God, why did you finish my life by taking my husband from me?'

The way I decided to deal with this blow was to exhaust myself physically and emotionally with my work. I also wanted to make sure my children lacked nothing, and in my endeavours to be a father and mother, my own healing process was at a standstill. As a result, I cried all too easily and the emotions that I kept suppressed often came out as misdirected anger towards other people or events.

In 1998, I met Shiamak Davar and, in the course of our conversation, he broached the topic of communicating with those who have passed on. My daughter was very keen to contact her father but at that point in time I was very hesitant about such matters, and was of the firm resolve that the dead should not be disturbed. We soon dropped the idea because I was not comfortable with it.

Earlier, my second crutch, my mother, was taken away from me and then my world really collapsed all around. Finally, push came to shove in April of 1996, when I faced what seemed to me as the most trying time of my life. A personal conflict had pushed me into a corner. I felt as if God really had no time for me. I felt like a helpless victim of circumstances that were beyond my control. I was in such a sorry emotional state that I was not able to think straight. As a last resort, I thought of communicating with Bruno although I was still apprehensive about disturbing departed souls.

I hesitatingly turned to my friend's mother who was a medium and I asked her if she would help me communicate with Bruno. She invited me to their meeting where she said the spirit of Meher Baba guided them on the ouija board. Meher Baba was not a new name for me. My paternal uncle who lived in Pune was Meher Baba's follower, and I had heard that Baba had not spoken for years before He dropped His body. At the meeting, the medium assured me that the whole experience would be an enlightening one and I should not feel guilty about communicating with departed souls or disturbing them, since she knew that they would not come to talk if they did not want to. With this assurance, I went ahead but I was still very apprehensive. Will Bruno come and answer my questions? What will happen? Will there be a burst of lights and maybe a gust of wind?

The ouija board, operated by the medium with a pointer, moved from person to person and then came to me. Immediately, Meher Baba addressed me and said a few words of welcome. Then Bruno came on the board and spoke to me. He was very slow at first since he had never communicated with us and, therefore, was not too practiced with the art of moving the pointer. I couldn't believe my eyes and ears when he spelt out his very personal message of love and comfort for us.

After the meeting, I wanted to know more about Meher Baba. It almost felt like an obsession. I went to the Centre at Lamington Road and picked up as many books as I could find; *Perfect Master, God Speaks,* and *Listen, Humanity.* I went through them one after another like a starving refugee. I continued to attend the meetings and felt at peace that Baba and Bruno were near to guide us every step of the way.

It was the season of Christmas 1996. Life was still full of thorns that pricked and pinched at every step. My children brought a new book for me as a Christmas present. On 24th December, at midnight, we opened our gifts. I read the book *Sounds of Silence* by Nan Umrigar till 3.30 am on 25th December. I cried, I laughed, I cheered, and I lived through the trials and tribulations of the people she wrote about; her experiences with Meher Baba, and her communications with her son Karl.

I have read thousands of books in my life, but *Sounds of Silence* has had the most profound effect on my life. It was the one book that not only fascinated me completely, but answered so many questions that had been confusing me since Bruno passed away. It drew me even closer to Baba.

I had never written to an author and expressed myself before, but on 26th December, I dashed off a letter to Nan Umrigar, vaguely remembering that we had modelled together at a Tata Textiles show in 1961. We fixed a day to meet and from that day my bond with Baba kept on increasing in strength.

Nan invited me to visit Meherabad for Baba's birthday in February 1997. It was a trip that I don't think I will be able to describe in mere words. It is an experience each person has to go through to know it. For me, Meherabad is what heaven will be like.

After that, I read more books on Baba's teachings and each book opened the inner doors of my heart and mind. Every word, every new page I read, opened up new horizons for me. The answers to all the questions that I had been asking God were revealed to me. Not only did it convince me that there is a life after death but it explained much more. In simple words I learned that the world is full of sorrow and misery but it is not God who does it to you. It is you who have chosen to go through that particular experience and God has come forward just to give you a helping hand. He is there, helping you to take a good look at your life and make it worth living. We have come to this earth with a purpose, we have chosen our own destinies, and everyone has a very special job to perform. It is how we perform this job that matters. It is how we balance our lives and try to achieve detachment (a very difficult lesson to practice), that will take us on a higher level of evolution and spirituality.

I've visited Meherabad several times after 1997 and each visit has been more beautiful and productive than the last. Each time I have returned with new thoughts – my horizons have expanded. I have learned to work hard, be true to myself and leave the rest to Him. I have learned that honesty is the only way, and love begets love. I have learned to go with the flow and not get frustrated if things don't go my way, because there is a reason for everything good and bad happening in one's life. I have learned about life here and on the other side. I have learned a little about birth and death.

I am now a much calmer person, more tranquil and peaceful, and ready to deal with the chores of the world.

I have learned why loved ones cannot be with me all my life. I have, in short, learned to cope with the highs and lows of life with Baba by my side. My only regret is I didn't meet or know about Baba earlier in my life. But then, as the saying goes, 'there is a time and place for everything, and when the student is ready... the Master will appear.'

CHAPTER 20

Changing Masters

Once we get on to the spiritual path and start looking for a Guru, there is a bigger meaning to life. Gurus also come in different forms, with different names and different teachings, and have varied thoughts about God. People go from ashram to ashram looking for peace, love and understanding, sometimes finding it and sometimes not.

I have been extremely lucky in this respect for I have found Meher Baba. I have found Him through a strange way, so tragic and yet a way that has later brought me much happiness. As you may know, I too went through days and nights of heartache, indecision and confusion, not knowing what or who Baba really was. At first I looked upon Him as a kind man with flowing hair and a heart of gold, who was there to take care of my son. Then I took Him as my constant companion, friend, and father in Heaven.

It was much later that Karl made me realise Him as God. Since that day, I have never really felt the need to look elsewhere for my heart is at rest. I have found a safe haven, a mission; something to live for. And although I am interested in reading and knowing about other Gurus and Masters, the focal point and the deep abiding love I have is now only for Baba.

But that does not mean that you do not have the free will to choose your own Master, knowing fully well that though the forms may differ, all rivers eventually run into to the same ocean.

Here, I will go straight into a story that beautifully deals with the burning guilt one feels when a Master sometimes moves you to another. This is how it all happened for Rupam Nangia.

It was just a simple conversation on the night of the 2nd of September 2000, that led to a most dramatic turn on my spiritual journey. It is what led me to a book, through the pages of which I found dear Meher Baba! The conversation was about communicating with the dead.

Reading *Sounds of Silence* was a gripping experience for me. I turned to the cover many times to read the words, 'a true story'. Could this really be true? Could it really happen? Could a dead son return to his family, as Karl had, and actually communicate from the other world? Could God enter into the lives and hearts of ordinary people, like Meher Baba had with the Umrigar family? What then about prayer and penance and meditation for lifetimes together, to catch a glimpse of the Almighty? Why was this story so simple and so beautiful?

While on the one hand there were these numerous doubts that were assailing me, on the other hand, paradoxically, there was a sense of empathy with the author, and a sense of joy in knowing that the dividing line between the living and the dead was so thin. My constant questioning on all matters relating to life and death seemed to have suddenly found a platform for discussion, and I was soon sharing the startling contents with my family.

It soon became a time of great turmoil for me. We have been devoted to Shirdi Sai Baba for as long as I can remember. The book explained, there had been a connection between Sai Baba and Meher Baba. It also told us that Meher Baba had looked upon Sai Baba as His Spiritual Master, but how could this person, this Meher Baba, call Himself the *Avatar* of the Age? Who could I turn to, to verify this audacious claim? Why had Sai Baba not acknowledged Meher Baba as his own, and why had Sai Baba not spoken about His advent as the Avatar any time later? It was no ordinary phenomenon. Why had Sai made no mention of it?

My family is extremely secular. Notwithstanding these rather progressive views and upbringing, I nevertheless went through a period of conflict. After reading *Sounds of Silence* and getting messages through Karl on some very urgent family issues, Meher Baba had made an entry into our lives as God, and not one of His numerous lieutenants! How does Sai Baba view this? Through the day, and at times at night, I would ask myself hundreds of times whether Sai Baba would approve of our looking upon Meher Baba as God. Will he be displeased? I decided the best and only way to stop my mind from running wild was to ask Sai Baba himself to give any hint, any indication that he understood my position on this matter and wanted me to go ahead and look upon Meher Baba with faith. I pleaded with Sai to show me the way.

I told him that if Meher Baba was really God, Sai Baba must give some clear indication of the same in the next twenty-four hours. He must, in his kindness, show us that Meher Baba and Krishna are one. I should be accorded a darshan of Krishna in some form or another. I made this rather fervent plea in all sincerity and asked for forgiveness if my questions were reeking of either disbelief in a higher power, or any arrogance on my part.

Later, delighted with the task set for Sai Baba, I awoke the next morning quite certain that all my doubts would have been well-founded and that I would safely put away *Sounds of Silence* and Meher Baba for good – forever! But the heavens had the last laugh, for lo and behold, the next morning we received a packet of prasad and a photo of Krishna from ISKCON with greetings for my sister's birthday, a few days later! The greetings do not always have a photograph of Krishna – this one had! We were taken aback, and a considerably chastened me decided I had received one proof which was equal to a million!

It was immediately after this that my mother found herself firmly ensconced between her two determined daughters, on her way to Ahmednagar and Meherabad. The Shirdi trips that we under-take at regular intervals are well planned and kind to her age, but this trip was hurried, unplanned and, perhaps because of this, very exciting! Not that my mother seemed to mind it. She was a real sport!

Placing our heads on His Samadhi was something we will never forget! It sent all the doubts flying out in a trice, and a sense of quietude descended on us. I found myself praying to Krishna as I normally do, and when I raised my head, I 'felt' Meher Baba. Through His picture He seemed to be telling me that it was alright. He had heard me. A torrent of tears greeted this signal from Him and I felt a sense of peace and calm all over me. My sister and mother had much the same experience. Karl has said in the book that Baba touches every soul that takes His darshan, and takes away their cares and worries. How true it seemed!

Thus began our interaction with Meher Baba which has grown closer by the day and opened a new spiritual horizon for us. This interactive web has drawn everyone to it – my father, my mother, my married sisters and their families, and a host of other relatives and friends. And very happily indeed!

Our love and faith in Meher Baba increased greatly after our trip to the Samadhi, with the proof of Baba's presence in our lives. Other than that, these last few years have been full of Baba incidents for me! A reassurance, some timely help, a phone call, a book I read – all these from unlikely sources and at times when I am at my lowest. To me these have been signs from Baba, signs which have brought solace to my troubled mind, signs which have made me exclaim, "I love you, Baba!"

More than any of these, what has struck me about Meher Baba is that nothing seems silly or insignificant to Him. I know that some of the concerns, in retrospect, appear rather trivial, even to me. But Baba is so humane that He has respected these and did not make me feel foolish for seeking answers to them. Fortunately for me, He has taken the challenges I have thrown at Him in such good spirit, that today when I start my mental game with Him with 'Baba if you are really God...' I not only stop short, but also feel I have lost it even before I complete the sentence!

Any rational human being, when confronted with this data, is apt to feel that my journey to finding God should have, by now, come to a logical and happy conclusion. Intellectually one understands that there is one God, but emotionally it is sometimes difficult to accept it. And there are moments when the mind is besieged with questions of the duality of God. So it was with me and although I was getting to love Baba more and more, these nagging thoughts refused to leave me.

Should one forsake the Master who has led one to the other, or should one pray to both? Should one ignore the earlier form because the newer one is also responsive? Is it possible to wipe out an old relationship with a new one, or can one be devoted to both interchangeably? If there is always a reason and time when Baba enters our lives, perhaps when we need Him most, why do doubts of duality and many-ness nag us? Does this reek of lack of faith, or is it the product of an overactive, mischievous mind? Or is it merely because of a strong sense of loyalty to the deity that one has worshipped for so long?

I did not have the answers to any of these questions but all along I did know that somehow Baba would resolve these for me soon. I had a feeling that the answers would appear, from one or many sources, by accident or through questioning, in a flash or over a period of time. Whatever be the means He employs, I was aware that my questions had been raised by Him and would finally be answered by Him too! He had a purpose in it and I just needed to wait and see what it was!

It is strange but while writing this story, and in the process of putting all my confusion down on paper, a sudden thought came to me. Why not ask Karl if he had anything to say on the subject? A call to Nan resulted in this message flashing on my computer screen the next morning.

Can a person have more than two Masters?

"Yes, it is possible, for all Masters are co-related and joined in harmony. They can pass you on from one to the other, whenever they feel it is necessary. There are impressions however in the human mind that make you aware of forms and names that you can identify them by, but the souls of all Masters are both fused together, and separate as well. According to circumstances, some will feel that Baba is Baba, someone else can feel that Baba is Krishna, and someone else that Baba is Jesus – but He is all of them rolled into ONE BIG, HUGE, compassionate universal ball of Spiritual LOVE and Energy. Actually the soul of the Master is faceless and formless, but shows itself to you in ways you can relate with in order to enter your consciousness, and gives you the happiness you experience when you first become aware of them. Love Karl."

A few days later, I came across something in Baba's own words which still further confirmed for me something my heart already knew, but what my mind needed to be convinced about. It read:

> ***"The supremacy of the claim of the Master is not to be challenged even by the reverence the disciple feels for Masters other than the one who has accepted him. All Masters are one in consciousness. One Master is not greater than another; the disciple must, however, place his own Master above other Masters, until he transcends the domain of duality and realises unity."***[1]

Now it was my turn again. So in order to close this issue, once and for all, I asked Baba my one last and final question. I said, "Dear Baba, You are aware of my spiritual past and the present. You, in your deep compassion, have responded to me in different forms at different times. Shankar, Mata, Krishna and Sai – they are all in You. Please guide me and tell me who is my Master and, though I may worship you in several forms, which is that 'one' form which is most recommended for me to concentrate upon?"

The answer through Karl was not long in coming. It is one that has so much meaning and gave me so much joy, that I would really like to share it with you. Karl's message from Baba said:

> *"Concentrate upon your own self, Rupam, for I reside within you. I am you and you are Me. So when you ask who your real Master is, know that it is both you and Me. When you look into your heart, you will see Me. When you listen to the voice within you, it is My voice you will hear. Therefore, concentrate on Love, concentrate on Hope, concentrate on Truth, and concentrate on the Self. All these combined will make up your heaven, and I will be there watching over you with love, hope, truth and through yourself. Be Happy. Love, Baba."*

After this, you must know that all my doubts have vanished and the dilemma of duality has now become a thing of the past. There is no confusion left and no searching for the 'real' God after this. Thank you Baba for filling our lives with the truth.

To end this chapter, I have to tell you about a time when I believe Baba was questioned on the issue of duality by a group of Christian devotees. They were keen to know if Baba wanted them to stop praying to Jesus, as they had been doing since birth, and replace it with worship for Baba. Baba had reassured them that they need not do so, that He and the Christ were One.

Baba sure has the knack to find the right source to reach us and a visit to His home in Meherazad a few weeks later confirmed this for me. As always, we had crowded around Baba's sister Mani who was entertaining us on the verandah with stories about her life with Baba. Sitting in the group that day, I noticed a very distinguished looking lady. She was middle-aged but looked very regal, proud, and strong. Her black hair was parted from the middle and pushed sleekly behind her ears which were weighed down with the weight of two beautiful hooped earrings. Large signet rings with family crests adorned her beautifully manicured fingers, which she kept tightly locked together as if she was holding back something. However, her voice was loud and clear as she asked Mani for permission to share her story.

She said: I come from Spain, and I am the proud owner of a large property, almost like a township, complete with its own residents, farmlands, schools, and entertainment. I live in a beautiful mansion and have a large family of my own. I make myself responsible for all those who live with me and around me too. I am a firm believer in the Christian religion, and have a beautiful big church of my own which is also open to all those that wish to visit. In there is a life-size statue of the Christ before whom I kneel and pray daily with all my heart.

My children grew up in these surroundings, but a day came when one of my sons decided to follow a Guru called Meher Baba. I was shattered! No amount of persuasion or threats could make him change his mind and I had no alternative but to ask him to leave. He left home with his family and I returned to my duties – heartbroken, but still strong in my own faith and beliefs.

Some years went by, years when I often wondered what could have impressed my son so much that he would turn his back on a faith he had believed in during his growing years. Till one day a terrible drought hit my village. Famine, disease, and a great deal of pain and unrest followed. Though I tried my best, many people died.

In desperation I knelt before the statue of Christ, closed my eyes, and cried out in anguish, "Dear Jesus, please save my people. If I have done anything wrong, please show it to me and I promise to make amends for it. Please show me the light."

I looked up, and on the statue I saw a strange glow. It became brighter and brighter, till suddenly there was a flash and, in that instant, in the heart of Jesus, I clearly saw another. It was Meher Baba.

I knelt there gazing in rapture for a long time, the tears streaming down my face.

My village recovered and was soon back to normal. I knew then that what I had done to my son was wrong, that the thoughts and beliefs I had clung on to all my life had really no meaning at all.

I have come all this way to apologise in person, to bow, and to acknowledge the fact that really there is no separation – they are all One.

CHAPTER 21

The King of Hearts

Baba's sister, Mani, once asked Baba, "What happens when we die and are reborn? How are we to recognise You? Do we have to look out for You, search for You? What about the lessons learned in this life? Do we have to start from scratch – all over again?" Baba nodded in the negative, gesturing, "It's always a moving forward, never backward... always forward... you pick up from where you have left."

It is often said that the good karma of past lives secures for you the benefit of having a Master. Once he comes into your life, then the best thing to do is to try and surrender to him, love him sincerely, and spend your life in serving him. The love and devotion that you may have felt for your Master in past lives, helps to form a deep association with the Master again, so that grace and help flows to you directly from him. In this way, you also win an opportunity to clear yourself of karmic entanglements.

The relationship between a Master and his disciples is utterly different from other mundane relationships that arise in the context of ordinary day-to-day life. It arises out of the basic laws of spiritual life. From the spiritual point of view, it is the most important relationship into which a person can enter. The Master is responsible for the spiritual development of his disciples and hence, whether they reincarnate or not, the relationship still carries on.

> Baba says, ***"The relationship between the Master and the disciple is often carried on from one life to another for several reincarnations. Those who have been connected with a Master in past lives are drawn to him by an unconscious magnetism, not knowing why they are thus drawn. There is usually a long history to the***

apparently unaccountable devotion that the disciple feels for his Master. The disciple is often beginning where he had left off in the last incarnation."[1]

The following story is very important for readers of this book but more so for me, because it was the beginning of a new chapter in my life. This has been described in detail in *Sounds of Silence,* but to tell you a little about this here, I have to take you back to a day in 1985 to the time when my communication with Karl had just started. It was a time when new doors opened up for me and I first heard the name Meher Baba. For a few days the writing repeatedly screamed, *"Message Meherbaba, Meherbaba message. Go, go wherever He is."* But who was He, and why should I go wherever He is?

Karl came out with a message that changed the course of not only my life but of my whole family, and of so many more to come. He said, *"I am waiting for you Mum. I am going to be there when you come, and will see you for sure. I promise you will know that it is me. I am a man and I am living there just now. I will come near you and sit down. I will be wearing a red shirt, brown pants and have no shoes on my feet. I am a foreigner – fair and good-looking, between the ages of eighteen and twenty-five, and my name is Hamma Maclane. I am Baba's right-hand man."*

How all this came to pass exactly as Karl had said, how we made contact with a young boy at the Samadhi, that is something I can never forget. He was a foreigner, fair and good-looking, in a red shirt and brown pants, and with no shoes on his feet. His name was Patrick.

What followed was still more amazing. At Mansari's room on the hill that day, and at the same time, we met up with a lovely lady. Moved by our story of Karl and the writing, she told us how her husband had died in a car crash and how she had come to Meherabad in order to find her own peace. She ended by assuring us that Baba would find some way of doing the same for us.

In all the excitement we had forgotten to ask her name, so after we reached Bombay, we called to ask. Over the crackle of the phone I heard the reply, "Her name is Mrs. Maclane. But actually she has two names – she calls herself Kristin Maclane Carlson." As I heard the last name CARL SON, the sun suddenly burst out of dark clouds for me.

Two years later we met her again, and related our amazing experience to her. I told her all about the boy 'in the red shirt, brown pants and no shoes on his feet' who was there to greet us at the Samadhi. In mid-sentence, she stopped me and said, "But why did you not ask his name?"

"I did," I answered. "His name was Patrick."

"Oh my God," she exclaimed. "My husband's name was Patrick, Patrick Carlson, and I had dressed him in a red shirt when I put him to rest!"

This was my first real proof that Karl's spirit really resided with Meher Baba, and that Baba was even then busy building a connection that carries on to this day.

Twenty-five years have passed, and now, after knowing even more details of Kristin's life with her husband, I cease to wonder why Karl had chosen to represent himself through Patrick. It was because of the beautiful, selfless, deep and abiding love, and absolute devotion he had for his Beloved Meher Baba.

The story you are about to read is entitled 'The King of Hearts' and is written by his wife Kristin Maclane Carlson.

I grew up in a New England intellectual family, with a father who claimed to be an atheist. Following my father's model, I expressed great contempt for religion when I was an adolescent and a young adult. Psychology interested me, and from a young age, I planned a career as a psychotherapist.

The first time I recall seeing a photograph of Meher Baba was in the early 70s. One day in Berkeley, I saw a poster of Meher Baba as an older man with a large round face and twinkling eyes. 'DON'T WORRY, BE HAPPY' was written in bold letters across the bottom. I reacted with usual distaste for those described as Gurus, barely looking at the photograph, and commenting angrily that 'Don't Worry, Be Happy' seemed to be a highly irresponsible message to write on a poster.

I continued to live for many years in Santa Cruz, California, working as a therapist without hearing anything more about Baba, until I met Patrick Carlson in 1978. The first time I visited Patrick's house, an odd photograph of a man lying on a bed, dressed in white, caught my eye. I asked who might this man be and was dismayed to hear the name Meher Baba. I was beginning to fall in love with Patrick and hoped this Meher Baba would not turn out to be important in his life.

I was disappointed to learn that Patrick was, in fact, extremely interested in Meher Baba. He even spent four months at Meherabad in 1970, describing it was the most wonderful experience in his life. I privately thought Patrick needed a father figure, since his own father was an alcoholic and the family life was very distressing.

Patrick and I started spending a lot of time together and he introduced me to several of his friends who also knew about Meher Baba. One night Beverly Smith showed slides of her trip to Meherabad. Other Baba friends came over to see them, and they all talked excitedly about Baba and India.

I listened silently, concluding that they all must have had unhappy childhoods to need such crutches in their adult life. I found their belief that Meher Baba had lived as God in human form particularly horrifying. The word God itself sounded like fingernails on a blackboard to me, something shouted by fundamentalist preachers.

"If you need a fantasy to live by," I told Patrick at one point, "Meher Baba sounds nice enough. I just don't happen to need a story to construct my life around. My childhood was not as unhappy as yours. I don't need a new family in India, or myths to live by." I waited defensively for Patrick and his friends to try and convert me, but they just listened politely to my objections and went on talking about Baba with the same enthusiasm. I found myself disturbed by the photographs and paintings of Baba that people had in their homes. When my eyes caught a glimpse of one, I would quickly turn away, almost in embarrassment. His eyes unsettled me; I didn't want to look at them.

One evening, Patrick and his friends wanted to attend a meeting. Everyone stood up to say a prayer at the end of the gathering and I felt strongly repulsed, vowing never again to come to a Meher Baba meeting. I told myself that these people suffered pathetic delusions and that their belief in this man indicated unresolved childhood traumas.

Although most of the time I was repelled by the conversations about Baba, I did experience occasional moments of softening. When Patrick played Cole Porter songs that Baba loved, or told stories of His sister, Mani, reading murder mysteries aloud to entertain Him in the evenings, I felt somewhat attracted to this strange person although I would never admit it to others.

One spring, I met Meher Baba's niece, Shireen, who had recently married Patrick's old friend. Sensing my conflicts, Shireen tried to reassure me with a story about Baba, forbidding her to read any books about Him. I felt immediately and strongly interested. He wanted Shireen to know Him in some other way, not influenced by words and ideas. She suggested that I need not read any books about Baba either and I felt strangely happy and relieved. No need anymore for me to decide if these ideas were right or wrong.

After a couple of years Patrick and I decided to get married and made plans for a wedding on the coast of Maine with family and a few friends. We sat down one day to write our wedding vows, preferring an informal personal ceremony, and almost immediately, I got into a conflict about the mention of God in the marriage. "I absolutely can't have the word God in this wedding," I protested vehemently. "I don't believe in God, my family doesn't believe in God, and my friends don't believe in God. God cannot be a part of this wedding. It would be incredibly embarrassing."

"Well, what do you think marriage is all about?" Patrick asked in some shock.

"I don't know, but it certainly isn't anything to do with God," I stated emphatically. "And I am definitely not having that 'until death do us part' thing either."

Patrick took a long walk on the beach to sort out his feelings. He told me much later that on this walk he had questioned the whole marriage, but eventually returned to present me with a possible compromise. "We'll leave out the word God, but I want a few passages of Meher Baba's to be read by Carl Ernst during the ceremony."

"Fine," I agreed, "but stick them somewhere in the middle and make them short." I privately hoped that no one would notice the passages if they were mixed in with enough music.

The wedding took place, and I managed to block my ears when

the Meher Baba words were read. Once happily married, we began making plans for a long trip abroad. Patrick often talked about wanting to revisit India which didn't interest me very much, but I agreed since it seemed very important to him. We agreed to travel in Europe for a couple of months and then head eastward.

"We can go to Meherabad for two weeks, from there to Sri Lanka and then on to Nepal," I explained. "I don't mind meeting the mandali since they seem important to you, but don't expect me to be going into Meher Baba's tomb or anything weird like that," I warned Patrick. He told me I could do whatever I liked. I planned to catch up on some reading.

In London, we stayed at a place called Meher Oceanic. I resisted many attempts to engage me in conversations about Baba, and at the time wished that I had never agreed to go to India with Patrick. But while I felt defensive and irritated most of the time, softer moments would occasionally creep up on me. Someone was watching a video on Baba one evening and I felt a curious tug, but I only watched a minute or so before I pushed myself away. Another person left Jean Adriel's book *Avatar* lying about, and I found myself reading a few pages with some interest before abruptly tossing it away. I was not going to be tricked into this Meher Baba cult, I told myself. It was only for desperate people clinging to false promises. I did not need this, I assured myself. I was already happy. My life was wonderful. I had married the man I loved, we were travelling together around the world, I had my work, family and friends that satisfied me, and I didn't need anything else.

The time eventually came for us to leave for India. I had noticed Patrick's unspoken impatience to be at Meherabad throughout our travels in France and England, and felt disappointed that he wasn't fully satisfied to remain in the French countryside forever. Why did he have to be so obsessed with this Meher Baba? In every other way he seemed to be the ideal partner.

We flew to Bombay one October evening in 1980, or at least tried to fly to Bombay, but were unable to land in the dense fog and thus forced to continue on to Madras for refuelling. The situation then grew worse. An engine failed during take off on our return to Bombay. Everyone sat buckled to their seats, knowing something to be gravely wrong, hoping to survive the flight. Many people prayed. I wished I believed in God.

The fog cleared and we landed amidst tremendous cheering and clapping. India seemed miraculous. I wanted to kiss the ground as we rushed out of the airplane prison. I immediately fell in love with Bombay, its vibrant pulse, noises and smells. It reminded me of West Africa where I had lived as a teenager and, in some odd way, I felt I had come home. We made our way to a place in Dadar. An Indian festival was in progress with many young people dancing in the streets, striking sticks against their partner's raised sticks. The noise was intoxicating. I felt a wild excitement, watching the streets from a small porch, hardly wanting to sleep. We stayed a few days making travel plans to Ahmednagar. I continued to feel very uncomfortable with the prayers and photos of Meher Baba, but the general environment thrilled me so much that I endured the rest. The lady who we lived with also seemed to be such a sweet woman that I hated to offend her by refusing to stand up for the prayers.

One evening, we boarded a bus for Ahmednagar. The whole night I remained wide awake filled with a strange excitement while Patrick dozed beside me. At 4 in the morning, we were dropped off at the Ashoka Hotel in Ahmednagar. A few people wandered around in the night, but the town seemed largely asleep. Patrick had not been there for over ten years, and felt disoriented. We staggered around in the dark with our luggage, looking for the trust office. Becoming more and more irritated, I wanted a hotel and sleep but Patrick pressed on in search of some sign of the Baba community.

We found the trust compound after half an hour of circling the area but the gates were shut, sleeping bodies lying on the ground in front. Patrick suggested we take a rickshaw out to Meherabad. We found a driver who knew no English and seemed never to have heard of Meherabad, but wagged his head from side to side at the mention of Arangaon.

"I think Meherabad is near Arangaon village," Patrick told me, "so if we go in that direction we will probably find it." I knew there was no point in arguing with Patrick, who could be very stubborn, and was clearly set on arriving at this Meherabad place. We set off into the night, soon turning on to a deserted country road, pinpoints of stars in a vast blue sky. Neither Patrick nor the driver seemed confident about the route and soon I wished I had argued more for staying in town, at least until daylight. Just as I began lobbying to return to town, Patrick shouted, "Meherabad! Meherabad!" and pointed the driver into a darkened driveway.

We pulled up outside a long, low building and peered out of the rickshaw. In the dark, a door banged open and an angry voice bellowed from the far end of the building. "What are you doing? What do you think you are doing waking everyone up so early? You stupid pilgrims. Why are you coming here? You are supposed to go to the Pilgrim Centre, but not in the middle of the night." A tall thin man with cushy white hair strode over pouring out a stream of abuse. Suddenly, he seemed to recognise Patrick and threw his arms around him, the torrent of angry words stopping mid-sentence. I still felt shaken and wished I could hop in a rickshaw and leave.

Another door opened and a woman rushed out. "Padri, Heather! Patrick!" Everyone seemed to be shouting and hugging in the dark. Between embraces, Patrick introduced me but I disliked the place already. Patrick inquired about Erico and, hearing that his old friend was still on the hill as the night watchman near the tomb, he wanted to rush off into the night. I, exasperated and miserably exhausted, now faced a choice of staying below with some Padri and Heather, or following Patrick up the hill to the tomb. I had been determined not to go near the tomb in case someone expected me to go inside and bow down, a thought I found particularly horrifying. The thought of remaining below in the dark with strangers alarmed me even more, so I accompanied Patrick up the hill in bad humour.

As we approached the tomb, Patrick spied Erico. They embraced and began talking in animated whispers. I stood immobile in the predawn, hoping I was invisible and wondering how soon we could leave. While waiting, I rehearsed a few conversations with Patrick. I would inform him that I didn't want to stay at Meherabad after all, suggesting that we leave for Sri Lanka, or at least for Ahmednagar, right away.

A woman carrying a small pot and a few rags opened the door of the tomb and went inside. From my spot outside I watched her begin to wipe the slab of marble, carefully pouring drops of water on her cloth. A few other women appeared out of the darkness, from the direction we had come, and began to help with the cleaning. I wished Patrick would finish his conversation so we could leave. The woman poked her head out of the door and seeing me standing in the dark beckoned me to come near. I smiled and shook my head. 'No thank you', I mimed. She tilted her head to one side, smiled and beckoned with more urgency. I wanted to tell her that I wasn't interested in Meher Baba and didn't want to be in His tomb, but a large sign outside the door read 'Silence'. I wanted to tell her that I hadn't meant to come here at all. I was just waiting for Patrick to finish talking to his friend. She kept beckoning silently, urging me to come inside.

Even more exasperated than I had been down below, I finally decided that it would be easier to just take the cloth, wipe up whatever she indicated, and be done with it. Maybe then she would leave me alone. Slipping off my shoes, I walked up to the stone porch, accepted the small brown cloth and stepped over the threshold of the tomb. The moment I found myself inside the small painted space, I began to weep. None of the others paid any attention, and the woman smilingly motioned for me to wipe the marble that I imagined covered Meher Baba's body. Feeling faint, I knelt down to wipe the surface.

I wiped and wept. I wondered why I was crying. I didn't feel sad but the tears streamed down my face. I decided I must be suffering from jet lag. One voice inside me said, 'This is what everyone in the world is looking for! This is the love everyone wants.' The other part of me argued for fatigue and jet lag, urging me to get out of the tomb and get some sleep. I stayed inside for what seemed like hours but when I emerged, Patrick and Erico stood in the same position talking. I walked down the hill later, dazed, forgetting all my plans to leave.

My resolve to stay away from the tomb disappeared completely. I was drawn like a magnet, returning several times a day to sit on the floor inside, even bowing down in the way that had previously horrified me. I found myself singing aarti, listening to the words of the prayers. The tears continued flowing, sometimes inside the tomb, sometimes at hearing the mention of Baba's name, seeing objects He used, or imagining Him having walked along the same paths I now walked. Jet lag, I told myself. Extreme exhaustion.

One morning I sat cross-legged inside the tomb and looked up to see Meher Baba standing, next to a vase of flowers in the corner. He looked very young, achingly beautiful in a long white *sadra*, smiling and watching me. The image was clear, although not solid. I could have put my hand through it. Hallucinations, I warned myself, but continued to gaze at Him. I must be still very exhausted from the trip. He seemed so beautiful I could barely breathe. I wanted to cry and cry.

I came back again and again, hoping to have more glimpses. Many times I could see Him in the corner between the windows, and once or twice saw Him pass by the right window, His sadra sweeping along. His eyes would meet mine through the window as He strode past and I felt dizzy. I must be imagining it, I told myself. It seemed that whenever I looked in the corner, I could make His image appear. I told Patrick who suggested that it might be better not to talk about it too much. I talked to a close Baba disciple, Bal Natu, who told me I was very fortunate to see Baba but I was not sure if I believed him. Sometimes I wondered if I was being brainwashed, because there were so many photos of Baba around, but I still loved to see Him.

One day I sat at the tomb and began to hear Him talk to me. It seemed to be a voice without sound, but I knew what He was saying. "You are troubled by the idea of an Avatar? You can't believe in this?"

"Yes, I can't accept all of this. It sounds crazy, someone being God. I don't even know what God is?"

"It doesn't make any difference. You don't have to use any words like those. You can just accept Me as your best friend. You are interested in psychology now, do you believe in the idea of highest self?"

"Yes that makes sense to me."

"Then that is all I am. I am your highest self. But the most important thing is to listen and obey this highest self."

I had always been bothered by people talking about obeying Meher Baba. I could not understand, with such a western background, the concept of obeying a Master. Now I felt caught in my own logic, simple and compelling.

"Stand up and go outside now."

"What? I just sat down in here," I protested.

"Learn to listen to this voice and obey it," He ordered, and I began to worry that I was now beginning to suffer auditory hallucinations, yet I obeyed Him. I knew from my psychology classes that auditory hallucinations indicated even more serious symptoms than the visual ones I had been experiencing, especially delusions of hearing the voice of God. I wondered if I was experiencing some type of mental breakdown. I felt happy however, and continued to follow the voice that led me to various seemingly meaningless exercises, practicing the art of listening and obeying. Eventually the voice became more internal, the words less distinct, until it became a knowing rather than an order.

Time passed, Patrick and I spent two months at Meherabad instead of two weeks. I didn't speak much of my experiences, often doubting the reality of them. I finally gave up the notion that I was having a psychotic episode and decided that I was just imagining things, making pleasant little games for myself.

We returned to the US and settled in New England. I carried a quiet and personal feeling of Baba inside me, still not liking to read books or discuss my metaphysical theories. At first my friends thought that I might be changed from this visit to India, but soon accepted that I was the same. Indeed I felt the same, yet utterly different.

A couple of years later, Patrick and I returned to India for Amartithi bringing a friend along. I looked forward to seeing Baba's image in the tomb once again since I had not been able to recreate it anywhere else. I sat and stared into the corner but no form came. 'Maybe I had lost my knack', I thought, disappointed to see only the painted walls. I tried many times to see Baba's image, but was unable. I enjoyed the trip nonetheless, a trip that was Patrick's last as he was killed in a car accident the following year. He carried the torch in the early morning run from Meherazad to Meherabad, lighting the Amartithi dhuni at dawn, saying afterward, "If nothing else happens in my life, it is complete now after this act."

On June 1st 1984, I came home from work to find a note on my door asking me to contact the police. I knew something had happened to Patrick. On the telephone, the officer asked me to come to the police station as Patrick had been in a car accident. My friend drove me to the police station. I repeated Baba's name all the way, knowing Patrick had died. Still in a state of numbness, I was aware of always having known this event would take place as if the souls now known as Patrick, Kristin, and the drunk driver (whose name I no longer remember), once agreed upon this intersection in our lives. I felt prepared in an odd way and knew that Meher Baba would help me get through the unimaginable pain that was due to follow.

Later in the day, I came to see his body arriving at the funeral home with friends, photographs of Meher Baba, and some ashes from a dhuni fire Baba once lit at Meherabad. I had never seen a dead body before, and when I first came into the room and saw Patrick lying on a hospital bed with hands uncharacteristically folded across his chest, I couldn't grasp what had taken place. Clearly this inert body was not Patrick or what I knew of him. I began silently to ask Baba what had become of Patrick. I stood by the side of the bed and touched his dull cold hands, looking up to the left as I saw a light near his head. Baba stood there, smiling and watching me, but this time as an old man clothed in a beautiful white sadra.

As images came into focus, I could also see Patrick clearly standing next to Baba. I was surprised he wore different clothes from the ones I had brought for the funeral director to clothe the body. Small irrelevant details seemed to stick to my mind. Why was he wearing blue jeans and a dark blue shirt? I had brought a crimson shirt.

Patrick stood next to Baba for several seconds, also smiling, relaxed and untroubled. Smoothly and silently, his form moved in front of Baba's and then disappeared. I remained absorbed, gazing at Baba for several minutes, His eyes mirroring everything that I had known and much, much more. He suffered all the pain I felt and all that I would come to feel in the days ahead. I understood at that moment that it never had been me creating those images in the tomb, but Baba who had given me those precious gifts. After a few minutes Baba's image faded, but I felt comforted by His response.

I had never been able to see His face or form again as I did in the early days at those moments when I most needed Him, but Baba sometimes makes His presence known in many other beautiful ways, teaching me to look everywhere for Him. One day, for example, not long after Patrick died, I went to a *sahavas* on the west coast near Los Angeles. I had wanted to be in the company of Baba lovers but knew very few people there. It was also the first time I had been away from family and friends since Patrick's death. At one moment, I suddenly felt very alone and unsure whether my coming had been a good idea. I begged Baba to stay very close to me, to let me know He was always with me as He had done many times in painful moments.

Hughie MacDonald suddenly walked up to me, a magician's hat on his head, and spread a pack of cards out in front of me face down. He wordlessly invited me to pick a card, any card. I touched them all, absorbed in the choice and anticipation of a trick, and pulled out one. When I turned over my card, I realised once again He was more than close. It was the king of hearts!

During my final trip to Meherabad with Patrick, I had written a song for Baba with the chorus line, 'I weep and I laugh, I hold out my hand, He's dealt me the king of hearts.'

CHAPTER 22

The Samadhi

"In the middle of an island there is always something that continues to give you hope that a ship will come your way. In the middle of a desert, there always remains a hope that sometime a camel will somehow walk your way. In the middle of an illness you feel confident that the doctor will make you feel better soon, and so, in the middle of a problem that seems insurmountable, you do feel that Baba is there and may change it all around for you. This will happen only if you have implicit trust and faith that God is in His heaven and will always look on you with love and compassion.

"The Samadhi at Meherabad is your ship, your camel, and your doctor. It is the anchor of your existence, and what takes you on to Baba. You have only to go there and ask in order to get.

"So I say to all – Love Him, and ask of His bountiful Grace. He wants to help you, to serve you, and to look after you. Give Him a chance to do so. Love Karl."

Perhaps you have noticed that in most of the stories written by people, the visit to the Samadhi becomes the central point of change or the point of transition in their lives. This is not planned and most certainly it is not coincidental.

You may have also noticed that being inside the Samadhi area, and putting their head on the marble tombstone, for some becomes a moment of catharsis. Some experience a time of equanimity and some feel an uncontrollable outpouring of love. That little mound on which the Samadhi is built seems to soak the tears of the countless that have come here. You could sit under one of the many gently swaying trees, unburden your heart or render your thanks, and the leaves of those trees will send forth comforting whispers. On that hill of serenity, each one finds his inner self.

Such is the peace and reconciliation you experience at Baba's Samadhi. You descend from the hill listening to the silence that speaks volumes and stays with you forever.

Baba's Samadhi is situated on a hill about nine kilometres south of the city of Ahmednagar. This property, known as Meherabad, lies near the village of Arangaon. A railway line runs through, dividing it into what is called lower Meherabad and upper Meherabad. In the 1920s, as Baba was once walking along this road, He rested under a neem tree close to a disbanded post office and decided to reside there, engaging Himself in activities connected with His own work. One day, as Baba was strolling on the hill, He suddenly picked out a spot on the top of the hill and ordered a pit to be dug six feet long, six feet deep and four feet wide at the designated spot. This crypt became a special place where Baba would spend many hours, days and weeks in seclusion, often accompanied by prolonged fasts, doing what he termed as His universal spiritual work. Later on when the post office where Baba had earlier resided was demolished, its stones were lovingly carried up the hill by His followers to be used for constructing a structure over the crypt.

Starting in August 1938, the Swiss artist, Helen Dahm, was asked by Baba to paint colourful murals on the inside walls of Meher Baba's underground crypt. She was absorbed in her work from morning to evening. Although Helen was not a young woman (she was sixty at the time), she worked on her back on top of scaffolding to paint the dome's ceiling. Hedi Mertens, who also was a painter, would assist Helen by mixing her paints but Helen did the actual painting of the figures. The results convey "an atmosphere of contemplation and mystical transfiguration" in a simple and primitive style.

A dome was subsequently built over the structure and the symbols of the four great religions were represented there – a cross for Christianity, a temple for Hinduism, a mosque for Islam, and a sacred fire urn for Zoroastrianism. Baba's motto, 'Mastery in Servitude' was inscribed over the door.

It was only when Baba ordered the mandali to build a dome over this 'crypt' or underground room in 1938, that everyone came to know this was to be the site of his future tomb. This was the room where Baba had secluded himself in 1927. It was also where he used to spend the night until the tin cabin was built on the hill in 1935. Now, all became aware that the 'underground pit' was to house His last physical remains and they all regarded this humble structure with sacredness.

Once in 1938 while strolling on the hill, Baba made a sweeping gesture and remarked, ***"This whole universe is Mine, but this place is specially Mine."***[1] This then was destined to become His final resting place – the Samadhi, the Tomb-Shrine – the place of world pilgrimage.

On the 31st of January 1969 at 12:15 pm, in His room at Meherazad, Baba breathed His last to 'live eternally in the hearts of those who love Him'. As per His wish, a record of His favourite song 'Begin the Beguine' was played seven times near His body. Baba's body was then brought from Meherazad to Meherabad, where it was kept in the open crypt for seven days with His face unshrouded, for His lovers to have a last glimpse of their Beloved. Thousands flocked from the East and the West for this last darshan of His physical form. Baba's body was finally covered on the 7th of February, which according to the Zoroastrian calendar, happened to be His birthday,

The Samadhi is open every day from 6 am to 8 pm. Anyone visiting the Samadhi receives an indelible impression of unconditional love from the Source, whether one is conscious of it at the time or not. Baba had indicated that of all the places on earth, Asia, and more particularly India, is closest to the 'creation point'. Hence the Samadhi at Meherabad has now become that unique site which is the source of His direct living and personal radiation, dispensing His love and compassion throughout the earth.

Through the years, I have taken so many to Baba's Samadhi and marvelled at the change in their lives. I have noticed that each one of them has found his or her own special way of relating to Him and that very soon He has become the nucleus of their lives. They have become convinced, verified by their own personal experiences, that Baba is watching over them, lovingly listening to their words, problems, pleas and complaints, and helping them to work everything out to a successful conclusion.

Baba's method in reaching the hearts of His lovers is matchless, and His responses to the needs of each of His dear ones are offered in the ways so personal that they can be wholeheartedly accepted. His love is unconditional and does not look for merits. It only waits for an excuse to flow.

Baba says, ***"I never come and I never go. I am present everywhere. Isn't it wonderful that I never leave?"***[2]

Now you may well say that if Baba is here, there and everywhere, in everyone and everything, then why do we need to travel the Samadhi to make contact with Him? What is the significance of the Samadhi, and why do we bow down and touch our heads to His feet? What is the benefit of all this?

When I first became aware of Meher Baba and through my auto writing with Karl, I received the first message saying, *"Message Meher Baba, go – go wherever He is,"* I was totally confused. Little did I know then what this little structure known as the Samadhi held in store for me. I did not fully understand that Baba's physical form was not there anymore, but hoped that may be His heart was ever alive to help me, to love me, and to listen to me. To tell you the truth, at that time, I made my way to Ahmednagar, the Pilgrim Centre, and the Samadhi, only because Karl asked me to do so. Who was this Meher Baba who was going to give me a message? I had never been to a place like this before.

I remember that it was early March, and although the sun was at its peak, my life was still full of dark clouds. Yet as soon as I climbed the hilltop that day, a certain sense of peace seemed to descend over me. I remember that I stepped over the threshold and stood staring at the tomb of Baba, trying to figure out what to do or say. The atmosphere was so overwhelming, that for a while, no words came. Then I knelt down, touched my head on the cool marble slab of the Samadhi and I questioned Baba about my son Karl. I have come – but why? Did my son's spirit really reside with this Baba?

I know that I said, "Dear Baba, who are You and where do You come from? All I can do at this moment is to thank You from the bottom of my heart just for making Yourself known to me. My Karl, my dearest son, he is so young and small, everyone that he knows and is close to is still here in this world. Please tell me, for I need to know, who will be there to look after him and to watch over him with love?"

And from the deep recesses of the tomb had come my answer:

"I will. I am here. Do not worry."

And then, my heart, for some inexplicable reason, had suddenly come to rest. This had been my first connection with Baba.

After that, Baba began taking on different proportions. A new happiness slowly began to flow through me, and soon looking for Karl did not seem to be a priority anymore. Every time I went, I wanted to get closer and closer to Baba. I guess, just being able to associate with those close to Baba, walk up the same path that He had walked, go into the room where He had stayed, and sit in the Samadhi touching His tombstone, began to make me feel closer to His physical presence. I needed His help to make me love Him more and more. I wanted to love Him the way He should be loved, but as yet I did not know how!

So, I went as often as I could to the Samadhi. It was such a comforting place to be in. I used to find the times of the day when very few would be up on the hill. I would then walk up there, stroll around the surrounding areas, or sit under a shady tree and just be with Him. It was a place where there were no rules and regulations, except that you kept absolutely quiet. There was freedom of thought and action, there were no questions asked, a place where I could do whatever I felt like doing – pray, meditate or just listen to the silence. It was a place where Baba had time for me. The funny thing was that I would prepare a whole lot of questions and things to ask of Baba but, when I went into the tomb area, all of them seemed to disappear, and all I would find myself saying was "Thank you Baba. I do love you, even if it is in my own way."

Many a time while sitting inside the Samadhi, and even now, I find myself unable to control the tears. Very often, I have also seen people weeping there profusely. Mani, Baba's sister, described this as 'melting' and told us that it was beneficial to "let go, for the candle to become wax under the fire of Baba's love."

Prayers and aarti are at 7 am and again at 7 pm at the Samadhi. First, the Universal or the Master's Prayer, followed by the Prayer of Repentance, and then the aartis. After this, one by one, you may step into the Samadhi for darshan, while people outside continue to sing *bhajans, kirtans, qawwalis,* and hymns in various Indian and foreign languages.

You may join everyone in saying prayers and aarti, or just stand there quietly till it is over. You may or may not attend at all. When pilgrims would question the value of going for prayers and aarti at Baba's Samadhi, Baba's sister Mani would often point out that it is a chance to remember Baba, to focus on Him with love. She called it one of those 'speed breakers' – things that remind you of Baba and break the headlong rush of the mind and its involvement in, and enchantment with, ephemeral things.

I remember that my first reaction to the Universal or Master's Prayer was, "Why is it not something easy, like the Lord's Prayer of the Christian religion, that we had learned in school? Why did Baba have to use such big words and lofty phrases and make it so difficult to remember?" Though Baba had encouraged His followers to do away with all rituals, He had obviously made it clear that He wanted His followers to recite these prayers daily. Why? There had to be a reason for this.

Reading through the books written by other Baba lovers, I gather that these prayers were not intended to glorify Baba. They were words picked out by Baba from all the different religious books of the world like the Bible, the Avesta, the Koran, and the Bhagvad Gita; words that had the strongest vibrations and that were most beneficial to mankind. I believe, at the time of recitation of these prayers, Baba Himself would wash His hands and face and straighten His coat or sadra, and then with great solemnity He would stand up, join His palms and listen with closed eyes and the utmost reverence to all these attributes of God in the Master's Prayer. Obviously, these superlatives were charged with deep significance and were very important to Baba in His universal work. So important that, even towards the end, when Baba could hardly stand, He would still call out to one of His disciples to support Him while the prayers were read out. ***"I have given these prayers to humanity to recite. They are for all posterity... All that matters is My having participated in the prayers. Anytime anyone repeats these prayers, I am there with them, and they will be helped spiritually."***[3]

Baba dictated the Prayer of Repentance at Meherabad in November 1952. At first I remember thinking, "Why should I say it, and what should I repent if I have not done anything wrong?" I used to just stand and listen to it, until one day what struck me was the use of the word 'we' in the prayer, and it dawned on me that Baba had also participated in my repentance, and since then my resentment vanished and it began to make sense to me. I believe there are so many things we unwittingly do, and the sanskaras build up daily. So if we make it a habit to give them up to Baba every day, it relieves us of future build-ups, and helps us to ease our sufferings.

And lastly, the 'Beloved God' prayer, which even to this day I find is the easiest, simplest and best of all. It entreats God to help us all to love Him more and more, "till we become worthy of union with You, and help us all to hold fast to Baba's daaman till the very end." I found no difficulty with that at all.

There is tomb-cleaning every morning at 6 am where newcomers are especially welcomed. It is quite exciting to get up at the crack of dawn, grab a quick cup of hot tea, and walk briskly up the hill in time to take part in cleaning the Samadhi area to dress the tomb with love and flowers. They say that if you do *seva* for the Master, it is greatly beneficial to your spiritual growth but apart from that, it leaves you with a beautiful feeling of participation and definitely makes you feel closer to Baba.

I often heard the residents of Meherabad and those close to Baba always say, "Go into the Samadhi while you can." When questioned about it, they explained that Baba had said that seventy years from the dropping of His body, His Tomb-Shrine on Meherabad hill would become a centre of world pilgrimage. They also said, "Put your head on the tomb as often as possible, for the benefits are plenty." I wondered why, till one day, my neighbour and dear friend, Freny Dadachanji, an old and ardent Baba lover, explained it all to me. Her thoughts are translated in the words of Delia Delon in her book *The Ocean of Love*. "When people come to a *Perfect Master* and touch His feet with their heads, they lay upon Him the burden of their sanskaras – those subtle impressions of thought and emotion and action which bind the individual soul to recurrent earthly lives. This is the burden to which Jesus referred when He said, 'Come unto Me all ye who labour and are heavy laden and I will give you rest.'"

What I deduce from this is that although this immense help may not be apparent in the 'now', it may reduce the burden of the sanskaras of your past in order to help you in the future. Sometimes, Baba may choose to hasten our sanskaras so that what we may have to undergo in several lifetimes is speeded up and spent in this lifetime. When this happens, one may get the feeling, though temporary, of facing more challenges. But eventually, the sanskaras become lighter and lighter. Thus it becomes that much easier and smoother to come close to Him and eventually become One with Him.

All humanity responds to the healing touch of love, and there is plenty available on that hill. A contact with the Master makes you feel that love. It helps you to carry that healing flame within you and then to spread it to those who need it. When you make a connection with Him, Baba sees your pain and distress and tries His best to transmute it into awareness, acceptance and joy.

The Samadhi is the source of His direct living and personal radiation, and where Meher Baba responds to the longings of the heart for His physical company. It is said that anyone who visits the Samadhi receives Baba's unconditional love, whether conscious of it at the time or not.

What then is Amartithi? Why is January 31st, the day Baba 'dropped His body', so important and special? Why is it that thousands go through discomforts, travelling miles in *tongas*, bullock carts, crowded buses and congested trains, taxis and overloaded cars, spending nights in make-shift tents, sleeping on hard bedding rolls, and standing for many hours in long queues, in order to be able to place their heads down on the Samadhi for just those few seconds. Why do people go through all this when, on an ordinary day, you can avail yourself of the opportunity to sit for hours at the Samadhi in peace without undergoing so much hardship?

I was sitting in my room one day talking to a new Baba friend, when he suddenly asked me this same question. I instinctively answered, "Because Baba's physical presence is felt all the more on that day, and His darshan is extremely strong and beneficial to all mankind." No sooner had I said these words than I clamped my hands to my mouth, wondering exactly how and why those words had slipped out. I had no authority to voice this, for I didn't really know if it was true!

After the person had gone, I regretted my outburst and asked Baba's forgiveness if I had inadvertently said something wrong. I realised that I had done exactly what I was constantly being reprimanded for by Jimmy – putting myself into a position of being all-knowing, without having any real authority to do so. I knew that this had come out spontaneously and I asked Baba if He could let me know, in some way, if what I had said had any real truth in it.

The next day, a very close Baba follower, Sam Patel, called me up and said that he would like to share an experience with me. He came. We sat over tea and sandwiches and he told me the following story.

During the Amartithi of 1999, I was doing some voluntary work around the Samadhi area and after that was over at around 11:30 am, I wanted to sit quietly to concentrate and focus on Baba, but being able to find a place to sit amongst the thousands gathered was quite difficult. With great difficulty I finally managed to sneak in amongst some people from Andhra. This was on the floor near Baba's cabin at the tin shed near the Samadhi, and was just perfect. They didn't know me and I couldn't understand what they were talking about.

At around 11:45 am, I closed my eyes and tried to visualise the events of that fateful day of 1969. How the Lord suffered those spasms when His whole body would tremble, how He asked if Dr. Ginde had arrived, how He asked Alobaji to read out these couplets from Hafiz:

> "Befitting a fortunate slave carry out every command of the Master, without any question of why and what.
>
> "About what you hear from the Master, never say it is wrong because my dear, the fault lies in your own incapacity to understand Him.
>
> "I am slave of the Master, Who has released me from ignorance. Whatever my Master does is of the highest benefit to all concerned."

All these thoughts of the Beloved's sufferings brought tears to my eyes and just then the final announcement for fifteen-minutes silence came on, from 12 noon to 12.15 pm. This is when my vision started.

I suddenly saw Meher Baba standing near the big green gate (leading towards Mansari's room). Baba looked very radiant in His white sadra and He had Eruch standing right beside Him. They keep looking at the thousands assembled there and then suddenly Baba nudges Eruch asking him to start marching in. Then they both somehow find their way through the crowds and get to the assembly platform. Eruch helps Baba to get on to the *mandap*. This is when I rush up there and tell Eruch, "What is Baba doing? If people see Him, there will be a stampede." Eruch tells me to be quiet and stand behind, and let Baba do His work. So I stand there quite perplexed.

Meher Baba's Samadhi at Meherabad.

Baba then starts flinging out both His arms, turning in all directions, showering His blessings to one and all gathered there. This goes on for a good ten minutes or so and there is complete silence amongst the thousands gathered there. Then some babies start crying and people begin clearing their throats. As soon as this begins to happen, Baba again nudges Eruch telling him it is time to go. Eruch helps Baba down and He starts rushing towards the Samadhi. I just trail behind. Baba goes in over the threshold, climbs up, and then coming towards the huge marble, He just lifts it as though it was a lid, gets in and lies down with His hands folded over His chest, and tells Eruch to quickly close everything. Eruch then calls me to help with the stone; this is when Baba gestures to me to 'tell people what you saw'. We then manage to close the crypt and cover it with flowers. Just then I wake up to reality when people start chanting "Avatar Meher Baba Ki Jai" and see myself sitting amongst the thousands of His lovers.

By the time Sam had come to the end of his story, I was almost in tears. For not only was it a beautiful experience but it had so truthfully and lovingly answered my own questions.

You can well understand that after seventeen years of knowing and loving Baba, of so many years of going to Meherabad and the Samadhi, the 31st of January 2000 found me standing, for the first time, in a line of thousands for Baba's Amartithi and His special darshan.

Crowds come to pay homage at Baba's Amartithi.

CHAPTER 23

I Forgive

In 1945, the following poem was found in the Ravensbruck concentration camp. It was written under the most adverse circumstances any human could be subjected to, and shows the triumph of the human spirit over seemingly insurmountable odds.

> "O Lord,
> Remember not only the men and women of good will,
> But also those of ill will.
> But do not remember all the suffering
> They have inflicted on us,
> Remember the fruits we have bought,
> Because of this suffering –
> Our comradeship, our loyalty, our humility,
> Our courage, our generosity, the greatness of heart
> That has grown out of all of this,
> And when they come to judgement,
> Let all the fruits we have borne
> Be their forgiveness."

It is difficult to comprehend how any human being, after being subjected to such atrocities, could find the generosity of heart to ask God for this. It shows us what we are capable of, if only we put in the effort. In this case, it shows us how the victim has overcome all odds and become the victor.

Carrying anger and resentment is like holding on to a very heavy boulder with fragile, delicate hands. Either you will carry this heavy load till at some point of time it becomes heavier still and it shatters you, or you can take the boulder and consciously throw it down the road which leads to the past, and move forward having freed yourself of this heavy burden. The choice is entirely yours.

Forgiveness is letting go of the pain and accepting what has happened, because it will not change. When we think of forgiveness, the fear may arise that in forgiving you are allowing the person who hurt you to go free. However, in actuality, with forgiveness one sets oneself free. In fact, we lose nothing but, on the contrary, receive a gift.

Our past is a series of lessons that help us to advance to higher levels of living and love. We can, if we choose to, emerge from the most painful circumstances with strong insights about who we are and what we want. Our mistakes, frustrations, disappointments and failures are all so necessary for our spiritual growth.

Once when Baba was at Guru Prasad in Pune during the summer months, the watchman at the gate came in to say that some dignitary had arrived to take His darshan. Baba asked that he be sent in. After the man paid his respects, Baba asked his name and profession. The man replied that he was a judge. Baba beamed a big smile and gestured, 'I too am a Judge, but with a difference.' His gestures continued, 'You establish the guilt of the person and punish him, I know the guilt of the person and forgive him.'

How often have we applied this principle in our lives? How often and how fast have we been able to forgive those who have wrecked our lives?

Now read on to know, how Zenda Marie Blair faced the many problems in her life and learned how to forgive.

In the past thirty years, I have struggled to find reasons to live and that is what I truly believe has brought me to the perfect moment to connect with Nan and her Karl, and their work through a beautiful spiritual Master who once lived on our earth, named Meher Baba. The irony of my life is that professionally I am a Registered Nurse. I could help others, but could not find my own way. My will to live came from one single purpose, the love of my beautiful daughter, Michelle. I share my heart song, and hope that you can follow the thread of my life that put together all the brokenness and pain, and took me to Baba.

As a child, I had many joys and many hardships, and what kept me alive was my love of God. I went to God with everything. The only problem though, as I see it today, was that I truly did not have a loving God. Everything in my life till then was taught with the intent to create fear and guilt of a punishing God; something that only served to create more lack of self-esteem and worth in a little girl already receiving abuse at home. But I stuck with God; He was all I had to lean on in times of desperation. I used every bit of will power I had to try to make the most of the holes in my shoes and the constant beatings, to try to be a perfect person, not make one single mistake, so that my home life would become better.

In high school, I met a wonderful person whose name was Robert Edward Caldwell. I not only loved his family but they all loved me, spent time with me, and never judged the poverty that my life represented. His family was home to me. In that state of happiness I not only became an honours student, but also received a scholarship, and I started college in August 1966. God finally loved me.

It was not much later that my Eddie and I were officially engaged. He had just finished boot camp and become a Marine, proud to serve his country. He soon received his orders for a thirteen-month tour of Vietnam. I was scared and devastated. The last thing he said to me before he was shipped out was a promise to come home.

He served twelve days short of his scheduled time to return home to us. He was killed in a medivac helicopter that was shot down by enemy fire; no remains, burnt to death. I remember screaming out to God, "I hate you! I will never come to you again." His parents' suffering was so much that they could not bear to continue with me, it was just too painful. So, I lost a family that loved me too. I just shut down and tried to finish school.

After graduation, I married a man called Jerry, who had obvious problems with alcohol, drugs, and violence. I married him with the belief that all he needed was someone to love him, and his life would change for the better, and I could stop feeling worthless.

We had our child Michelle twelve months later, an absolutely beautiful little red-headed, blue-eyed child. But very soon my husband's problems escalated, and consequently he became more physically violent. Needless to say, I became a target for his abuse till I appealed to the courts for help and it was not long before he was shot and killed by the police, in his efforts to kill us.

The next thirty years was a cycle of drifting between jobs, relationships, and spirituality – all unsuccessfully. I tried my best to make the fear go away, but it did not happen.

Then something did happen. I was working as a Registered Nurse in a psychiatric hospital unit, where I had a very nice connection with a nurse who went by the spiritual name Biskra. Shortly afterwards I lost my father, and because I had great love and also great anguish with regard to our relationship, I felt totally at a loss with his passing, and a sense that the place of forgiveness was lost to me forever. Then Biskra mentioned a spiritual retreat centre in Myrtle Beach, South Carolina, and shared with me about her Avatar Meher Baba. I knew instinctively that I was to go to Him.

So arrangements were made, and I went to The Meher Spiritual Centre. I was home. Two nights after being in my beautiful cabin – in the most beautiful surroundings ever seen, I had a kind of vision. Baba came to me, holding my departed father by the hand, and showed me with a pointed finger and by gestures on His face, 'See he is with Me now!' Not only was it a revelation to discover that my father had actually heard my request to give me a sign that he was alright, but I also later found out that Baba did not speak in His life on earth as the Avatar. This was such a powerful awakening moment in my soul's journey.

I had more awakenings over the next ten years. My relationship with Baba grew stronger by the day, and though much was better in my life and things more stable in all ways, I longed for Eddie and his love, but even more, wanted desperately to learn to forgive Jerry. I remember thinking that my longing for happiness would never dissipate or lessen. I had Baba, my daughter, and my life, but the hole in my heart with the cold wind blowing through was always just there.

Through Jerry Watson (a devoted Baba lover for most of his life), I learned about Nan, Karl and her book *Sounds of Silence.*

I just knew and trusted that I had to contact her. I also purchased the book, and nothing has meant more to me than the journey of love I learned, and read about, with this beautiful family.

And so I followed my heart and e-mailed her. I wish that I could include here the communications that I have received from Eddie and Jerry through Karl, for then you would be able to see clearly the beautiful thread of gold of my life.

With the grace of Baba, my Eddie has now come back to me, as he promised before he left. My Jerry is now with our Beloved, and I can live knowing in my heart, that through this communication, very slowly I learned how to forgive him and lead him to the help and love he so sorely needed. My heart had always promised him in my marriage vows to help him, and now he will never have to walk alone. Baba has proved to me in no uncertain way that nothing we love can ever leave us; that it is never too late or impossible to forgive, to heal our wounds, and to be there to help those we love.

In the past two years, Baba led me on a journey to clear out and release all that was not real. Suffice it to say, I experienced a depth of complete surrender of my will and my life, clinging only to the knowingness of Baba walking with me, hand in hand, and heart to heart. I give thanks every day that Nan trusted Baba and 'walked her walk' as that has helped so many like me. I understood the aloneness of developing a spiritual gift that is not so easily accepted by all – and the absolute trust you have in your God to do it!

I have to tell you about another experience that really moved me. One day, sitting on the hill at Meherabad, I noticed a lady sitting alone, away from the crowd, in silent contemplation of her love for Baba. I was drawn to her because she looked so serene and peaceful. Her face was familiar. And then, I remembered that some time ago she had contacted me after reading *Sounds of Silence*. She had lost her mother when she was a tiny girl, and grew up missing her love and care. The pages of the book had touched her heart, and she had become closer to her mother again because of the messages of love that came through for her from Baba via Karl. Our eyes met in recognition, and she smiled. Much later that day, she walked up to me and told me the most amazing story:

Dear Nan, I made my way to Meherabad only because I wanted to thank Baba for letting me know about my mother. I entered the Samadhi and sat down in that little space at the foot of His tomb. But as I sat and talked to Him, instead of the problems of my present life unfolding, my soul seemed to drift away, and I suddenly went back in time, back to the days when I was a young girl, to the harrowing days when I had conceived a child out of wedlock, and been forced to give the baby up for adoption. At that time, I had gone through a terrible hell of my own making, and I really do not know why this part of my life, which I had buried a long time ago, suddenly raised its serpent head in the peaceful confines of the Samadhi.

I looked around as the silent tears dripped from my eyes. No one was there except Baba and me. It was then that I decided to tell Him all that I had kept hidden for so long.

I spoke out aloud in my agony. I unburdened my secret to Baba, and after I had told Him everything, I knelt before Him and begged, "Baba, my heart cries out to you. Where is my child? Where is the little son I bore so long ago, whose sweet face I saw just once? Baba, please, please tell me, where is he? How is he? Is he well, is he happy? I just want to know. I desperately want his forgiveness through you Baba."

I sat there and I cried for I do not know how long, at the same time wondering at myself for having told Baba the secret I had locked away for so long.

By the time I came out of the Samadhi, I was back in the present, and the problems of the everyday world came crowding back, problems of husband and children, of health and happiness, and my little secret went back to being the permanent pain I carried inside of me. Only this time, it had become a little lighter for the sharing.

Some months later, I was attending a business seminar and happened to meet up with some ladies from Scandinavia. I do not really recall how the topic of unwed mothers and adoption agencies came under discussion, but in the course of this, something one of them said struck a bell. It was as if Baba took hold of the rope and swung it with His own two hands – loud and clear.

It sent me on a wild goose chase, for it started a chain of events that led from one revealing fact to another. It led me back to the place where, as a frightened teenager, I had first hidden away to give birth to my baby, to the day when, with a heart full of love, I had first set eyes on his little form for the first time, to the day when my father had taken him from my arms to give him away, and how with him a piece of myself had also gone forever.

Now suddenly, out of nowhere a path seemed to have lit up – a path that had me floundering through red tape and so many rules and regulations. To checking up in different adoption agencies, and searching in different countries, through a maze of people and places, till finally I came to the doorstep of a couple who had adopted a little boy child from India, many, many years ago. It was not easy, and Baba really did make me work for it, but...

Yes, I found my son. I found him eventually in Scandinavia, but as per my promise to Baba, I will not tell him who I am or what he means to me. He is happy, successful, and dearly loved, and my heart is at rest. I do not wish to trouble or complicate his life in any way. I know Baba would not wish me to do so. I know also that this is my karma, and it has to be completed.

In the depths of despair and sorrow, I had asked for help and forgiveness, and in His infinite compassion, Baba has given it to me with all His love.

Now, a little bit more about myself. One of my latest trips to Meherabad and the Samadhi was a real eye-opener for me. When I was in the hall of the Pilgrim Centre at dinner that night, my daughter Tina called to tell me that one of their horses in their stable, called 'Colour Bearer', had passed away that morning. He was a real favourite, and they felt it a lot. So would I please ask Baba and Karl to watch over his soul, and help him on his way?

The next morning at 7 am, it was aarti time. Prayers were just over, and songs were about to begin. The person before me had just gone into the Samadhi to take darshan. I was waiting next in line, very deep in thought, when I suddenly remembered what Tina had asked of me. I rested my head on the stone wall just outside the Samadhi and said to Baba, "Please Baba, watch over this horse and keep him with You."

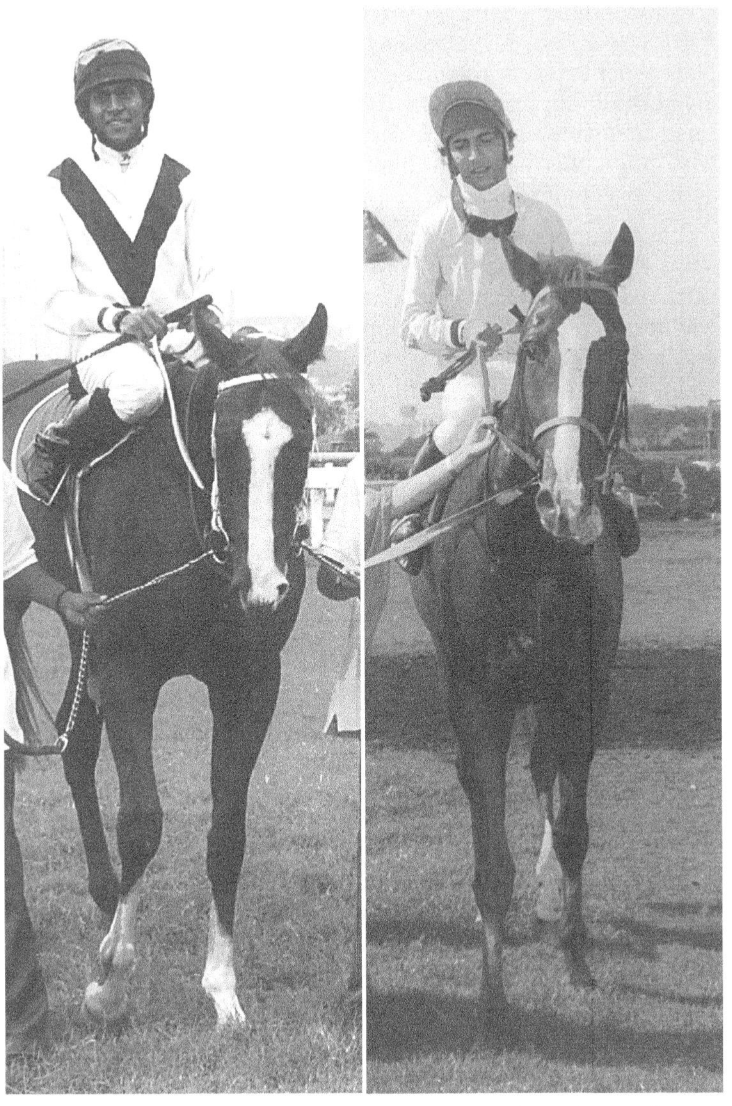

A jockey rides Colour Bearer.

My son Karl astride Vasudha.

Just then it was my turn, and as I stepped over the threshold a new song began, "Vasudha – Vasudha – Vasudha – Vasudha." The words rang out in increasing volume, shattering the silence of my soul.

I stepped into the Samadhi shivering from head to toe. Vasudha was the horse that Karl had fallen off, whose hoof marks remained like those of a searing red-hot iron on his lean muscular chest. It was the horse responsible for his death.

My mind in a whirl, I knelt down at the tomb and from somewhere inside of me I heard my voice burst out and say, "Baba, I forgive. Yes Baba, I forgive, and I will carry nothing more in my heart from this day forth."

I was so shaken that I had to take support of the door to make my way out of the Samadhi. I sat down on the bench outside and found it difficult to breathe. It took some time for me to still my heartbeats and look at it in a more rational way. What did it all mean? What was Baba trying to tell me?

Yes, maybe I had been unconsciously carrying this inside of me for a long, long time. Maybe I really needed to forgive that horse so that the karmic ties between the horse, Karl, and me could be finally resolved.

However, on my return home, when I finally shared this experience with the family, it was Neville who pointed out the astonishing similarity between the two horses concerned. They both had the same galloping action, they were the same shape and size, they were both chestnut and with the identical white blaze!

Could it possibly have been the same soul reborn?

CHAPTER 24

Food for Thought

I woke up one morning with the strong intuitive feeling that it was time I made a trip to Bombay again to catch up with old Baba friends, and also to make personal contact with the new ones that Baba had sent my way. But even before I could finish my morning coffee, the phone rang. It was Ranjana Salvi, from my old group of Baba followers. "Good morning Nan," she said, "I awoke today with the desire to talk you into coming to Bombay. We would all love to meet with you again so please do come, and let us share our love for Baba together."

There, I knew it! As always, Baba had it all planned from the very beginning and had wasted no time in shooting His thoughts down through the first flashing meteor He could find!

I finally met everyone for lunch at Ranjana's beautiful, spacious Bombay home. After the entire initial hi's and hello's, hugs and tugs were over, we settled down to some serious discussions.

The first, of course, was how both Ranjana and I had both intuitively received this urgent message that we all needed to meet. What would we call that? Would we term it as intuition or coincidence, or just imagination? And if so, how would one recognise it?

We looked at each other, at a loss how to begin. Some came up with one explanation and some with another. Nisha Ghosh quoted a beautiful sentence from the Pune Times, which very pertinently states: 'Beyond the chasm of silence that separates life and the other world, there are sounds. Most of us hear them in our dreams as intuition or sometimes even in our hearts – but only a few listen to them.'

An animated discussion on this followed, till eventually Cyrus Khambata of the Bombay Baba Centre, who was fortunately present with us that day, called for a copy of *Lord Meher* by Bhau Kalchuri, and helped us to find it all there in Baba's own words:

> ***"When you feel something as intuition and have no doubt about it, then know it is real. Passing doubtful thoughts and temporary emotional feelings should not be given importance. But when you feel it touches your heart, follow it. When it comes from the mind it is not intuition. Intuition means that which comes from the heart. In the divine path, first there is intuition, then inspiration, then illumination, and finally Realization..."***[1]

This seemed to answer that question for the time being, and the next topic that came up for discussion was 'fate and destiny vs. free will' and the difference between the two.

The subject being fairly intricate, and in order to understand its functioning at deeper levels, it needed to be discussed in much detail. So we again started by reading out some quotes from the books we had on hand which gave us a fairly good idea about the relationship between fate, luck, or chance, and the exercise of free will.

> It read: ***"Fate is man's own creation pursuing him from past lives; and just as it has been shaped by past karma, it can also be modified, remolded, and even undone through karma in the present life... Proper understanding and use of the law of karma enable man to become master of his own destiny through intelligent and wise action."***[2]

Cyrus elucidated that the message conclusively puts to rest the conflict between whether the events in our life are predestined, or whether we have a free choice to alter the course. He elaborated that we could all see in the 'here and now' a meeting point between the fruits of our past karma, which we call fate or luck, that crop up in our lives as our environment, conditions, occurrences, events, circumstances, or occasions, and the opportunity to exercise free will which is always available to us at every given moment in the eternal now. The past may impel us to take a certain course of action – a sort of habit pattern or mental tendency – but it can never compel us to take that action. Herein lies the power of choice or free will in the present moment to modify, remould and undo our past, and unshackle ourselves from its results.

So then, what is Destiny?

"Destiny is the divine law or will which guides us through our numerous existences. Every soul must experience happiness and unhappiness, virtue and vice, from the very commencement of its evolution till it achieves its final goal, which is the Realization of God... Destiny, or the goal that souls have to attain, is the Realization of God... We can compare destiny to a load of seven hundred tons of happiness and unhappiness, vice or virtue, which every soul has to carry throughout its existence. One soul carries seven hundred tons of iron, another soul the same weight in steel, others lead or gold. The weight is always the same, only the kind of matter changes. The impressions of each individual vary, and the acquired sanskaras form the structure and the condition of the future life of every individual. Hence, destiny is one, but fate is varied and different for each."[3]

This was definitely food for thought, but our attention was now suddenly interrupted by a call from the hostess saying, "Attention please – present destination – food for the stomach and, if you do not come now, your fate will be to go hungry!" So we made our choice and off we rushed to feast on a variety of soups and salads followed by delicious brownies, fruits, and ice cream.

Stomachs full, the discussions began again, but this time in a completely different vein; the sharing of personal experiences. The result was that two really beautiful stories were shared that day. I do not know whether to label them as extraordinary, entrancing, exhilarating or enlightening.

Jimmy Mody terms his experience as 'strange'. Padmini Sathe terms hers as 'unbelievable but true'. Here they are for you, exactly as they were told that day.

Jimmy Mody says: I had never heard the name 'Meher Baba' until a few years ago. He was one of the greatest Saints, I was told.

But what did He teach? I would ask.

Someone finally suggested that I might read Nan Umrigar's

book and my friend Firoo kindly lent me her copy. Wonderful! Nan's experiences were wonderful. But it is one thing to read about it, quite another to experience it yourself. I wondered at that moment how many people reading this book must have also felt the same way. What is it that always seems to separate us from 'belief' or from what some might call 'faith'? If we have to experience something first-hand each time in order to believe in it, then surely Meher Baba must have a huge task ahead of Him! After all, can we help it if we are born with these body-mind limitations?

The only time I have ever missed a train in my life was on the morning we decided to go to Meherabad. Strange! Nevertheless, with a little grit, determination, and a lot of running, we finally managed to get there, albeit an hour late.

During this trip, I met up with a young Mother, Sunita, who had lost her husband just a year ago. She was accompanied by her very lovely fifteen-year-old daughter, Puja. Both of them still seemed to be in a state of loss and mourning.

We sat together and over lunch I listened sadly to their story. They told me how they had contacted Karl through Nan, made a connection with their beloved one, and at last received a message but were still doubting, for as I pointed out earlier, the human mind needs some sign or proof.

Nan explained to them that she was not a medium in the strict sense of the word, that all her messages came through with the grace of Meher Baba, and that they normally took the shape of help and guidance from the spirit world, so it would be difficult for her to get a specific name but, "I am more than sure that Baba will find a way to set your heart at rest," she said.

So, the trip to Meherabad was arranged. Just before leaving for Meherabad they asked for one more message with the all-important question, 'Please Karl, where will our loved one be? Please help us, give us a sign.' Karl answered and said, *"When you go under an archway, that will be the time and place where and when you will be united with him. You will know."*

I was intrigued and joined in the search. We looked around us – the Pilgrim Centre was full of archways. Now which one? Where could we look? Where was the sign? Where and how were we going to feel his presence?

In the evening all of us decided to walk up the hill to the Samadhi. I found myself walking alone with Sunita, for the others were a few paces behind. We followed the road and started up the path that led to a railway crossing. As we slowly approached, still deep in conversation, we came to an iron rail which was used as a kind of gate to fence off the brown and stony rail tracks. The only way to cross was to bend under to get to the other side. Just as we were about twenty feet away from the rail, Sunita screamed out aloud and stood as if frozen, pointing and staring at the iron bar in front of her, "Look, Look!" she cried. I did not know what was happening. The rusty old rail was shaped like an archway and there, on the left in large letters written in white chalk, were the letters S-O-N-U. It was the name her husband always used to call her by. It was Sunita's pet name. How could anyone have known? Strange!

Baba had just killed not two, but three birds with one stone! He had pierced three hearts with His arrow of love, and had used their experience to reach my heart.

By the time we reached the Samadhi, we needed to sit for a while to assimilate all that had taken place but there was not much time, for the evening aarti soon started. It was a very powerful experience for me. The music, the people – people from faraway lands to the locals – blind musicians, orphan children, the reddening sunset, the barren landscape, the acacia trees, all felt like we were one. For a moment I did not seem to exist.

As we climbed down the hill in the growing darkness, I walked behind my friends. I was almost in a trance-like state trying to recover from the ecstasy I had just experienced. I soon noticed that the young fifteen-year-old daughter had slowed her pace so as to walk with me. I hoped she would be silent as I was in no mood to talk. I turned my head to my left and for a brief moment our eyes met and something very strange happened; I completely lost all consciousness! To this day, I still have no idea what happened to me! I have no idea how long I was unconscious! I only know that when I regained consciousness I found myself still walking down the path. I had not even fallen down! The experience was the most mind-blowing experience I had ever had in my life! Words cannot describe it.

In the silence that then continued, I felt compelled to ask her if she had noticed anything or experienced anything and she then said softly to me, "You know what happened? Meher Baba sent my father to be with me. He was walking alongside with me – I am sure of it – for that moment, you were him!"

This was no miracle. I wondered if we could have, for a brief moment, transcended the separateness or duality of 'I' and 'You'. Could we have for a brief moment been one with 'Divine Love'?

I probably would never have been able to recognise 'Divine Love' even if it had fallen in my lap! Instead, I would have probably recognised it only as a miraculous union, a mystical coincidence, an act of heaven, or as a demonstration of the power of Baba. But this time, for me, it was simply something that I could not explain. I felt no need to explain the experience. Strange? Thank you Baba.

Padmini Sathe says: I was not the kind of person that goes to such places but when my friend Salome mentioned that she was going with some friends to a place called Meherabad, on a whim I just said "Yes, book me in, I'm also coming." That is how I eventually landed up at Pune station and met Nan for the first time. She knew me by name, that's all, and yet as soon as I saw her something stirred inside of me.

After the initial hellos and introductions, we all piled into the bus and when we were on our way, Nan handed us messages that she had received from Karl that morning. Some were personal, some general, and some just welcoming ones, but all highlighted Baba's love, help, and support.

Never before having received a message from the spirit world, I opened mine with shaking fingers. It read, *"Dear friend, we have not met before, but I can see and know that you carry a sadness in your heart. Your father says, 'I want you to know that Baba is the kindest, most gentle and compassionate friend you can ever have. Because you and I have been not only father and daughter but also good friends, I will now arrange that you find a friend in Meherabad who will be forever your right hand, and through this right hand, you will find your happiness, for it will be my right hand helping you.'"* My father went on to tell me that our hearts had been joined together and that we had been spiritually connected through many lifetimes. He assured me that this trip of mine to Baba's Samadhi would be a memorable one, for it would help me never to be sad again.

When I finished reading, I just sat and stared at the piece of paper, not really knowing what to make of it. However, after some initial hesitancy, I admitted that Karl was right and that I was carrying sadness in my heart. It was because my beloved father, whom I loved and revered above all else, had passed away a little while ago. I was totally lost without him. I missed him so much, for he had not only been a father to me, but also my friend, philosopher, and guide. My life was not the same anymore.

However, I left all these thoughts behind as we approached the Centre and as everyone seemed in a jovial mood I also joined in, smiling at the light-hearted banter of my friends who teased me saying, "Come on Paddy, let's ask Baba to find a good husband for you!"

The first day in Meherabad was beautiful and exhilarating and the energy at the Samadhi had a strong impact on us all, even though we were curious and looking desperately for clues from the messages received. In the end, however, not really finding any answers I decided to leave it to Baba and enjoy the peace and calm that pervaded my entire being. The whole feeling of the place was just so beautiful!

The next day a strange thing happened to me. It was evening aarti, the prayers were over, my eyes were closed, and I was listening with joy to the beautiful songs. All of a sudden everything around me just seemed to fade away and I found myself alone with Baba – all alone – everyone else seemed to have disappeared and there was no one there anymore!

I do know what I was doing for I remember going into the Samadhi, bowing and touching Baba's tomb, then going to Beloved Mehera's and Mani's tombstones. Later, I even remember walking to Baba's room a few feet away and paying my respects at the stretcher on which Baba had made His last journey – and yet it all seemed so unreal.

Darkness was falling, I looked around for my companions but there were none. Where had they all gone?

I slowly walked down the slope still in that semi-entranced state and soon became aware of a strange light-shadow next to me and, all of a sudden, it seemed to be my father walking down with me. He asked me how I was, he asked after my mother's health and about my career and I told him everything, but before

I could do any asking, I somehow became aware of a lone man actually walking next to me and just at that instant, he stumbled. I watched in disbelief, as I seemed to come back to consciousness, and instinctively caught hold of his left hand. "No," he said, "I am paralysed on my left side."

It hit me right in the middle of my solar plexus. My father had been paralysed on his left side before he passed away!

With a palpitating heart, I somehow held him by his right hand and walked with him across the railway line. Thus we reached the Pilgrim Centre and parted. I was completely shaken, my face drained of blood. I do not know how I got through dinner and for a long while after, I still lived in the euphoria of my beautiful experience. It was much later that I was able to share it with my friend Ranjana, and then with Nan.

The message had said, *"and through this right hand, you will find your happiness."*

What was the significance of these words? I wondered and pondered, I asked over and over, 'Papa, did I really see you? Did Baba really bring you to me? Were you really there?'

All that night, as I half-slept, I went over it again and again, yet I knew for sure in my heart that I had not imagined it all. I looked up at the sky and begged, 'Oh God, will I ever really get an answer to this?'

Our three-day stay came to an end and our last stop was a visit to Mohammed, Baba's mast. A mast is a God-intoxicated soul who was used by Meher Baba for His Universal work. "Masts hold the power to affect the laws of nature, performing miraculous feats at will. Their ability to subsist in first class health, without food, in unsanitary sites, without bathing, without a roof overhead, defies all medical wisdom."[4] In His lifetime, Baba tried hard to contact and gathered many masts from all over India. Mohammed was one of the masts brought by Baba back to Meherabad to help Him with His work.

On this day, Mohammed was not in the best of moods, his head was hanging down and he was flatly refusing to look at or acknowledge those already gathered there. I walked into the room, and stopped dead! The very sight of him took my breath away and left me stunned. He looked exactly like my father just before he

Mohammed – the 'mast'.

passed away – the same fragile form, saliva dripping from the mouth, a white sheet covering his legs, same bald head and ears. I could not believe my eyes.

Without thinking, I ran and knelt down at his feet. I burst out in Marathi, "Papa, papa, mala olakthai kai?" (Father, father, do you recognise me?)

His head shot up and there was a smile in his eyes as they locked into mine. He said, "JAI BABA."

I will never forget the look on his face for it was the same soulful look of love my father gave me just before he died.

My trip to Meherabad turned out to be an enlightened journey, engulfing me with a love beyond expression – a love for Baba. I want to thank you Karl for you have a unique way of touching people's hearts, but for me you have lifted it out of my physical body and placed it at Baba's feet. I came to pay my respects to God, not really expecting anything in return, but came away in body form, leaving my heart and soul at Baba's Samadhi with a strong yearning to keep returning to my Baba.

Thank you for making it happen.

Padmini had finished speaking and there was silence in the hall. You could hear a pin drop. It seemed like all of us sitting there that day had also been transported by Baba into His Never-Never Land. Sometimes in life there are some instances such as these that defy definition. Then again why do we human beings want to put everything in a box and label it? There is more that we don't know about the mysteries of life and the connection between the two worlds. It is also at times such as these when you feel that those in the other world – our loved ones – do reach out through the thin veil. Only a shadow separates them and us. We feel their presence, we almost touch them, almost, and they touch us, but almost.

Hot tea and chocolate brownies gave us time to slowly recover enough to ask more questions about Mohammed the mast. Did anyone know more details about him?

An old Baba follower, Dara Katrak, who happened to be with us at Ranjana's house that day, came forward with the following story.

Mohammed's real name was Tukaram. He was the son of a potter who lived by the banks of a stream in a small village named Sonawadi in the Ratnagiri District. He grew up in these simple surroundings, soon married, and had two children. Then he began playing gambling games for fun and winning everything he touched. He could hardly ever lose – so much so that they had great difficulty carrying home his winnings.

Shortly after this stroke of luck began, a strange thing happened. He awoke one morning, stood up, stretched his arms directly over his head and remained standing in his hut, dazed and ecstatically entranced in that position, clad only in his underwear, for almost twelve days. At the end of that time, as the trance weakened, he put on his sandals, gave all the money to his wife, said goodbye, and left.

But what happened to him?

In his own words, "I became a deva."

He had not been a seeker in this life, but in his previous life he had been a priest in a small Khandoba temple. I guess something had been suddenly revived and now he had obviously received his calling. Eventually when he met Baba, they both embraced and were filled with great happiness. Since then he has remained forever in love with his *dharma cha dada* – the respected elder brother of all humanity's faiths.

The story goes that during the period of World War II, Baba had an ashram built for the masts at Meherabad. Several masts were brought from various places and He would be with them hours on end, day and night, helping them on their spiritual journey in the inner spheres, and in turn use their spiritual energy for His universal spiritual work of helping humanity. One day, Baba closeted Himself with Mohammed in the seclusion cabin.

He instructed Eruch to stand guard outside and not allow anyone inside under any circumstances. Baba said that the work was imperative for the good of humanity and He did not want to be disturbed at all. Eruch waited patiently, hour after hour, when suddenly the door of the cabin burst open and Mohammed came hurtling out. He rushed through the now open door and as he passed by, Eruch was thrown violently to the ground. With the passing of the mast, an electric current seared through Eruch's whole body leaving him almost unconscious.

He came to his senses just in time to see Baba struggle to the door; He was sweating profusely and had tears in His eyes. He looked at Eruch and shook His head sadly, as if to say, 'I tried, I really tried but I could not do it, I could not.' The next day, the morning papers were splashed with the headlines of the massacre at Dunkirk, and the world went into mourning with Baba.

When questioned, Dara Katrak clarified that Mohammed was deeply connected with Germany during the war and very often Baba worked through him to try and avert such tragedies. However, it is important to note here that while nothing is impossible for Baba to achieve, He usually binds Himself to the natural laws and works within them.

I have now been going to Meherabad for almost twenty-four years and, every time I went, I made it a point to visit Mohammed, even if it was for a minute or two. For as long as I can remember, I have seen him sitting on that verandah outside Baba's Mandali Hall. He was like 'an exalted ET', hardly ever talked, sometimes shouted *jao* – go away, sometimes just smiled, and more than usual when he saw soap! He loved his bath and the fresh smell of soap, especially I believe, when Baba lovingly bathed him. He was such a simple and special soul. Just how special can be seen by the amount of people who have benefited by contact with him.

I remembered the day I got the news that Mohammed was sick and that he had stopped breathing. Baba followers and close disciples made preparations for his internment, they even dug his grave, but he revived! He lived on for a couple of years till finally he went to join His Beloved Baba.

Eric Nadel, who always looked after Mohammed says, "He clearly knew he was dying and accomplished this fairly quickly, gracefully, without any agitation, anxiety, fear or distress, and with occasional outbursts of humour and cheerful nagging. He was beautiful and loving to the end. I could never exaggerate nor do justice to either his generosity and loving kindness, or the love he inspired in us for his beloved 'Dada' – our Beloved Lord Meher Baba."

Mohammed passed away on 17th June 2003 and went to Baba. A few days after, many noticed a change in a picture of Baba that is on the *gaddi* – throne, under the tin shed just outside Mansari's room; it now clearly showed an image that had not ever been noticed before – an image of Mohammed. His head is resting on Baba's shoulder and he is embracing his Beloved.

CHAPTER 25

Gone Forever?

Gary Kleiner and I have been friends for twenty-five years since the time I wrote my first letter to Meherabad, asking for an appointment with Meher Baba. And he wrote back to me saying that since Baba had already 'dropped His body', I could not have a meeting with Him, but he gave me instructions on how to get to the Samadhi, and that is how I went there for the very first time.

Gary was born in Russia after World War II. His father was a Jew who became a direct victim of the Holocaust. His mother lived in the city of Stalingrad when it was bombed and levelled to the ground. When Gary was a little boy, he used to go to school through the bombed-out areas and buildings in Poland. Eventually, when they came to America, his dad had just eighteen dollars in his pocket to start a new life. So, as he so often says, if he could be happy, anyone could be happy! He took many steps to make sure that he did not become a victim of life. The biggest step that he took was a choice of voluntarily opening the door, when love knocked on his heart in the name of Meher Baba.

Gary has been in the service of Baba since 1978, sharing his happiness with all who come. He is happily married and has his own little house on the outskirts of Meherabad.

About four years ago, Gary Kleiner invited me to attend a workshop in Meherabad. I received his call and invitation with some trepidation. A workshop in Meherabad? I found it hard to believe till he explained that it was going to be held at his residence, that it had nothing really to do with the Trust, but was a first effort on his part to encourage a spirit of closeness and togetherness in the residents and pilgrims of Meherabad. Originally, it was always Baba's mandali who performed this loving service; who gathered everyone together in the halls of Meherazad and held our attention with wondrous tales about Baba and their life with Him. Now, over the years, so many people close to Baba (Mehera, Mani, Mansari, Goher, Arnavaz, Katy, Eruch, Aloba and Bal Natu) were all gone – they had earned their eternal rest with Baba. What really had Baba got in mind for the future?

This getting together of people in a spirit of fellowship and sharing was a brave effort by the younger generation to help the remaining mandali fulfil their task and, although it did go into a slightly new direction, I felt that it deserved our consideration and support. We were all leaves of the same tree, Baba's Tree, reaching for the light, even though finding expression could be through different ways.

I asked Gary what the workshop was all about and was surprised to hear that the topic was 'How to address the issues of death and dying'.

My first reaction was, 'Death and dying – no, no, I cannot go!' As it is, I spent my day sending comforting messages from Baba and Karl to so many and I felt that I did not need to face this more than was necessary. However, as the day approached, my curiosity got the better of me and the appointed morning saw me speeding to Meherabad. I arrived well in time to join the workshop. After greetings, we met up with the facilitator Ann Speirs, a charming lady who introduced herself as being under the tutelage of Elizabeth Kubler Ross, M.D., a Swiss-born psychiatrist, who is a 2007-inductee into the National Women's Hall of Fame. Her extensive work with the dying led to the publication of *On Death and Dying* in 1969. She later wrote over twenty books on the subject of dying.

Ann settled us in with a small explanation about the different aspects and approaches to death and dying, and then took us through a guided meditation to experience the facing of our own death. Well, that was something new!

There were many tears and much sobbing and clinging to one another by the younger generation, but I found that the older ones faced the exercise with much more acceptance. After we recovered from this rather difficult and emotional exercise, we got into a lighter frame of mind and were asked to put down our impressions on paper. With the help of magazine cut outs, coloured pencils, paints and crayons, we had to create a collage of our own perception, our own concept of death. The results were quite fascinating. For one it was the end of suffering on earth, to another it was a reminder of cars crashing, of accidents, and tragic endings. To some it was the sad termination of a relationship. And as it happened, there were many closures.

After that we got ten minutes to write a poem on death and, what the heck I thought, what could you write in ten minutes! But to my surprise, what came out on my paper was a revelation to me. My poem said:

"Death means putting everything aside,
To know that I have smiled, that I have cried.
To know that I have done my best,
and now the time has come to rest.
To meet my loved ones face-to-face,
and know that I have won my race.
That God has helped me through my life,
to be a loving mother and a wife.
That God has made my life worthwhile,
and walked with me mile after mile.
And then, at last, to see Him smiling there,
With sparkling eyes and golden hair,
That, to me is happiness beyond compare,
and death is going to lead me there."

When I read it out, I could hardly believe what I had written. This really made me look back on my life. My God! How far had I come?

Karl went to Baba on the 3rd of May 1979. Yet it seems like only yesterday that I said goodbye to him in the lift, and he left for the races for the last time on the 15th of April 1979. The eighteen days he suffered in hospital after his accident will always remain a nightmare for me – yes, they were long dark days. Then after he passed away, although I was really painfully 'awake' most of the day and night, I never wanted to physically open my eyes to see the dawn light. With the vanishing of the physical form of Karl that was dear to me, it took a long, long time to come to terms with, and to accept, the fact that he was not physically present with us anymore. I became a victim of unending sorrow, not realising at the time that the streams of life are ever-advancing like the waves of the ocean. I thought, or maybe I wanted to think, that after a person is gone there was just darkness – no tomorrow –

just nothing. It used to hurt and make me cry through the long night to think that there was no chance of ever seeing my son again. How very unfair!

But thanks to Baba, those days have now slowly lost their horror. I no longer shut them out but have learned to face them and, more importantly, let go of them. The many signs and proofs that I have received along the way have definitely helped towards this. I keep telling Baba that I believe everything now but still, year after year and time after time, He keeps sending me wonderful confirmations that really astound me. I feel so beholden to Him, knowing so well how a mother can long to know about her child.

Here are some more incidents for you to think about.

Pune, 1997: The phone rang. "Excuse me Mrs. Umrigar, you do not know me, but such a strange thing happened that I had to call you to tell you about it."

She continued: I have a daughter called Dilnavaz, about five years old, who seems to be quite psychic. She sees imaginary friends, talks to them, plays with them, and is so totally happy with them that she never seems to miss real people or children of her own age. I really worry for her, for she arranges imaginary tea parties and holds long conversations with imaginary children, when actually there is no one there at all. I keep asking her what she is doing and whom she is talking to, but she just smiles blissfully and says, "I am playing with my friends." One day, as she happily skipped and ran about in the garden, I joined her and began to pester her to at least tell me the name of one of her playmates. For the first time, Dilnavaz suddenly stopped her game, cocked her head on one side, looked straight at me and gave a direct answer. "His name is Karl," she said, and I had to be content with that.

A few days later, I was reading a book given to me by a friend and at the same time keeping a watchful eye on my daughter who was playing in the garden. The doorbell rang. I put the book down on the table and went to answer the call. When I returned, Dilnavaz had come in and was staring at the cover of the book. Her cheeks were pink with excitement, her eyes sparkled like jewels and there was a look of such indescribable joy on her face that I was stunned. "What is it Dilnavaz, what is it?" I asked.

"My friend, my friend," she screamed in delight. "This is my friend, mummy!" Mrs. Umrigar, I just wanted to tell you that the book I was reading was *Sounds of Silence*, and the face on the cover was the face of your son Karl.

1998. A soft and gentle voice told me over the phone that she was Dimple (name changed) from Bombay. Her husband had recently passed away. She was left to shoulder the responsibility of looking after not only the children and old parents, but also the family business. She heard about *Sounds of Silence*, bought it, read it and came to ask if it was possible to get a message through to her husband.

Soon a link was established, and with the grace of Baba and the efforts of Karl, Dimple was comforted and happy with what she received, for a while. She even went on to learn to do auto writing on her own. There were times of depression when the writing was weak, and also times of elation when something he said would suddenly click and she would be able to feel his presence clearly. He would also talk incessantly of Baba and it was more because of this that Dimple learned to love Baba and greatly depend on Him.

As her sensitivity increased, she began to have a strong feeling that her husband Ramesh (name changed) and Karl had become friends and were closely linked with one another. Was there any way to be sure? It is quite normal in this kind of situation that there comes a time when we tend to doubt our own capabilities and feel that the writing is not really from the spirit world, but just a product of our own subconscious mind. This also happened to Dimple and she began to wonder if it was really Ramesh, or just plain Dimple! It got to a time when she really needed to be convinced. She wanted more proof, more answers, more words of love, and was willing to try different ways and means to get them. How can anyone blame her? Hadn't I done the same thing myself? Shortly afterwards, Dimple went to visit her relatives in a small, remote village. Someone there told her of a *bai* who claimed to have a sixth sense and was a good clairvoyant. Dimple could not resist the temptation and went to visit the lady.

She was welcomed and made to sit and meditate on her husband, while the bai made necessary preparations. In a few moments Dimple's thoughts were interrupted. Through a cloud of smoke and incense, she heard the words, "Han, dictai, dictai, toomara patti dictai" (yes, I can see him, I can see your husband), and the lady went on to describe him quite perfectly, till suddenly she stopped. She screwed up her eyes as if looking for something more and added, "Theheryai, aur bhi koi sath mein hai, aur bhi koi dicta hai, koi chhota, patla jaisa, jaukey-type jaisa dicta hai. Koi aisa dost hai kya?" (wait, I can see something more, someone else is with him, someone thin and small like a jockey – does he have a friend like that?). Dimple was more than just startled. How could this village lady ever know what a jockey looked like?

Dimple had got her proof.

1999: Through the grace of Baba, two sisters were able to connect with their father, through Karl. This is their story:

On a trip to the UK, they made their way to the Spiritual Centre at 33 Belgrave Square, and walked into a general demonstration of mediumship in the main hall. Not really expecting much, they were surprised when almost towards the end of the session, the medium pointed her finger at the little family and said, "I see someone here who wants very much to connect with you. He is in a hurry but wants you to know just how much he loves you and wait – wait – what do I see? I also see someone young with him, rushing up and down the stairs. His clothes show me he is definitely connected with horses, and they both say they are together and want to help you in every way."

A young five-year-old in a garden, a bai in a sparsely inhabited village, and a professional medium in the UK, had all seen Karl in different ways at different times – and always dressed in his jockey clothes!

I thought I had lost my son but now I know that Karl has not really gone anywhere. Baba, in His infinite compassion, has proved over and over again that when your loved ones die, they are not gone forever.

Karl in his jockey dress.

CHAPTER 26

Difficult Decisions

In the course of our lives, many of us go through traumatic times and find it difficult to deal with situations that come our way. So many go through near-death experiences and find them hard to explain away. Some have to just stand by and watch loved ones being in a coma. Most of us find it difficult to 'let go' when the time comes. Sometimes we are faced with the most traumatic situation of all – the guilt of having to make a decision to end suffering. Talking about it all and sharing the burden with others helps, so here I will try my best to tell you about a few instances where friends have so kindly shared their trials and experiences.

One day, I was on my way to Meherazad in the bus with some friends and we happened to be discussing Alobaji, one of Baba's trusted mandali. He was a Muslim Irani gentleman who ran away from his home in Iran at a very young age to join Baba. He had a fanatical love for Baba and made no bones about telling anyone, that it was Baba and only Baba who should be the centre of one's life. He was so forthright in his way of speaking that newcomers took a little time to get used to him. And although he was a little different, he definitely had a charm that was all his own.

I happened to be seated next to a lady who I believe had come all the way from a small suburb in France. She seemed to have overheard our conversation because she suddenly piped in and said, "No, no. Do not say anything about Aloba. He is a very, very special person and I will tell you why."

The first words of her story made me sit bolt upright!

I died.

I was ill in the hospital and I died. I was soon speeding through a deep tunnel, faster and faster, till suddenly I came to the end. I saw an ethereal figure in a thin, white, long gown standing there surrounded by a beautiful light. He held up His hand, palm-up, and said, "Stop! You have to go back. It is not your time. You have to go back."

I soon found myself coming back again through that deep tunnel, faster and faster, till suddenly I was floating into the room again. I saw my body on the bed, machines beeping, the doctors pumping my heart furiously – and thump! I was back in my body once more.

I revived, survived, and was discharged from the hospital some time later. However, this whole experience lived with me. I lived and relived it again and again till one day, a few years later, I walked into a book shop. A book fell on my head. I picked it up and flipping through the pages I came across a picture that made my heart stop. I thought I was going to collapse. Yes it was Him! It was the same beautiful figure in the long white gown that had stopped me at the end of the tunnel. A caption below the picture said 'Avatar Meher Baba'.

It took me a long while to find out more about Him, and eventually here I am.

I arrived in Meherabad after a long and exhausting journey. It was 10 am and, just like now, the bus was leaving for Meherazad. Since it was the very last day that pilgrims would be allowed to visit there, the receptionist in the office advised me to leave my bags there and join the bus so that I could see Baba's home and meet the mandali before it closed. The bus rattled across the hot and dusty road. I sat quietly, not knowing a soul therein. I alighted at Meherazad and was walking into the gates when a figure in white came flying out at me, with arms outstretched, and enveloped me in a great big hug.

"Welcome, welcome," he said. "I know exactly why you have come. I know what happened to you, I know how and why you had to return. I also know who stopped you!"

Aloba

I was speechless. How could he ever know? It was Aloba. So please don't ever say anything about him. He is very special.

However, it was an eye-opener for us. We clearly understood that Baba chose all the members of His mandali for a reason, and by now we had learned never to question the ways of a Master.

There are times when you are faced with difficult decisions and do not know how to cope with them. These are the times when Baba comes forward to lend a hand.

Priya Pardiwalla's mother stayed in hospital for more than three and a half years without much hope of a recovery. She was mostly in an unconscious state, hardly able to open her eyes, or really to focus on her daughter's kind and loving face. Maybe she was holding onto life because she felt that her only child would be left alone in this world. What should Priya do? Should she take her mother home or let her remain in the hospital? Should she let her live out her time this way or put her on a life-support machine? Karl told Priya to sit by her mother's bedside, and constantly help to release her by saying, "Mum, I am alright. Go in peace and love. All is well. Go to Baba."

He kept stressing on the importance of not holding on and getting verbose or hysterical at the bedside of one who needs to let go of life and move on. Karl explains, *"Coma does not mean that the soul has left the body. It just means that the physical body is comatose and cannot in any way pass a message to the brain. Consequently the brain cannot react to any of the sensory organs in the body. No recognition in eyes, no movement of the lips, no expression on the face. Noise registers, sounds register, voices vibrate but do not make sense. So no amount of shouting or saying something loudly will help. There is a feeling of neither being here or there – it is like being in limbo. It is a state from where you either opt to come back again, or want to slip away. However, if you just sit quietly and touch the hand, and send out a lot of gentle love, it helps the person to know that they are not alone, that someone cares enough to be there. It helps."*

"Coma is a period where God allows the soul to rest and then to make its karmic choice whether to stay or leave. It is a time to decide whether to prolong the days, or limit the days, or finish the days – according to its karmic plan. Whichever way it is, this plan has to be completed before the soul leaves the body. Baba makes the soul realise everything the moment it passes, to then carry on with the normal procedure from there."

Although earlier Priya kept crying and urging her mother to fight, she soon started doing her best to follow what Karl had told her. In the process, she found herself so much more at peace knowing that her decision to entrust her mother into Baba's care was for the best, and that all would be well when the time came.

The time came eight months later and on the 17th of September, 2008, Priya's mother peacefully passed away and went to Baba. After all the last rites were over Priya and her good friend Steve, made their way to Meherabad to thank Baba for all His help in her time of need. She sat inside the Samadhi and with tears in her eyes offered sincere gratitude to her Beloved Divine Master. Could Baba please show a sign that He had heard her?

She got up and sprinkled a handful of her mother's ashes behind the Samadhi, with a wish that everyone in the family would always merge with Baba in every way. Then she seated herself with Steve, on the bench in front of the tomb, to sit in silence for a while. She felt someone giving her a nudge. A young girl came and literally pushed her way to sit beside them. Wondering why this little girl wanted to be near them, they looked closely at her. She was wearing a T-shirt with a heart printed in the middle and KARL written in bold letters across it.

Priya says: Karl is my special beloved friend and guide and he too traveled the journey with mum and me these last three years and eight months. Through Karl, Baba had made a promise to my mummy while she was well. He had promised her that He would always take care of me. He has, and continues to do so even now. When the young girl with the word KARL printed on her T-shirt came and sat right next to us, it was as if Karl was saying to me, "Look Baba is keeping His promise to mum. And please know that I am also with you and all who ever need Baba, always and forever."

I cannot close this chapter without telling you about another time that was most difficult for me.

My son Karl passed away in May 1979. Then, just when I wanted to stay away from doctors, hospitals and crematoriums, when I needed time and space to get over the tragedy, it seemed to me at that time that God had other ideas. My beloved father died in January 1980, my precious mother in October 1980, and my mother-in-law, who I was also very close to, in 1981. This was a most traumatic time in my life. A huge void opened up. Not only were those whom I loved and depended on suddenly taken away from me, but the day and the way my mother went left a horrible guilty feeling that lived with me till just a short time ago.

My parents had a beautiful and close relationship with each other and when my father died, I somehow knew that my mother would not be able to survive long without him. She was a brave lady and struggled on, till she threw up one morning and complained of slight pain in the chest. We took her to the hospital and the family took turns to be with her. A few afternoons later it was my turn to be with her. I was happy to see that she had recovered and looked well. I sat on the bed close to her and we talked for a long time. Then she patted my head and said, "Zia will be coming soon to take over and I am quite well now, so I want you to go home and rest, my darling, and come back tomorrow." She insisted and would not take no for an answer, so I kissed her and left.

Hardly had I entered the door of my home which was just a few minutes away, when the phone rang. My mother had just passed away!

I was mortified and grief-stricken. The fact that my niece Zia entered the hospital just a few seconds later did nothing for me. Oh, why had I left? After she had spent her whole life looking after us, why in the end did my Mum have to go when there was no one with her?

I lived with this remorse for many years, till just the other day I was reading a book by Neal Donald Walsch. I was reading about his *Conversations with God*, and he says, "Have you ever noticed how many people wait until the room is empty before they die? Some even have to tell their loved ones, 'No, really, go. Get a bite to eat,' or 'Go, get some sleep. I'm fine. I'll see you in the morning.'

And then, when the loyal guard leaves, so does the soul from the body of the guarded. The greatest gift you can give to the dying is to leave them in peace and let them die with dignity."

Oh, what a relief! Maybe that is exactly what had happened, maybe that is exactly what my mother wanted. She needed her own space to go and rest with my father, in peace.

Reading about all this on a regular basis now, I seem to have lost my fear of death. Sure, I do realise that most people are not really afraid of death itself but about the manner of dying. As one grows older, one always has a special sentence to add to their prayer, "God, please do not let me suffer." It is the suffering that is frightening to think of and not the actual passing. And yet, if we pause for a moment and think about it, we will realise that suffering too is our choice. A choice we have consciously made to balance out our karma. Before we began this earthly life, we actually made choices about every experience we wished to undergo so that we may grow, and for many of us physical pain is one such experience. It is possible that we hope to learn endurance from it, or tolerance, or mind control, or we have simply chosen it as a tool to come closer to a Higher Source. This pain may well be the reason for many of us to take that first step on the spiritual path. Baba through His *Discourses* asks us to consider mental and physical sufferings as gifts from God which, when accepted gracefully, lead to everlasting happiness. So even our suffering, when viewed from this perspective, can be more tolerable and easier to deal with. We just have to continue to keep faith and know that whatever happens, it is what we have chosen for our own highest good and the highest good of all concerned.

C H A P T E R 2 7

Merging with the Light

The moment of our merging with the Light has been described very beautifully by Neale Donald Walsch in his book *Home with God*. He describes it as a feeling of being "warmly embraced, deeply comforted... and unconditionally loved – all at once."

What really happens to you when you pass over? What is the procedure when you get there? How does the soul live on? So much information was coming to me from somewhere outside of myself that I wanted to know more, especially Baba's views on the same.

So, one day during my writing sessions, I asked Karl what exactly happens at the time of death and this is what he said:

"Mum, the last day on earth is the most difficult for anyone to cope with, because on that day you are neither here or there. You kind of hang by a thread, not knowing when it will be broken – willing it to be and yet not too sure of what lies ahead of you. However, when Baba is in your life, this thread becomes a thread of gold because as soon as it is broken, it is caught hold of by Baba with Love in His heart. Immediately you can sense Baba's presence near you, and feel the strength that flows through Him. He then guides you towards the Light, making you secure in the knowledge that because someone is holding you, you will never fall or drift away into the unknown. You have no idea how good that makes you feel."

Could this be really true? Would God really be there to greet and help us?

Reading all this, and especially Karl's message, made me delve still deeper into the subject in question. I started asking Karl more questions and voraciously going through books by various authors on the subject of death and the life after, but the topic is so vast and the opinions expressed therein so varied that the more I read, the more confused I became. Frustrated, I appealed to Baba and said, "Baba please help me to know the real truth."

Out of the blue, a sudden thought came to me.

Besides going periodically to Meherabad, I sometimes made my way to the Baba Centre at Lamington Road in Mumbai. It felt good to interact with other Baba lovers, to try and understand the many things that intrigued me but just seemed to be outside my limited understanding. Group meetings were often conducted there by either Cyrus Khambata or someone leading the discourses. I knew that Thursdays were dedicated to free exchange of Baba stories, personal experiences, for sharing information of Baba activities around the world, and the asking of questions. That is where I now made my way with all my questions in mind.

I was late and the session had already begun but, as always, I was welcomed with many smiles and hugs. When it came to my turn, I asked Cyrus the question that was uppermost in my mind. "Can you please tell us something in simple language of what Baba has to say about this phenomenon called Death, and the soul's journey thereafter?"

Cyrus thought long and hard, cleared his throat as if he was preparing himself for a long session and said, "Before I begin, I wish to clarify that whatever I say here is my understanding, my interpretation of what Baba – the very Source of Knowledge – has given in His various books. My attempt would be to make His words more understandable as you request. Also, when I quote Baba from memory it may not be the exact words but it would convey the meaning generally. This needs to be understood clearly.

"In order to understand death, and life after death, a certain spiritual understanding is necessary. We need to know these basic facts: we are composed of not just a physical body but of a number of distinct yet interdependent bodies. Besides the physical body with its physical senses, we also possess a subtle body with subtle senses, and a mental body with its mental senses. These finer aspects of nature are not perceptible to us. They are not remote but are inaccessible to the consciousness that is functioning through the physical senses.

"Ordinary, gross conscious man is unconscious of these inner spheres or worlds, just as a deaf man is unconscious of sounds, and he cannot deal with them consciously. Therefore, they are the 'other worlds' for him. Because most of us are conscious only through the physical body and thus are not conscious of these other bodies, we have no personal knowledge of life independent of the physical body. Hence, as Baba says, ***"Life through the medium of the gross body is only a section of the continuous life of the individualised soul; the other sections of its life have their expression in other spheres."***[1] Others joined in and the next question asked was, 'Why is death considered the end of existence?'"

Cyrus thought for a while; he seemed to be drawing from his vast knowledge of Baba literature.

"Man, in all spheres of his activities deals only with the outer form which is the gross physical body. He is, therefore, attached to it and gives undue importance to it. Hence, he considers the beginning and the end of bodily existence as the beginning and the end of the individualised soul. On account of this, he is naturally impelled to believe that life ends with the end of bodily existence. But this view is incorrect."

By now everyone's interest was thoroughly aroused and the questions continued to flow. Cyrus patiently and attentively proceeded to answer them.

Q: At what point in time does death normally occur in an individual's life?

"In normal cases, death occurs when all the sanskaras released for expression in that incarnation are worked out. That means, when the purpose of that particular body is accomplished, the soul dissociates itself from that form or body as it is no more useful for its purpose. Although the soul drops its physical body, the subtle (energy) body and the mental (mind) body are retained with all the fresh impressions accumulated in the just-dissociated earthly career."

Q: Is death painful?

"However painful life may have been, the experience of dying itself is completely painless and brings release from whatever physical pain that may have been endured in the body before death."

Q: What about emotional pain?

"Yes, severing of an individual's emotional entanglement with the gross world may sometimes be difficult. It is for this reason that various religious rites are observed immediately after death, to help the soul to proceed towards its onward journey."

It was my turn again. My head was already spinning but I just had to know more. I heard my own voice as if it was speaking from afar, "And what happens then?"

> Cyrus explained what Baba had to say, *"The individualised soul sinks into a state of subjectivity in which a new process of mentally reviewing the experiences of the dissociated earthly career begins... If the lessons inherent in a single death were to be thoroughly assimilated by the individual, he would benefit by the equivalent of several lifetimes of patient spiritual effort. Unfortunately this does not happen in most cases, because after death the individual usually tries to revive his accumulated sanskaras. Through these revived sanskaras he recaptures the experiences through which he has already lived. The period immediately following death usually becomes therefore an occasion for the repetition of all that has previously been lived through, rather than a period of emancipation through understanding all that has been lived out...*[2]
>
> *"Heaven and hell would, however, serve no specially useful purpose in the life of the individual soul if they were to consist merely of mental revival of the earthly past. That would mean bare repetition of what has already occurred. Consciousness in these after-death states is in a position to make a leisurely and effective survey of the animated record of earthly life. Through intensification of experiences, it can observe their nature with better facility and results... The lessons learned by the soul through such stocktaking and reflection are confirmed in the mental body by the power of their magnified suffering or happiness. They become, for the next incarnation, an integral part of the intuitive makeup of active consciousness, without in any way involving detailed revival of the individual events of the previous incarnation. The truths absorbed by the mind*

in the life after death become, in the next incarnation, a part of inborn wisdom.

"Developed intuition is consolidated and compressed understanding, distilled through a multitude of diverse experiences gathered in previous lives."[3]

The session came to an end. Although no one wanted to go home, Cyrus very wisely thought he should give us time to digest all the wondrous things he had said. He promised to continue next week. He was right, for although he had simplified Baba's words as much as he could without changing the meaning, it was rather difficult for someone like me to assimilate it all at one go. I needed time and maybe more explanations on the same.

So, the next day during my communication with Karl, I repeated that last question to him. "Karl, please explain to me again, in the light of what was already told to us, what is the next step after we pass on?"

Karl very simply said, *"What happens after? We bring you to Baba. Then we see that you are very, very comfortably sleeping, with lots of your own angels and guides around you to attend to you with love. You have no cause to worry at all, because you will now go into deep, deep slumber, where in the first stage, all your wants and desires will be complied with. After that, the second stage will begin, where with gentle and loving guidance, you will be shown all your life the way you have lived it, and what you have done with the opportunities that came your way. All this is of an extremely personal nature, and cannot be revealed to anyone. Then the third stage will begin where the recuperation starts, and then all will be over. This is the cycle of help that comes for a soul after we pass on.*

"After that, then the choices remain as to where we want to stay – with who and how, and then last of all, when, where, and with whom we want to reincarnate.

"You know, all this is quite beautiful to behold, because we, as spirit helpers, see the changes that come over a soul. We see how they are affected by the love that is given to them by Baba, who is here monitoring every step of the way.

"So, those left behind in the physical world must try to continue on with their daily life, and not worry about their loved ones anymore. They are completely and absolutely happy in their sleep state just now. So if those in the world are also at rest, it will help the soul here.

"They must however, know that even at this stage, they can still meet with the soul in its sleep state. They meet regardless of anything anyone thinks or feels, and may tell you to the contrary. When the soul is in deep sleep, the meeting takes place, and please know that in His compassion, in this way, Baba is keeping a watchful eye on both. Love Karl."

CHAPTER 28

Born Again

A couple of Thursdays later saw me rushing to the Baba Centre again. I did not want to miss a single moment of the session – everything was so interesting and absorbing. Most of those gathered there seemed to have the same idea, for the expectant crowd was larger than what it normally was.

"Well, who is going to ask the first question?" asked Cyrus.

Almost twenty hands went up at the same time but, of course, only one could be answered. The question? Reincarnation!

To tell you the truth, I never believed in the theory of reincarnation till Baba came into my life. In spite of all the messages received in my communication with Karl, I still needed to know and to understand much more. So it was I who started the day's session by asking, "Cyrus, there are still many people who do not believe in reincarnation – like me at one point in time. What have you to say to them?"

Cyrus replied, quoting Meher Baba:

"Reincarnation has been an immutable, divine fact from the first manifestation of creation; it is so now and will continue to be, regardless of whether man, in his unawareness, refuses to accept it as a fact. In the course of spiritual evolution, all human beings reach a point of consciousness when the fact of reincarnation becomes vividly clear to them; and when it does, the phenomenon of death assumes an entirely new aspect: it reveals the innate beauty and sublimity of its creative place in the divine pattern of life."[1]

Hearing this in Meher Baba's own words was certainly very convincing. The group, sensing the importance of what was being said and going to be said, were all eyes and ears.

The questions continued, and Cyrus continued to answer.

Q: If that is so, an immutable divine fact, then how come the Divine Beings like Zoroaster, Jesus and Muhammad taught that there is only one life, whereas the Vedantists believe in several lives?

"There is no difference between what Rama, Krishna or Buddha taught and what Zoroaster, Jesus or Muhammad taught. They all meant the same thing. The apparent difference is not of fact but of interpretation by individuals who lived after them.

"In truth, there is only one 'real' birth and one 'real' death. We are really born once and we really die only once.

"The one 'real birth' is the birth of our ego-mind when the consciousness impressed by the first most-finite sanskaras makes us experience ourselves as individuals – separate, distinct, different, limited and other than the whole (God).

"The one 'real death' is when the consciousness, after undergoing varied and diverse experiences through varied and various species, ultimately emancipates itself from all illusory bindings and limitations and experiences the unlimited Reality eternally. That is, it consciously experiences its Oneness with God.

"In between this one 'real birth' and one 'real death' of the ego-mind, there are innumerable so-called births and deaths of the body forms which the Vedantists term as reincarnation. The soul is eternal and can never die."

> Quoting Baba from *God Speaks*, ***"All the so-called births and deaths are only sleeps and wakings. The difference between sleep and death is that after you sleep you awake and find yourself in the same body; but after death you awake in a different body. You never die. Only the blessed ones die and become one with God."***[2]

Q: But why do we have to be reborn?

"To balance our karmic debts and dues with our previous connections and to undertake a fresh set of experiences in the divine game, to progress from unconscious divinity to conscious divinity are we reborn. Till such time as our consciousness is unburdened and becomes devoid of any impressions or sanskaras – till they are totally wiped out, we continue to be reborn."

Q: Is it true that you undergo various experiences in your life, not because God has willed it but because you yourself have chosen it? If that be true, why would anyone choose a negative, miserable, difficult life? Do we also choose when, where, and to whom we are born, and our race, religion, the circumstances of our birth and the manner of our death?

"God's Will operates in this world through the institution of the Law of Karma. This law is inexorable and seeks to balance itself at all times. All our experiences are the outcome of our own previous choices, and the relentless operation of this law helps us to balance our karmas. Hence, it is the accumulated impressions or sanskaras that determine whether we take incarnation in the east or the west, in male or female form, in this or that family etc. When the individualised soul is ready for reincarnation, it automatically gravitates toward its future parents, brothers and sisters, and others depending upon its past *sanskaric* connections. It is in this sense that we, meaning our sanskaras, choose our own life and its circumstances to speed up the balancing of our karmas."

Q: When we reincarnate as you say, with an agenda of experiencing and balancing our sanskaras, why do we not remember that? Why do we not retain the memory of past lives?

> Baba says, ***"The memories of all past lives are stored and preserved in the mental body of the individual soul, but they are not accessible to the consciousness of ordinary persons because a veil is drawn over them. When the soul changes its physical body, it gets a new brain; and its normal waking consciousness functions in close association with the brain processes. Under ordinary circumstances, only the memories of the present life can appear in consciousness because the new brain acts as a hindrance to the release of the memories of those experiences, that had been gathered through the medium of other brains in past lives... At first view it might seem that the loss of memory of previous lives is a total loss, but this is far from being so. For most purposes, knowledge about past lives is not at all necessary for the guidance of the onward course of spiritual evolution...***

Life would be infinitely more complicated if one who is not spiritually advanced were burdened by the conscious memory of numberless past lives... Spiritual evolution consists in guiding life in the light of the highest values perceived through intuition, and not in allowing it to be determined by the past."[3]

Q: It is now clear that the primary reason for reincarnation is balancing out of the accumulated sanskaras through experiencing of opposites – right? But when will this process end? Will it ever end and how?

"As long as the ego-mind with its accumulated sanskaras desiring expression exists, there is an inevitable and irresistible urge for incarnation. When all forms of craving disappear, the sanskaras that create and enliven the ego-mind disappear. And with the disappearance of these impressions, the ego-mind itself is shed, with the result that there is cessation of incarnations."

Q: This answers 'when', but 'how' do we go about that?

"The *Discourses* by Meher Baba has a chapter on the removal of sanskaras, wherein He has given five ways of securing release from sanskaras. But it is to be understood that any self-effort on the part of the aspirant can lead him only up to the sixth (mental) plane of consciousness. Beyond that, he cannot proceed of his own accord. Only the grace of a living Perfect Master, or the Avatar who is the Eternal Perfect Master, can effect the final wiping out of the sanskaras."

Q: Is there no other simpler way of coming out of the recurrent cycle of birth and death?

"Yes, there is, but that requires the Grace of the Avatar or a living Perfect Master. On our part, with continuous remembrance and repetition of God's name, particularly at the time of breathing our last, we end up liberated from the rounds of birth and death and experience Infinite Bliss eternally."

That certainly did wonders for all those who were listening. We seemed to be mesmerised by what we heard and knew we were about to touch deep waters. In spite of the fact that the clock was ticking by, the questions kept pouring in. So, what is destiny and who 'writes' the fate of different individuals? What is the place of free will in our life? What about the law of karma, the Divine Will, the Grace of God, and so on?

But darkness was falling and since the subjects were all fairly intricate, Cyrus explained, that in order that all this is really understood, it would all have to be discussed in much greater detail. That though this was all given clearly in Baba's *Discourses, God Speaks* and *Beams*, we would have to leave all the explanations on these topics for another session, another day.

I really wanted to thank Cyrus for all his extensive explanations and could not fail to be amazed at the clarity of his understanding of Baba's messages on such complex subjects, and the lucidity and ease with which he responded to all the questions, quoting Baba exhaustively from memory.

"Thank you Cyrus, that was really wonderful," I said in appreciation. "Before we end, is there anything else you would like us to know that you think is important to you personally and would be beneficial to all of us?"

Cyrus replied, "My wife Soumya and I feel that we are all extremely fortunate to have been born during the period of the Avatar's Advent. It now rests upon each of us to make the most of it by following His Wish so as to reach our Goal in the quickest possible time. We endeavour to achieve this by loving Baba more and more, and cultivating a direct relatedness with Him through His remembrance and making Him our constant companion in all that we think, feel, speak and do. Baba says that, that is the high road of all roads leading to inner development.

"And we also beseech Baba to help us remember Him in our last moments. *'Yeh hai hamari arzi; aage aapki marzi.'* (This is our supplication; the rest is Your Wish.)"

I left the Centre that day fantasising about my next life! The choice was going to be mine – oh, how exciting! Of course, I would so dearly love to spend my time there with Baba and never come back again. But if that were not to be, then where would I choose to go? Whom would I choose to be with?

One thing was for certain, I was not going to leave the memory of Baba behind me this time!

So happily, I jogged my way home. Then, while mulling over how fortunate I was to have received all this guidance and knowledge, I suddenly remembered one such personal experience on the subject in question that had taken place in my own communication with Karl. Why hadn't I thought of it earlier – I could have shared it with them at the Centre! However, now I will share it with you.

Dina's (name changed) parents separated when she was barely a teenager, and she shifted with her mother from India to the UK. Therefore she grew up away from the proximity and influence of her real father, Andy (name changed). Yet she kept up a relationship with him, meeting only when she could join him for holidays. She did not realise just how much she loved him, till he passed away.

She then came down to India, wanting to spend some time in his environment and also to put his affairs in order. Having already read *Sounds of Silence*, loving Baba and having been to Meherabad more than once, Dina came to ask if we could get a message through to her Father. She just wanted to tell him how much she loved him and missed him.

So, although we had to wait a while, very soon we were able to establish a connection and messages began to flow to and fro, from the physical world to the spirit world, from father to daughter, and from India to the UK. Although Dina was more than happy to receive them, there still remained some measure of doubt. Were they really from her father? She needed some positive proof. She asked if he could tell her what she put near his picture every day.

Karl said, "*He cannot answer that question. Baba says he must not be disturbed. He has gone into seclusion and is in deep contemplation, for he wishes to go back into the world again. He wants to be close to his daughter – in her family once again, and so, at this moment, he is in preparation for this.*"

In all these years, I had never before received a message like this! Hoping that it was not one of Karl's excuses to avoid giving a direct answer, I wrote it down and sent it to her in the hope that she would understand the contents. The letter never reached her! She called again after a while, "Aunty, where is my message?" Strange, I thought, for I remember posting it myself. I promised her I would rewrite it and send it to her once more but, this being a Sunday – a race day and a busy one for me – I decided I would do so at the very next opportunity.

Off I went to the races and who should I meet as soon as I entered? Andy's closest girlfriend and companion during the last few years of his life. She came up to me and took me by surprise, for she asked, "Any messages from Andy lately?" Seeing the shock on my face, she hastened to add, "You know why I am asking, because in the last two days I have repeatedly had the same dream. I dreamt of Andy looking strong and healthy again, and he tells me, 'Do not try to contact me anymore because I am going back. I am going back, but this time I am going to the cool, green planes of England.' Aunty, would you by any chance be knowing what Andy means?"

You could have knocked me down with a feather! I wrote it all down and sent it to Dina. She had asked for one kind of proof and Baba gave it, not only to her but also to me, in His own inimitable way.

After all this, I now do believe that life, karma and reincarnation are linked. That the pathway chosen has to be the pathway marched, with all its preordained lessons, and the theory of reincarnation offers an explanation, an answer to all the unanswerable questions of life, and to the seeming unfairness of it all. It allows for the possibility that one who is born rich in this life, may have to experience being poor in the next one and so on. It explains the phenomenon of the child prodigy who demonstrates talents that he or she has not had time to develop in this lifetime. It provides a unique answer to Job's age-old question, "Why do bad things happen to good people?" It puts premature death, illness and suffering in context, and assures us that some kind of balance will come our way. Each life that we have is one piece of that main puzzle, and all the pieces have to fall into place before it is complete – before we finally become one with our Maker. So, it is about time we understood that this life we are living is but one of many, that we do have an immortal element; we do have the God within, and a soul that lives on.

All this has now become a part of personal knowledge to me. I look forward to whatever is in store for me, knowing that Baba is there, and that He will look after me in every way. I know He will. I realise now that the individualised soul is not the same as the physical body, that we all have to come and go, again and again. Hope is definitely there, that I will actually meet Baba. I want so much to see Him face to face, and to give Him the biggest hug possible. I know that I will also see my Karl again, whatever the form, for he has to be there with Baba. I know he is.

CHAPTER 29

And I Still Listen

It is said that prayer is when we talk to God, and meditation is when we listen.

From the beginning of *Sounds of Silence* to the end of this book has been a long journey for me, from turning away from God to learning to love Him again. It has taken me through twenty-five years, to meeting a lot of lovely people and of growing to know and love them all. In this way, Baba has given me an even larger family and I sincerely thank Him for it. My many trips to the Samadhi, the signs that I received and still continue to receive, as well as Karl's beautiful messages from the other world, continue to still enlighten me.

It is only time that tells whether one has been traversing the right path, and how far one has progressed. Baba says that spirituality is not an accumulation from without, but rather an unfolding from within. That unfolding, slow but steady, eventually leads one to fulfillment and brings about a state of equanimity in one's being.

Although in my search for God I came across so much that was utterly new, it helped me to uproot my ignorance concerning life and myself. Oh, how I used to flounder through it all and doubt everything! I still do flounder, but I do not doubt anymore. Deep in the recesses of my heart, I now know that there is definitely much more to life than just looking for answers; of living day-to-day, thinking only of the problems and of the complexities of life. I used to worry about making the correct choices, now I know that the choice of road is not really that important. It is the goal of life that you have to work towards, and the goal is to be eventually one with God.

God is love personified. His love for all of us is unconditional. It needs no excuse to flow to us, and requires no qualification on our part to have it. What needs to be done on our part is only to stay connected with Him. And how do we do that? By remembering Him, loving Him, involving Him in our moment-to-moment living, by making Him our constant companion in whatever we are doing, and in whichever role or capacity we invite Him to be with us. We must realise that we are all one, and all we have to do to be happy is to tap into the source of all love and bliss.

My progress has been slow. There have been so many moments of pain, but so many moments of happiness too. I have gone through the gamut of a hundred emotions and, through it all, have eventually come to depend on Baba for understanding, then friendship, companionship and guidance. From there I have moved on to trust in His compassion, have faith in His love, and finally been convinced of His divinity.

Baba came into my life exactly at a time when I desperately needed Him – I entered His Samadhi and my life changed. Through all the years of struggle and suffering, all the years of pain, Baba has stood by me, just like that 'Almighty Rock' that manifested itself in my garden one August afternoon and, as Karl said, all I had to really do was *"to hang on to Him."*

Today, I am still the same person, the same Nan, still attending to my home and family, going everywhere and doing everything just the way I used to. The difference is that I have learned to listen to that voiceless Voice that is deep within my soul – the Voice of inspiration, of intuition, of guidance.

I have learned to listen to the sounds of silence.

The Song of Karl

Beautiful Dreamer, wake up and see,
Meher Baba's love is waiting for thee.
Sufferings of the rude world felt in the day
Lulled by His love-light will soon pass away.

Beautiful Dreamer, sleep off your fears,
Let go the past and dry up your tears.
Baba sends this book for a reason,
Not for just a day, but for all seasons.

Beautiful Dreamer, wake up and see,
Thoughts of a new world are waiting for thee.
Sounds from His Silence will ring in your heart,
And dawn will herald the song of the lark.

All you have read is real and true,
Available to many but known to so few.
So listen well – and don't take too long,
Beautiful Dreamer, please join in my song.

– Love, Karl

APPENDIX A

Meher Baba

A Biographical Note

Merwan Sheriar Irani was born in Pune, India, on February 25, 1894 at 5 am, to Zoroastrian parents of Persian descent. His father Sheriar, an ardent seeker of God, left his family at the age of twelve and began wandering through Iran in search of the Truth. For eight years, he led a penitent and ascetic life without any results. Frustrated and disappointed, he sailed for the port of Bombay. In India too, he wandered around with a staff and a bowl in his hands. His path crossed many sadhus and fakirs, and he took refuge at various places of pilgrimage. He only longed for the sight of his Beloved God – Yezdan. To achieve that, he went to the extent of undertaking *chilla-nashini*, a severe penance of forty days and nights, within a secluded circle, without food, water or sleep. After thirty days, unable to endure the torture a moment longer, he dragged himself away, collapsed near a river and fell into a deep slumber.

A divine voice then spoke, "He whom you seek, He whom you wish to see, His attainment is not destined for you. Your son, it is your son who will attain it, and through your son – you."

Failing to achieve the enlightenment he sought, his steps eventually led him to Pune, to the home of his sister Piroja, who urged him to marry and settle down. Following his sister's advice, Sheriar married a girl in her early teens, Shireen Dorab Irani, who eventually bore him seven children.

Merwan was their second son and Sheriar knew that He was the one through whom his heart's longing would be fulfilled. A few early instances took place which confirmed his intuition.

In the early morning of the day Merwan was born, His mother Shireen saw a vision which she narrated to her mother.

"I saw a glorious person, like the sun sitting in a chariot, and His cool brilliance pervaded the atmosphere. A few people were pulling His chariot while thousands of people led Him in a procession. Tens of thousands of eyes were gazing at Him consoled by His divine radiance."

A few months after Merwan was born, Shireen had a dream. She dreamt that she was standing at the doorway of their home, holding Merog (Merwan's affectionate family name) in her arms. Nearby was a well and out of it rose a beautiful Devi, like a Hindu goddess. She was dressed in a lavish green sari, her arms were covered from wrist to elbow with green glass bangles which tinkled as she held out her hands to Shireen and said, "Give me your son; give Him to me." Frightened, Shireen held on to Merog all the more tightly and, awakened from her dream, was relieved to see Merog sleeping by her side.

As He grew, there were many such instances but, all in all, Merwan had an active and happy childhood. He was very alert, fast and mischievous. His friends called him "Electricity." He was kind and helped the poor and needy. He was a soft-hearted and mystical child with a deep interest in literature and poetry. He loved playing cricket, playing with marbles, flying kites, and listening to music. He was a good runner and a strong walker. He was a natural leader but never craved name or fame. He matriculated in 1911 from St. Vincent's High School, one of the finest in town, and later attended the Deccan College. However, His academic career came to an abrupt end in 1913 on a day that changed the entire course of His life.

Merwan used to cycle daily from His home to college and back. His daily route took Him past a neem tree under which sat Hazrat Babajan, a Muslim Perfect Master, around one hundred and twenty years of age. One day in May 1913, as Merwan passed by the tree, she suddenly looked at Him and beckoned. He got off His bicycle and walked over to her. He was drawn to her like steel to a magnet. Their eyes met. Babajan stood up and engulfed Him in her embrace with the fervour of a mother finding her lost son. Tears streamed down her wrinkled cheeks as she kept repeating, "Mera pyara beta..." my beloved son. Merwan was dazed. What He then experienced is indescribable – His individual consciousness was merged in the Ocean of Bliss. He walked home leaving His bicycle behind.

In due course, Merwan lost all interest in life. He was unable to concentrate on anything and could not express to anyone what He was experiencing. The only thing Merwan regularly did for the next seven months was to visit Babajan every day and sit by her side for long hours, sometimes late into the night. Then one fateful night in January 1914, just as Merwan was about to leave, He kissed Babajan's hand and she, in turn, held His face in her hands. The time had come. Babajan looked deeply into His eyes with all her love and kissed Him on the forehead. Turning to her followers gathered there she declared, "This is my beloved son. He will one day shake the world and all humanity will be benefited by Him." The divinely ordained task of Babajan was accomplished. Merwan began experiencing the infinite bliss of God-realisation. In Baba's own words, given out later, ***"At the time Babajan gave Me the nirvikalp experience of My own reality, the illusory physical, subtle and mental bodies – mind, worlds and one and all created things – ceased to exist for Me even as illusion. Then I began to see that only I, and nothing else, existed."***[1]

His mother, Shireen, worried endlessly as cruel neighbours jeered at Merwan's vacant looks. What had happened to her Merog? His father looked on with patience and sympathy at his young son. He knew all along what was happening but did not speak. Merwan's eyes were open but they did not see. His ears were open but they did not hear. He was in the world, but not of it. He had gone somewhere far, far away. For the following nine months, He lived without sleep, staring vacantly into space. He never ate solid food and He grew gaunt and pale. If He sat, He would sit at one place for hours without moving. If He walked, he would continue doing it for hours until someone stopped Him. Much of His time would be spent sitting in solitude and total darkness in a tiny cubicle upstairs in the attic of His home.

In November 1914, Merwan started becoming somewhat normal and began recognising people and places around Him. He also started eating a very small quantity of food. He began singing Persian songs with deep fervour – He sang to the glory of God. He conversed with friends about God, the inner path, the need for a Guru, and other such spiritual subjects. The glow on His face became a halo, for He was absorbed in the highest state of spiritual consciousness.

Then He began visiting places of pilgrimage and saintly personages.

He visited Narayan Maharaj, the Perfect Master in Khedgaon. Darshan was on at his palace and Maharaj, wearing a gold crown, was seated on the silver throne of Dattatrey. Upon seeing Merwan, Maharaj stopped the darshan and had all the people disperse. He came down from his throne and taking Merwan by the hand, gently led Him to his throne where he made Him sit. Maharaj then removed a garland from his own neck and placed it around Merwan's and offered Him mango juice to drink. They talked for a while and then Merwan left the place. After this meeting, Merwan began to feel the glory of His Godhood.

Next, Merwan met another Perfect Master, Tajuddin Baba of Nagpur. Although Tajuddin was in a bad mood that day, not allowing anyone to come close to him, he became silent the moment he saw Merwan and walked towards Him with roses in his hands. Their eyes met and their gaze locked. Not a word was spoken. Tajuddin waved roses on Merwan's cheeks and forehead and, when Merwan turned to leave, he waved roses in a farewell gesture and muttered, "My rose, my heavenly rose!" Merwan had received His 'Taj' (Crown).

In the month of December 1915, He went to Shirdi to meet Sai Baba, the *Qutub-e-Irshad* – the head of the five Perfect Masters. As Sai Baba was returning from his *lendi* procession, Merwan stretched Himself full length on the ground in front of his feet. Paying obeisance to the young lad in return and in a deep resounding voice, Sai Baba uttered one majestic word, *Parvardigar*, meaning 'God the Almighty' – the Sustainer. In that instant, Sai Baba conferred Infinite Power upon Merwan.

Sai Baba then beckoned Merwan to walk down the road. There was an old Khandoba temple some three hundred yards away where Upasni Maharaj was living. When Merwan approached Maharaj with folded hands, Maharaj stood up and greeted Merwan, so to speak, with a stone, which he threw with such great force that it drew blood. It hit Merwan at the exact spot where Babajan had so lovingly kissed Him. That was the stroke of *Dnyan – Marefat of Haquiqat* or Divine Knowledge. With the force of this impact, Merwan's consciousness began returning to the gross world. But it took seven more years for Maharaj, who by now had shifted to Sakori, to help Merwan completely regain gross human consciousness.

The day finally arrived. The Avatar's divine mission was to begin. In January 1922, a few minutes before Merwan's departure from Sakori, Upasni Maharaj called Him into his hut and with folded hands proclaimed, "Merwan, You are Adi Shakti – the Primal Force! You are the Avatar and I salute You." Merwan wept tears of bliss and bowed down at the feet of the Perfect Master. For a long time, until the tonga went out of sight, Upasni Maharaj gazed as the dust stirred on the road. As Merwan departed from the 'King of the Yogis' to begin His mission, silent tears caressed the *Sadguru's* cheeks. They were tears of joy. And so at age twenty-seven, Merwan, young, strong and handsome, began His work for mankind.

Drawn by His divinity and magnetic personality, a small group of men started collecting around Him and this formed the nucleus of His mandali. One among them started addressing Him as Meher Baba, meaning the 'compassionate father'. Baba was most loving, but He was also a very strict disciplinarian. He emphasised love for God and selfless service as the twin divine qualities to annihilate the false separative ego. His motto was 'Mastery In Servitude'. His lovers are from all walks of life and from every community. He allowed each one to follow his or her own religion, but emphasised the need to understand and live by the crux of it rather than cling to its crust embodied in rites, rituals, ceremonies and dogmas. As for Himself, He said, ***"I belong to no religion. Every religion belongs to Me. My own personal religion is of My being the Ancient Infinite One and the religion I teach to all is love for God, which is the truth of all religions."***[2]

Meher Baba established a community near Arangaon village in the Ahmednagar District of Maharashtra, which is called Meherabad. It is this place that He chose as His final resting place up on a hill. He Himself supervised the construction of the tomb and spent many days and weeks, at intermittent periods, sitting inside its crypt in prayer and meditation, to send forth the vibrations that have since brought much happiness and comfort to so many. His Tomb-Shrine or Samadhi, as it is now called, has become a place of pilgrimage for His lovers and for seekers of God throughout the world.

In Meherabad, His work embraced a free school where spiritual training was stressed. He opened a free dispensary and hospital to give medical assistance as well as shelter and food to the poor.

He inaugurated ashrams for the mad and the mast. A unique characteristic feature of Baba's activities in Meherabad, as well as at other places, was the manner in which He would suddenly and without any warning or any cogent reason stop a project midway regardless of time, money, energy spent on it, and regardless of its success. Baba considered all such external activities and projects as a mere scaffolding for His inner spiritual work. Just as the scaffolding is brought down once the building is constructed, Baba disbanded His external activities once His inner work was accomplished.

From July 10, 1925, Meher Baba began observing silence. This was not undertaken as a sort of penance. Baba says, ***"My outward silence is no spiritual exercise. It has been undertaken and maintained solely for the good of others."***[3] He communicated initially by pointing at the letters and figures on the English alphabet board, which also He discontinued from October 7, 1954. Later on, He communicated by means of His unique hand gestures and facial expressions which His mandali members were quite adept at interpreting. Through His silence, He dictated several books and messages; chief among them are *Discourses* and *God Speaks*. He had given up writing from January 1, 1927 and also stopped touching money, except when distributing it to the poor.

Meher Baba worked extensively with what He termed as masts. Masts are spiritually advanced souls intoxicated in their intense love and longing for God. They are so absorbed in their direct awareness of God that they have lost consciousness of their physical bodies, actions and surroundings. Baba regarded these meetings with the masts as most crucial to His work on the earth plane – ***"I work for the masts, and knowingly or unknowingly, they work for Me."***[4]

On the 16th of October 1949, Baba, together with selected companions – sixteen men and four women – embarked upon what He termed as the "New Life" – a life of absolute purity, a total lack of desire, a complete reliance on God, of remaining cheerful under all circumstances, and giving no importance to rites, rituals and ceremonies. During this phase, Baba bulldozed individual barriers of temper, habit patterns, attachments, hopes, desires, longing, and security. The Master-disciple relationship was relinquished and Baba, as the elder brother to all His companions, exemplified the life of a true seeker.

Meher Baba travelled several times throughout the world to 'lay cables' for His spiritual work. On one of His visits to the West in 1952, He inaugurated the Meher Spiritual Centre in Myrtle Beach, South Carolina, USA. Baba referred to it as His home in the West. He also established a new Sufi Order, which is devoid of the *Shariat* – external rites, rituals, ceremonies, and He named it 'Sufism Reoriented'. It is based on love and longing for God and the eventual experiential union. In His later visits in 1956 and 1958, Baba visited various places in Australia and established the 'Avatar's Abode' in Woombye, Queensland, Australia.

Baba underwent two, self-imposed, automobile accidents and suffered immensely without a single sound. These were foretold by Him as a necessary part of His Universal Spiritual Work of taking upon Himself the sufferings of the world.

In spite of His pain and discomfort, He continued His work with the poor. He spent many hours washing the feet of lepers and distributing grain, cloth and money to thousands of poor and destitute people. Suffering did not deter Him from His work of 'awakening' people and sowing the seed of His love in their heart. He opened the floodgate of His love through travelling to remote parts of India and giving His public darshan to tens of thousands of His lovers. After one such darshan programme, Baba remarked, ***"When you see Me giving darshan and prasad to thousands of people, it is neither mechanical nor meaningless. These are the means by which My love flows to humanity."***[5]

The last years of His life were spent in strict seclusion. It was a time for complete absorption into inner universal spiritual work. On the evening of July 30, 1968, Baba declared, ***"My work is done. It is completed one hundred percent to My satisfaction..."***[6] Later on, Baba said, ***"I have been saying: the Time is near, it is fast approaching, it is close at hand. Today I say: The Time has come. Remember this!"***[7]

On Friday, the 31st of January 1969, Meher Baba dropped His physical form at His residence at Meherazad at 12.15 pm. All those who sincerely love Him and have faith in Him can always feel His presence and His love. Thousands congregate at His Samadhi on that day which is called Amartithi, to perpetuate the memory of the Eternal Beloved. His tombstone reads – **"I HAVE COME NOT TO TEACH BUT TO AWAKEN."**

Meher Baba's approach to spiritual development transcends differences between the various factions of religious philosophy. He never sought to form a sect or proclaim a dogma. He attracted and welcomed people of all faiths and every social class. And so His lovers, without establishing any cult, or religion, continue to gather to discuss and read His works and express their reflections on His life and message through music, poetry, dance, drama, painting and other forms of art.

"I am nearer to you than your own breath. Remember Me and I Am with you and My love will guide you."[8]

"Real happiness lies in making others happy." – Avatar Meher Baba

APPENDIX B

The Wall of Love at Meherabad

Early in 2006, over two thousand hand-painted tiles were installed onto the large courtyard wall facing the dining room of the new Meher Pilgrim Retreat (MPR) at Meherabad.

The tile wall project was conceived as a fun way for large numbers of people to make an artistic contribution to the building. As many people as possible were given an opportunity to participate and there were no restrictions on how many tiles each could make. The instructions were simply to use the provided six-inch square tiles and colourful under-glazes to illustrate the theme: Welcome To My World.

Beginning in 2003, over a thousand tiles were painted by Baba lovers from the USA, Canada, Mexico, and Australia. Over a thousand more were made right at Meherabad by those living nearby, visitors from other parts of India, and hundreds of foreign pilgrims from other countries. It was truly an international project. The tile wall was envisioned as a colourful 'family album' of Baba's amazing world.

By late 2005, all the tiles were gathered in a large room at the MPR ready to be organised into a single, cohesive piece of artwork that would become the Welcome To My World tile wall. Seeing all of the tiles together in one place was breathtaking! All the beautiful colours, the imagination and unique expression and sincere intention in each tile was awesome. But even more than that was the heartfelt effort and love that radiated from each one. Even scattered haphazardly across the floor, the presence of so much feeling from so many of His lovers from far and wide was powerful and moving.

A month was spent arranging all the tiles on boards on which an outline of the wall had been drawn. One of many challenges faced during the design process lay in ascertaining whether there were enough tiles to fill the wall, or if there were too many. After final measurements were taken of the wall and decisions were made about how to space the tiles, it was calculated that 2145 hand-painted tiles would fit on the wall. Determining the exact number of tiles that had been made was difficult: The tiles were counted again and again; each time a different total was reached.

It wasn't until the design began to take shape on the boards that counting the tiles became easier. When an accurate count was finally obtained, it was only two tiles short. Or so it seemed. Little did anyone know that behind the scenes Meher Baba had made His own calculations. He had been keeping careful track, and all along He knew exactly where each tile would come from and where each would go. This became stunningly clear one morning as the last tiles were incorporated into the design on the boards. Miraculously, every space was filled. The total number of hand-painted tiles was not two tiles short after all, but just right. There were exactly 2145.

At long last, all of the tiles were moved to the courtyard where masons affixed them to the wall within a beautiful blue border. A week before Baba's Birthday the installation was completed without a hitch. Every tile was on the wall - each individual six-inch square truly splendid in its expression of love for Him, and the hundreds together making a spectacular Wall of Love. But best of all was that Meher Baba kept careful count and arranged it all so perfectly.

– Dot Lesnik

Dot Lesnik was the main facilitator for the Tile Wall project. She was responsible for the artistic arrangement of the tile collection.

APPENDIX C

Those Who Serve Baba

I am giving you a few details of those who are still serving Baba at Meherabad and Meharazad. These are people who have been associated with me through the years and have always helped make my stay a memorable one. As time goes by, there are so many more additions, but I leave that to Baba. I am sure that when you go, He will lead you to those you are meant to meet.

Only one of Baba's women mandali is alive today – Meheru Irani. You can meet her every Tuesday, Thursday and Sunday at Baba's home in Meherazad. It is an honour and a great privilege to spend time with her. She has as loving helpers, Kaycee, Davana and Shelly, who have been present in Baba's beautiful home as long as I can remember. They look after the mandali, show you around Baba's home and make your day a memorable one.

Bhau Kalchuri is the only one of Baba's Eastern Men Mandali who is still there today. Bhauji was Baba's night watchman for several years and never hesitates to share his personal experiences of Baba with all of us. He is the present Chairman of the Avatar Meher Baba Perpetual Public Charitable Trust. His assistant Craig, is always there to answer your calls, in case you want to contact Bhauji.

Tall and stately Ted Judson can be seen every day, without fail, singing with his guitar at the morning aarti, with the same fervour and love that drew me to him in the first place. He is married to a lovely lady called Janet who looks after the plants and garden there. She also looks after the archival work and loves Baba as much as he does.

Gary Kleiner was one of the first Baba friends I made when I first went to Meherabad, and we have been friends ever since. He is married to a beautiful young lady, Mehera. You can usually meet him at mealtimes when he will readily share all his experiences with you.

Strong and sturdy Alan Wagner has been in charge of the kitchen for as long as I can remember. The Baba prayer Alan recites at the Samadhi every day around noon, will resonate in your ears even after you have gone home.

Heather Nadel of the beautiful voice, and her husband Erico have spent their lives in Baba's service. Erico, who also looked after Mohammed, Baba's mast, recently passed away.

Judy will take you on a guided tour of the Samadhi and the entire Meherabad area. Adair, Suzy and Laurel will welcome you at the reception with smiles. Dr. Anne is always around in case you are feeling unwell. The always cheerful and smiling Roxanne Jessia is in charge of housekeeping and goes out of her way to see that you are comfortable at the Pilgrim Retreat.

If you need a booking at the Pilgrim Retreat, all you have to do is ring up Pat Summers and her co-workers, Irene and Meredith. They will not only make a reservation for you but help you with travel arrangements as well. If you need someone at the Ahmednagar Trust Office, you can contact Ward Parks, or Mehernath who is in charge of the bookshop.

Amrit and Dara (Baba's nephew) have shifted their residence from Ahmednagar to a lovely home in Meherabad. Apart from their usual appearance in the dining hall at teatime, Amrit can now be seen every morning at Samadhi duty helping newcomers to dress all the tombs with flowers.

Last but not least are Dolly and Jal Dastur. It is Dolly who normally starts the aarti now and welcomes you at 6 am for tomb cleaning. Jal is also a Trustee, and looks after the Dharamshala. He also prepares and makes all the arrangements of the dhuni on the 12th of every month.

All these wonderful people live at Meherazad and Meherabad They not only love and serve Baba, but also make it a point to help and serve all those who find their way there to Him. They do it with so much love and understanding that the pilgrim's progress becomes assured, and the journey to the Samadhi always remains an unforgettable experience.

The list is endless, and Baba's reach is endless and His love is endless for everyone and everything.

APPENDIX D

Information for Pilgrims to Meherabad

MEHERABAD

Meher Baba's Tomb-Shrine (Samadhi) situated in Upper Meherabad is open for darshan throughout the year from 6.30 am to 8.00 pm. Prayer and aarti are performed every day at 7.00 am and 7.00 pm.

Accommodations for the pilgrims, separate for men and women, are given at the Meher Pilgrim Retreat (MPR) at Upper Meherabad, the Dharamshala and the Hostels at Lower Meherabad. Accommodation is available from 15th June to 15th March each year. Prior reservation is necessary. With the opening of the new Meher Pilgrim Retreat in June 2006, the old Meher Pilgrim Centre (MPC) now functions as a Pilgrim Registration Centre and meeting hall.

MEHERAZAD

Home of Meher Baba where He lived with some of His mandali. It continues to be the private residence of the existing mandali members. It is open for pilgrims on Tuesdays, Thursdays and Sundays, during the posted timings.

RESERVATIONS AND CHECK-IN

Request for reservations in Meher Pilgrim Retreat (MPR) should contain full name of each person, date of birth, mailing/email address, phone numbers, date and time of arrival/departure.

For Meher Pilgrim Retreat, send to: pimco@mail.ambppct.org

Pilgrim Reservation, Avatar Meher Baba Trust, P.O. Bag 31, King's Road, Ahmednagar 414 001, Maharashtra, India.

Reservations can be confirmed maximum 6 weeks in advance. Telephone reservations are not accepted, but the office can be phoned to check on status, make changes, etc. Tel: 0241 2548733, 0241 2548736.

Check-in at Meher Pilgrim Retreat is available between the hours 10:00 am to 7:00 pm.

HOW TO GET TO MEHERABAD

From anywhere in India: Meherabad is outside Ahmednagar, Maharashtra State, and is accessible by rail and road from various parts of the country. The nearest airports are at Pune and Aurangabad, both about 2.5 hours away by road. Once you reach Ahmednagar Railway Station or the Bus Depot, you could cover the 6 kms distance to Meherabad by auto rickshaw or by local transport going towards Arangaon village.

From Mumbai (Bombay): By train, state transport buses or private coaches or taxis. By road, Mumbai-Meherabad distance is around 300 kms and can be covered in about 5 hours using the express highway and the Chalkan bypass, without entering Pune.

From Pune (Poona): By train, state transport buses, private coaches or taxis. Pune-Meherabad distance is around 100 kms and can be covered in 2.5 hours.

The Pilgrim Reservation Office provides information and help regarding travelling, and may also arrange for private pick-up from airports at Mumbai and Pune.

From MPC to MPR.
Left on Main Road (0.3 km)
Right to 1st Road. Follow around curves, parallel tracks to RR crossing. Right across tracks. Right 0.2 km to 1st road, take Left ... go straight.

Follow over bund. At top of hill, road goes right. Keep to the right. Continue on the curvy road until the MPR is on your right.

Distances:
MPC to Garden Condo turnoff 2.0 km
MPC to Stone Terrace 2.6 km
MPC to Bus entry sign 3.0 km
MPC to MPR parking/staff entry 3.2 km

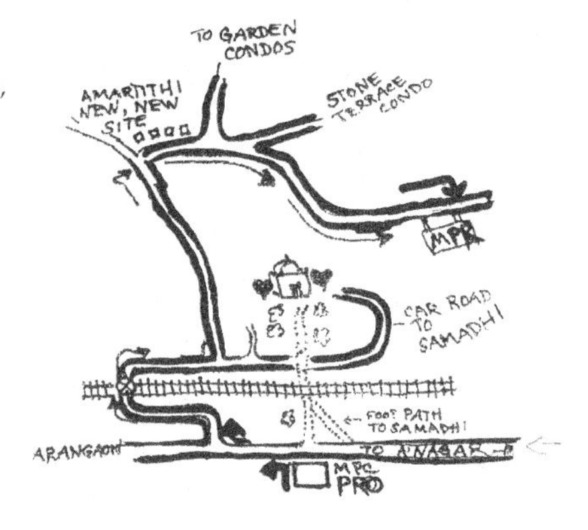

APPENDIX E

Centres of Information about Meher Baba

INDIA

Avatar Meher Baba Perpetual Public Charitable Trust,
P.O. Bag 31, King's Road,
Ahmednagar-414 001, Maharashtra.
Contact for Trust matters:
Mehernath Kalchuri.
Tel: 0241 2343666/7419/7093

Reservations at
Meher Pilgrim Retreat (MPR):
Contacts: Pat, Irene, Meredith.
Tel: 0241 2548733/36

Meher Pilgrim Retreat
Contacts: Heather Nadel, Adair, Suzy. Tel: 0241 2548211

Avatar Meher Baba Bombay Centre,
Navyug Nivas, 'A' Block, 3rd flr.,
Dr. D. Bhadkamkar Marg, Opp. Minerva Theatre, Mumbai 400 007.
E: avatarmeherbababombaycentre @rediffmail.com
Contact: Cyrus Khambata
022 28117639, 9821009715

Avatar Meher Baba Poona Centre,
441/1, Somwar Peth, Near K.E.M. Hospital, Pune 411 011.
Contact: Pratap Ahir, 9763701780

Avatar Meher Baba Delhi Centre,
50A, Tughlakhabad Industrial Area,
M.B. Road, Near Batra Hospital,
New Delhi 110 062.
Contact: Manoj Sethi, 9810123853
Kusum Singh, 9313879011

Avatar Meher Baba Hyderabad Centre,
Esamia Bazar, Koti, Hyderabad 500 027,
Andhra Pradesh.
Contact: Balaji, 9849090417

Avatar Meher Baba PPC Trust,
Meher Dham Nauranga,
Taluka Rath, District Hamirpur,
Uttar Pradesh.
Contact:
Shaligram Sharma, 05282-22217
Mobile: 9415145978

Avatar Meher Baba
Tamil Nadu Centre,
22, Moorthy Nagar, Villivakkam,
Chennai 600 049.
Contact: Dinesh, 9840032490

OVERSEAS

Meher Spiritual Centre On The Lake,
10200 Highway 17, North Myrtle
Beach, South Carolina 29577, USA.

Sufism Reoriented Inc.,
1300 Boulevard Way, Walnut Creek,
California 94595, USA.

Avatar Meher Baba Centre of
Southern California,
1214 South Van Ness Avenue,
Los Angeles CA 90019-3520, USA.

Meher Baba Association,
1/228 Hammersmith Grove,
London W6 7HG, England, UK.

Meher Baba Foundation Australia,
P.O.B. 22, Woomby, Queensland
4559, Australia.

Meher Baba Information,
Anthony Thorpe, 3 Flowers Track,
Christchurch 8, New Zealand.

SOME WEBSITES

avatarmeherbabatrust.org
avatarmeherbaba.org
meherbaba.com
meherabode.org
jaibaba.com
lovestreetbookstore.com

For a detailed list, please visit: www.trustmeher.com/files/centers.htm

APPENDIX F

Glossary

Aarti A traditional Hindu way of devotion and worship to God. A song or prayer with a refrain or theme which expresses the yearning for the offering of one's self to the One worshipped, or a song sung in God's praise describing His divine attributes and seeking His blessings.

Amartithi Immortal Date. The day when Baba dropped His physical body – 31st January 1969.

Ashram A simple, humble, unostentatious abode of a spiritual teacher.

Auto writing An occult phenomenon where the writing is inspired by a spirit source other than the self.

Avatar The total manifestation of God in human form on earth; descent of God; also called the God-Man, the Messiah, the Buddha, the Christ, the Saviour, the Rasool, the Saheb-e-Zaman.

Avataric The Age during which the Avatar, as the supreme God-realised One, heads the spiritual hierarchy. He awakens contemporary humanity to a realisation of its true spiritual nature. He brings about a new release of power, a new awakening of consciousness, a new experience of life, not merely for a few, but for all.

Avestan Sacred scriptures of the Zoroastrians.

Bai Elderly woman.

Bhajan A bhajan is any type of Indian devotional song. It has no fixed form: it may be as simple as a mantra.

Chilla-nashini Spiritual practice of penance and solitude, known mostly in Indian and Persian folklore. In this ritual, a mendicant or ascetic attempts to remain seated in a circle without food, water, or sleep for forty days and nights.

Daaman Hem of a garment. When Baba says "Hold on to My daaman," it connotes love, obedience and surrender to Him.

Dargahs A Sufi shrine built over the grave of a revered religious figure, often a Sufi saint.

Darshan An audience with the Master. An act of seeing, folding of hands in adoration or bowing at the feet of one's Master to express devotion. The spiritual presence of the Master at His Samadhi.

Dhuni A ceremonial fire lit on special occasions. As per Baba's wish, the dhuni is lit on every 12th of the month at Meherabad.

Diya Oil lamp.

Dnyan Gnosis, knowledge of spiritual truths. In Sufism it is called Irfan.

Gaddi A seat or throne.

Ganesh The God of the Hindus having the head of an elephant.

Gulchedi A sweet-smelling flower.

Guru A teacher. Generally referred to as a spiritual preceptor or Master.

Karma Action. Also, the working of the law of action and reaction – effect, fate. The natural and necessary happenings of one's lifetime, preconditioned by one's past lives and actions in this life.

Kirtan Call-and-response chanting performed in India's devotional traditions.

Kurta-pyjama A traditional Indian male garment; draw-string trousers over which a long-sleeved, knee-length shirt is worn.

Lendi A ceremony in which Sai Baba of Shirdi would be taken in a procession with pomp and adoration to defecate every day at a fixed time. Sai Baba explained, "When I pass my stool, I direct my 'abdals' – spiritual agents on the inner planes – about their duties to the world. I call upon them through the sound of the music during the parade."

Mandali Close ones; used to describe Baba's close disciples.

Mandap A sacred structure supported by four pillars under which the auspicious ceremony takes place.

Mast A God-intoxicated person on the spiritual path.

Nazar To see. The Master's protective watch over His disciples.

Nirvikalp The experience of the "I am God" state of the Perfect Ones.

Ouija board Board lettered with alphabets and other signs, used with movable pointers to obtain messages in spiritualistic séances.

Parvardigar Vishnu. The Preserver or Sustainer.

Perfect Master A God-realised soul who retains God-consciousness and creation-consciousness simultaneously, and who has a duty in creation to help other souls towards the realisation of God. Also known as Qutub, Man-God or Sadguru.

Prasad A gift, usually edible, given by the Master which is symbolic of the inner spiritual gift that it conveys.

Qawwali Islamic devotional song in praise of Allah.

Reiki Universal energy. An ancient touch-healing system through the laying of hands.

Sadguru Perfect Master, Qutub, Man-God

Sadra A shirt of very fine muslin.

Sahavas Intimate companionship. A gathering held by the Master or in His honour where the lovers and followers intimately feel His physical or spiritual presence.

Salwar-kameez A traditional ethnic Indian female garment; draw-string trousers over which a long-sleeved, knee-length shirt is worn with a long scarf or shawl (called a 'dupatta') around the head or neck.

Samadhi The Tomb-Shrine of a Spiritual Master. Baba's Samadhi is at Meherabad, Ahmednagar, Maharashtra, India.

Sanskaras Accumulated imprints of past experiences which determine one's desires and actions in one's present life.

Sanskaric Links between persons, places or things forged through past sanskaras.

Sari A traditional female Indian garment of around five to six metres in length wrapped around the body.

Seva Service.

Shariat The esoteric path, orthodoxy, external conformity to religious injunctions and traditions.

Sufi Movement A mystic discipline whose origins are lost in antiquity. It is known to have existed at the time of Zoroaster, who is Himself said to be a Sufi. It is an expression of the way of life in which the goal is to purge the heart of everything but God through spiritual contemplation and ecstasy and to eventually achieve total absorption in God. It was revitalised by various Avatars. Adherents of the esoteric teachings of Prophet Muhammad came to be called Sufis. Sufism Reoriented, which is functioning in the West, follows Baba's Charter.

Tikka A circular dot usually made on the forehead by Indian women using a bright vermilion pigment.

Tonga A horse-carriage used for transporting people.

APPENDIX G

Source Notes

Introduction

[1] *Lord Meher,* Copyright Bhau Kalchuri, author in Hindi; English translation by Lawrence Reiter, Vol. 16, p. 5652.

[2] *Silent Teachings of Meher Baba,* Beloved Archives, Inc. 2001, compiled and edited by Naosherwan Anzar, pp. 13-14.

CHAPTER 1 – The Ocean of Love

[1] *Sparks of the Truth from dissertations of Meher Baba.* A version by C. D. Deshmukh. Sheriar Press Inc., Copyright The Universal Spiritual League in America, Inc., p. 40.

[2] *God Speaks,* Meher Mownavani Publications, Indian Edition of Revised and Enlarged Second Edition, Sufism Reoriented, p. 39.

CHAPTER 2 – The Family Grows

[1] *Discourses,* Meher Baba, Seventh revised edition, 1987, Copyright Avatar Meher Baba Perpetual Public Charitable Trust, Ahmednagar, India. p. 106.

CHAPTER 4 – Piloting the Uncertainties of Life

[1] *Discourses,* Meher Baba, Seventh revised edition, 1987, Copyright Avatar Meher Baba Perpetual Public Charitable Trust, Ahmednagar, India. pp. 1-2.

CHAPTER 5 – I am Here

[1] *The Silent Master,* Copyright Meher Baba Archives, 1967, p. 7.

[2] Information, excerpts and quotes taken from *Meher Baba – The Awakener of the Age,* Don Stevens, pp. 141-146.

CHAPTER 9 – The Young Ones

[1] *The Book of Mirdad,* Milhail Naimy.

CHAPTER 10 – More Tests for Me

[1] *Glow International,* Naosherwan Anzar, February 1887, Remembering Mansari, p. 9.

CHAPTER 11 – A Channel to the Other Side

[1] *Mediums and their Work,* Linda Williamson, p. 166.

CHAPTER 12 – Rays of Angels

[1] *Extraordinary Encounters,* George Chapman.

CHAPTER 13 – Guidelines

[1] *Brochure on the extracts from the teachings of Avatar Meher Baba,* Copyright Avatar Meher Baba Perpetual Public Charitable Trust.

[2] *How to Do Autowriting,* Edain McCoy, pp. 95-96.

[3] *The Samadhi: Star of Infinity,* Bal Natu, Copyright Sheriar Foundation, 1997, p. 57.

CHAPTER 14 – Shopping Around

[1] *The Samadhi: Star of Infinity,* Bal Natu, Copyright Sheriar Foundation, 1997, p. 115.

CHAPTER 15 – Laughing with Baba

[1] *Lord Meher,* Copyright Bhau Kalchuri, author in Hindi; English translation by Lawrence Reiter, Vol. 13, p. 4444.

CHAPTER 16 – Howzzat!

[1] *Lord Meher,* Copyright Bhau Kalchuri, author in Hindi; English translation by Lawrence Reiter, Vol. 15, pp. 5341-5342.

[2] *Message given by Baba to Naosherwan Anzar.*

CHAPTER 17 – The Compassionate Father

[1] *Lord Meher,* Copyright Bhau Kalchuri, author in Hindi; English translation by Lawrence Reiter, Vol. 20, p. 6531.

[2] *Meher Baba's Call,* Copyright Avatar Meher Baba Perpetual Public Charitable Trust.

CHAPTER 19 – "God, Why Me?"

[1] *Discourses*, Meher Baba, Seventh revised edition, 1987 Copyright Avatar Meher Baba Perpetual Public Charitable Trust, Ahmednagar, India, pp. 327-330.

CHAPTER 20 – Changing Masters

[1] *God to Man and Man to God*, ed. C. B. Purdom, Copyright 1975 Avatar Meher Baba Perpetual Public Charitable Trust, pp. 47-48.

CHAPTER 21 – The King of Hearts

[1] *Discourses*, Meher Baba, Seventh revised edition, 1987 Copyright Avatar Meher Baba Perpetual Public Charitable Trust, Ahmednagar, India, p. 335.

CHAPTER 22 – The Samadhi

Note: Information/excerpts in this chapter are all taken from *The Samadhi: Star of Infinity*, by Bal Natu.

[1] *The Samadhi: Star of Infinity*, Bal Natu. Copyright Sheriar Foundation 1997, p. 39.

[2] *The Samadhi: Star of Infinity*, Bal Natu, Copyright Sheriar Foundation 1997, p. 15.

[3] *The Samadhi: Star of Infinity*, Bal Natu, Copyright Sheriar Foundation 1997, p. 68.

CHAPTER 24 – Food for Thought

[1] *Lord Meher*, Copyright Bhau Kalchuri, author in Hindi; English translation by Lawrence Reiter, Vol. 11, p. 3812.

[2] *Discourses*, Meher Baba, Seventh revised edition, 1987 Copyright Avatar Meher Baba Perpetual Public Charitable Trust, Ahmednagar, India, pp. 330-331.

[3] *Lord Meher*, Copyright Bhau Kalchuri, author in Hindi; English translation by Lawrence Reiter, Vol. 6, p. 2172.

[4] *Memoires of a Zetetic*, by Amia Kumar Hazra.

CHAPTER 27 – Merging with the Light

[1] *Discourses*, Meher Baba, Seventh revised edition, 1987 Copyright Avatar Meher Baba Perpetual Public Charitable Trust, Ahmednagar, India, p. 304.

[2] *Listen, Humanity*, Meher Baba, narrated and edited by D. E. Stevens, 1957 Copyright Avatar Meher Baba Perpetual Public Charitable Trust, Ahmednagar, pp. 102-103

[3] *Discourses*, Meher Baba, Seventh revised edition, 1987 Copyright Avatar Meher Baba Perpetual Public Charitable Trust, Ahmednagar, India, pp. 311-312.

CHAPTER 28 – Born Again

[1] *Silent Teachings of Meher Baba*, Beloved Archives, Inc., 2001, compiled and edited by Naosherwan Anzar p. 49.

[2] *God Speaks*, Meher Mownavani Publications, Indian Edition of Revised and Enlarged Second Edition, Sufism Reoriented, pp. 238-239.

[3] *Discourses*, Meher Baba, Seventh revised edition, 1987 Copyright Avatar Meher Baba Perpetual Public Charitable Trust, Ahmednagar, India, pp. 314-316.

Appendix A – Meher Baba

[1] *Listen, Humanity*, Meher Baba, narrated and edited by D. E. Stevens, 1957 Copyright Avatar Meher Baba Perpetual Public Charitable Trust, Ahmednagar, Appendix II, p. 245

[2] *Lord Meher*, Copyright Bhau Kalchuri, author in Hindi; English translation by Lawrence Reiter, Vol. 12, p. 4341.

[3] *Lord Meher*, Copyright Bhau Kalchuri, author in Hindi; English translation Lawrence Reiter, Vol. 20, p. 6533.

[4] *The Silent Master*, Copyright Meher Baba Archives, 1967, p. 36

[5] *Lord Meher*, Copyright Bhau Kalchuri, author in Hindi; English translation by Lawrence Reiter, Vol. 11, p. 4062.

[6] *Lord Meher*, Copyright Bhau Kalchuri, author in Hindi; English translation by Lawrence Reiter, Vol. 20, p. 6641.

[7] *Last Sahavas*, Copyright Dr. H. P. Bharucha.

[8] *Meher Baba Calling*, Copyright Avatar Meher Baba Perpetual Public Charitable Trust, Ahmednagar, p. 29.

APPENDIX H

Copyright Details

1. Copyright © All rights reserved. With permission from Bhau Kalchuri, Chairman, Avatar Meher Baba Perpetual Public Charitable Trust, Ahmednagar, M.S. 414001, India for all of Meher Baba's words, messages, and discourses quoted in this book, as also for photographs and paintings of Meher Baba, photographs of His mandali members and the *Tile Wall – Welcome To My World.*
2. Copyright © All rights reserved. With permission from Bhau Kalchuri, Author of *Lord Meher, The Biography of the Avatar of the Age Meher Baba* for use of excerpts and photographs.
3. Copyright © 1957 All rights reserved. With permission from Avatar Meher Baba Perpetual Public Charitable Trust to quote excerpts from *Listen, Humanity.*
4. Copyright © 1999 All rights reserved. With permission from D. E. Stevens to quote excerpts from *Meher Baba The Awakener Of The Age.*
5. Copyright © 1973 All rights reserved. With permission from Sufism Reoriented, Inc. Walnut Creek, California to quote from *God Speaks – The Theme of Creation and Its Purpose by Meher Baba.*
6. Copyright © 2008 Beloved Archives. With permission from Naosherwan Anzar to quote from Meher Baba's letter to him in 1966. Extracts from *Glow International – A Journal Devoted to Meher Baba* and *Silent Teachings of Meher Baba.*
7. Copyright © 2009 Dot Lesnik. With permission to use the article on *Welcome to My World. The Wall of Love.*
8. Copyright © Homyar J. Mistry, Homzprints, for the use of Inside Samadhi Image.
9. Photo of Bhau Kalchuri courtesy of Lynwood Sawyer (Shiva).

APPENDIX I

Recommended Reading

The following books on Meher Baba are available at Avatar Meher Baba Perpetual Public Charitable Trust, Ahmednagar, and the Bombay Centre, Navyug Nivas, Bhadkamkar Marg, A-wing, 3rd floor, Mumbai 400 007. Also available are brooches, lockets, audio CDs, VCDs/DVDs.

Avatar, *Jean Adriel*

Conversations with the Awakener (Series), *Bal Natu*

Discourses, *Meher Baba*

God Brother, *Manija S. Irani*

God Speaks, *Meher Baba*

How a Master Works, *Ivy O Duce*

Listen, Humanity Meher Baba, *Don Stevens*

Meher Baba The Awakener of the Age, *Don Stevens*

Mehera, *Compiled by Janet Judson*

Much Silence, *Tom & Dorothy Hopkinson*

The Everything and the Nothing, *Meher Baba*

The Samadhi: Star of Infinity, *Bal Natu*

That's How It Was, *Eruch Jessawala*

The Beloved, *Naosherwan Anzar*

Wayfarers, *William Donkin*

Lord Meher, *Bhau Kalchuri*

Mehera-Meher, *David* Fenster

The author may be contacted on email:
umrigar@vsnl.com

For further details, contact:
Yogi Impressions Books Pvt. Ltd.
1711, Centre 1, World Trade Centre,
Cuffe Parade, Mumbai 400 005, India.

Fill in the Mailing List form on our website
and receive, via email, information on
books, authors, events and more.
Visit: www.yogiimpressions.com

Telephone: (022) 61541500, 61541541
Fax: (022) 61541542
E-mail: yogi@yogiimpressions.com

Join us on Facebook:
www.facebook.com/yogiimpressions

The Sacred India Tarot

Inspired by Indian Mythology and Epics

78 cards + 4 bonus cards + 350 page handbook

The Sacred India Tarot is truly an offering from India to the world. It is the first and only Tarot deck that works solely within the parameters of sacred Indian mythology – almost the world's only living mythology today.